SPECIAL MESSAGE TO READERS

This book is published under the auspices of

THE ULVERSCROFT FOUNDATION

(registered charity No. 264873 UK)

Established in 1972 to provide funds for research, diagnosis and treatment of eye diseases. Examples of contributions made are: —

A Children's Assessment Unit at Moorfield's Hospital, London.

•

Twin operating theatres at the Western Ophthalmic Hospital, London.

•

A Chair of Ophthalmology at the Royal Australian College of Ophthalmologists.

•

A new Children's Eye Unit at the Great Ormond Street Hospital For Sick Children, London.

You can help further the work of the Foundation by making a donation or leaving a legacy. Every contribution, no matter how small, is received with gratitude. Please write for details to:

**THE ULVERSCROFT FOUNDATION,
The Green, Bradgate Road, Anstey,
Leicester LE7 7FU, England.
Telephone: (0116) 236 4325**

**In Australia write to:
THE ULVERSCROFT FOUNDATION,
c/o The Royal Australian College of
Ophthalmologists,
27, Commonwealth Street, Sydney,
N.S.W. 2010.**

Susan Kelly was born in the Chilterns and brought up in Oxford. After reading French and English at London University, she trained as a computer consultant and worked in this field as a freelancer during the eighties before giving it up to write full-time. She lives in west London with her solicitor husband.

THE GHOSTS OF ALBI

When Malcolm Dawson's only daughter Robyn is reported missing from her archaeological dig in south-west France, he immediately sets out to look for her — but he doesn't speak a word of French. Fortunately, he encounters Janey Silverman, who offers to accompany him as his chauffeur and interpreter. Travelling to Albi, they meet Robyn's boss, Professor Clements, and his team. Malcolm soon discovers that all six of Robyn's colleagues seem to have a reason to wish her out of the way. But the truth is stranger — and more dangerous — than anyone could have imagined . . .

SUSAN KELLY

THE GHOSTS OF ALBI

Complete and Unabridged

ULVERSCROFT
Leicester

First published in Great Britain in 1998 by
Severn House Publishers Limited
Surrey

First Large Print Edition
published 1999
by arrangement with
Severn House Publishers Limited
Surrey

British Library CIP Data

Kelly, Susan, *1955*–
The ghosts of Albi.—Large print ed.—
Ulverscroft large print series: mystery
1. Albi (France)—Fiction
2. Detective and mystery stories
3. Large type books
I. Title
823.9'14 [F]

ISBN 0–7089–4035–8

Published by
F. A. Thorpe (Publishing) Ltd.
Anstey, Leicestershire
Set by Words & Graphics Ltd.
Anstey, Leicestershire
Printed and bound in Great Britain by
T. J. International Ltd., Padstow, Cornwall

This book is printed on acid-free paper

For Francis Clarke, as always

Acts 2:28

A Brief History of Montprimeur

The Albigeois hill town of Montprimeur was settled as early as the tenth century by a group of perhaps six families, expanding over the next two centuries so that by the time of its sudden and tragic demise in 1211 the town was home to some two hundred and fifty people. The attractions of the site are obvious, even to modern eyes: a steep hill with only one accessible slope, easily defended against outlaws and, in extremis, the Spanish Moors; countryside which, while not the best arable land, is well suited to the grazing of sheep and cattle and with the sweet waters of the River Agout in the valley to provide both transport and fresh water should the wells dry up in summer.

Since this was a lawless age, the settlers' first task was the building of the protective stone walls, typical of hill towns in the Midi, some twenty feet high, with walkways running the whole circuit. Stout wooden gates could be closed each sunset to exclude unwanted strangers. Ironically, the first major building to be begun after the walls was the village church — dedicated to St Denis.

Ironically, since by early in the twelfth century the Cathar heresy had taken root among the townspeople and the church was left deserted in favour of an unadorned meeting-room.

By 1208 Montprimeur was a thriving trade centre, holding a market in the town square four days a week. It was a mixed society with prosperous merchants providing work and, if necessary, charity to peasant workers and artisans. The townspeople had everything to lose when, in January of that year, the papal legate, Pierre de Castelnau, sent to reason the Cathars back to Rome, was brutally murdered on the banks of the Rhône outside Arles. Within weeks a crusade had mustered to crush the heresy. The man chosen to lead the crusade was one Simon de Montfort, Earl of Leicester, whose youngest son and namesake is claimed by the English as the father of democracy.

De Montfort senior was a fanatically pious man who would stop at nothing to destroy the threat to Catholicism. During 1208, 1209 and 1210 town after town fell to his army, the townspeople suffering the most horrific and merciless deaths, usually by being burnt alive. Starting at the Mediterranean coast near Béziers, by 1211 the crusaders had reached the northernmost parts of the Albigeois and in the spring of that year Lavaur fell after a two-month siege with the loss of four hundred Cathar lives.

That left Montprimeur as de Montfort's logical next prey. The townspeople were ready for him. Their hill was steep and their walls high and well defended. They had laid in food to withstand a siege of three months, even allowing for the two hundred refugees who had sought sanctuary within their walls. But disaster struck on the night of 4 May 1211 and the town fell without an arrow being exchanged. De Montfort and his men were guided up a hidden pathway and in at a secret door left open for them.

Not a man, woman or child survived the massacre. Almost five hundred people died that night, betrayed by one of their own.

The site has been left derelict for almost eight hundred years as the local people believe there is a curse on the place. Tourists — even the most blasé — to this quiet memorial to man's intolerance are often left speechless at the sight of it, standing, as it seems to do, outside time. At twilight, particularly, it has a stark and evil beauty, a black hulk against the blood-red sky. The locals say that on the anniversary of the massacre the ruins seem to moan as the wind snakes through the remains of what was once a happy, peaceful little town where people went about their business and asked only to be left in peace with their beliefs . . . of what was once Montprimeur.

1

*'For we are not of this world, and this
world is not of us, and we fear lest we
meet death in this realm of the alien.'*
                                    Cathar prayer

It was almost without surprise that Malcolm
learned that his only daughter had disappeared
off the face of the earth.

He'd never understood why Robyn wanted
to leave Belfast; to him it was the most
beautiful city in the world, sitting in the
grey North Channel in a bowl of hills made
green by the frequent rain.

Earth, air, rock and water.

She broke it to him gently that she
was going to Durham to do her degree
in French and archaeology, not staying
at home and attending Queens daily as
he'd assumed. He worried about her while
she was away: you heard so many stories
about girls being attacked, raped, even
murdered on the mainland. In Belfast a
woman could safely walk the streets at
night.

After Durham she spent a year at a

university in Paris which was called Nanterre and not the Sorbonne as he'd thought. She asked him often to come and visit her there, offered to show him the sights, introduce him to her friends, take him for delicious meals in bistros the tourists hadn't discovered. He always found a plausible excuse not to go.

Then she moved further south in pursuit of the distant past, emitting her regular letters, her cheery postcards, her infrequent phone calls, from towns he'd never heard of: dusty-sounding towns like Albi, Carcassonne and Nîmes. 'Sunshine, Dad!' she would chide, her occasional voice thin and distant over the narrow bandwidth of the telephone. 'Warmth, heat! Come and get it.'

What was sunshine, he wondered, compared to the cold grey sea and the hills of Antrim where, on a blustery day, the dark volcanic basalt of its plateau was drawn in the sky like a low black curtain?

Soon she came only once a year and despite the regular letters, which took so long to reach him that they often arrived out of sequence, he watched her float further and further away from home so that the news, when it came, seemed inevitable.

★ ★ ★

'She was working for this archaeologist,' he explained again, this time to an inspector, having told his story to a constable and then to a patient sergeant. 'Professor Clements. From Oxford University. They were doing excavations at a place in the south-west of France called Montprimeur, near some town called Albi, researching some people who lived there — I don't know — *hundreds* of years ago, in the Middle Ages. Then Professor Clements rang me late last night. Around midnight.'

★ ★ ★

'Am I speaking to Mr Dawson?' The voice had been soft and hesitant, academic, with traces of a northern English accent. 'We haven't met but my name's James Clements. I work with Robyn. I suppose you could say I'm her boss. I'm sorry to call so late.'

'Yes?' The ringing of the telephone had wakened Malcolm and he was still groggy. 'She hasn't . . . she hasn't had an accident?'

Since her mother's premature death it was the one thing he dreaded, the first thing he thought of.

'I don't know,' the other man said unhappily. 'I hope not. I hope to God not. The thing is, Mr Dawson, not to beat

7

about the bush, we've lost her.'

'*Lost* her?'

'She's disappeared.'

★ ★ ★

'And she's how old?' the inspector asked.

'Twenty-four,' he said, for the third time.

'If she's disappeared abroad, it's a job for the local police, I'm afraid.' He looked at Malcolm with a tired pity. He was a young man, not much over thirty, but his eyes were old. Girls ran off from Belfast all the time, the eyes said, mostly to London, mostly because they were pregnant. Lots of paperwork and no impact on the crime statistics. He was glad this one wasn't his problem. He continued, intending to be kind. 'She may just have decided to take off, you know, mate. Young women do. They meet some man, don't think about the worry and distress they're causing to the old parents.'

'She's not like that,' Malcolm insisted. 'She's mature. She's ... ' He looked for another word to reinforce this concept. 'Responsible.'

'She'll be back,' the inspector said. 'You see if I'm not right. Bright-eyed and bushy-tailed, wondering what the fuss is about.'

'That's it,' the sergeant put in. 'Ninety

per cent of missing persons turn up within twenty-four hours, sir.'

The constable nodded wordless solidarity. Malcolm felt outnumbered. He knew they meant well, these three stocky men with their scratchy uniforms and their undertakers' smiles and their empty statistics.

Ninety per cent left ten per cent who didn't turn up. He thought that was ten per cent too many.

★ ★ ★

The travel agent glanced at her watch. 'There's a Jersey Airways flight to Gatwick leaving Belfast at eleven-fifteen, connecting with a British Airways flight to Toulouse at five past two — sorry, 1405 hours. Arriving Toulouse at 1645 — quarter to five — local time. They're an hour ahead of us, of course.'

'I prefer five past two,' Malcolm said, 'and quarter to five. What if I can't catch the eleven-fifteen?'

She tapped a few times on her computer keyboard and watched as her display changed. 'Then there's nothing until ten a.m. tomorrow, not by that direct a route, anyway. Maybe via Heathrow and Bordeaux . . . Heathrow and Paris — '

He held up a hand to stop her. Enough data. 'I'll make the eleven-fifteen if it kills me.'

No problem then, she said, pick up a hire car at Toulouse. Change currency here or at any of the airports. Take your credit cards, your Eurocheques.

They made it sound so simple although he hadn't got a credit card and didn't know what Eurocheques were, thinking they were somehow connected with the Ecu, of which he had heard. But he nodded and paid her with the money from his newly emptied building society account. He'd said, and his wife had said before him, that those few hundred pounds were for emergencies and what was this if not an emergency? He had perhaps thought more in terms of roof repairs and broken windows, of subsidence and new guttering, but it seemed risible now that he should have pictured such mundane matters as emergencies.

Pick up a hire car? He didn't like to say that he hadn't driven a car in more than fifteen years, not since Ann's death, and certainly never on the wrong side of the road. But he'd kept up his licence. He wouldn't stop to think about it. He would just do it.

It was only when he was halfway to the

bus stop on his way home to pack that he realised he had no passport. His rare holidays had been passed in England or Scotland, or in the Republic in the peaceful, pretty resorts of Connemara and Galway.

Malcolm turned reluctantly back, sure that the travel agent would think him an old fool, but the young woman in the bright orange lipstick and the neat black suit was kind and sympathetic. She was blessedly uncurious, too, about this whimsical desire for an out-of-season holiday to a place no Belfast holidaymaker went. She gave him an application form.

'You'll need two photos,' she explained. 'There's a booth at the station. You'll need someone to sign them and the form, vouch that you are who you say you are — your priest, say, or solicitor or a doctor. Then you'll have to go and queue, I'm afraid.' He was grateful and she smiled and wished him *bon voyage* once more.

The queue at the passport office wasn't long. It was mid-April and few were thinking about summer holidays yet. He'd been expecting a stiff blue document in which the queen demanded that he, her subject, be allowed to travel without let or hindrance, on pain of her displeasure; instead he got a small bendy, burgundy passport of the European Union. It was more practical, he told himself, to hide his disappointment, took up less space.

Honi soit qui mal y pense.

Malcolm put it in the inside pocket of his jacket and patted it at intervals on the way home to make sure it was still there.

★ ★ ★

He packed a small case at high speed. He wrote a note, 'No milk until further notice', contemplated it, added an afterthought 'thank you' and left it in a washed bottle on the doorstep. He emptied the perishables from the fridge and put the bags out for the binmen. He unplugged the TV and the radio, the toaster and the twin-tub in case of fire. He made sure the doors and windows were shut and fastened. He rang for a minicab to take him to the airport. Robyn was in danger. She was all he had. He must go to her.

3 February
'Darling Dad,
Before I forget, happy birthday! I saw the most perfect present for you today except that I can never give it to you, not if I become a squillionaire, because it's not for sale.

Picture an exquisitely beautiful chess piece — a black figure of a man in an apron and cap, a pawn presumably, butcher? baker? — lovingly carved by long-dead hands in the cold evenings by the light of a log fire in a Cathar hill town almost eight hundred years ago.

And the feel of it, Dad. Your fingers slide the length of it, never catching on the sheerness of it. I held it enclosed in my hands for several minutes, then rubbed it against my face; then I licked it gently and it tasted of time itself. If ever I begin to ask myself what I'm doing here, living out of suitcases in scruffy hotels, I need only remember that three-inch manikin.

He must have been an educated man, Father Hugues, a civilised man, to play at chess. It was in his house that I found it, or what remains of his house, which is about three stones in a not very straight line. I was on my own when I came across it and would have given anything to drop it in my pocket and keep it — anything, before you say it, except my integrity.

Who do you play chess with now that I am gone? Why have I never thought to ask? Why am I such a selfish brat that I never thought to ask before?

. . . Speaking of which, the answer to

your question is, I'm afraid, no, I shan't be able to make it home at Easter. We're only taking a couple of days off work and a group of us are nipping over to Barcelona to admire the eccentric outpourings of an architect aptly named Gaudi.

Sorry. Sorry. Sorry.

Your real birthday present is on its way and should arrive by the vagaries of the French and Royal Ulster postal services some time before Christmas.

How I wish I could give you the pawn, though. Imagine what the kings and queens and bishops must have been like! What I wouldn't give to see them. But it must sit in some museum behind glass for the world to admire; but never touch, never smell, never taste.

In haste and with much love, as ever,
Robyn.'

★ ★ ★

Malcolm made the eleven-fifteen shuttle with five minutes to spare. On the plane he found that his hands were shaking. He'd busied himself since hearing the news — acting, not giving himself time to speculate. Now at last he had leisure to think and little to occupy him except magazines containing nothing but advertisements, overt or covert.

He'd seen reports on television over the years when babies were snatched or older children went missing on the way back from school, had seen the inarticulate pain of the parents as they appealed to the abductor for the child's safe return: the mother in tears, gulping out her plea; the father beside her, a volcano of silent fury.

It was the nightmare of everyone with a young child.

Except that what they didn't tell you, when you embarked on the long road of parenthood, was that it never ended, that worry, that it didn't fade away when they reached the age of eighteen and got the vote.

So Malcolm sat on the plane, a volcano of silent fury and anguish. He knew he ought to be numb with worry and disbelief — wasn't that how it was in books? — but, if anything, his mind was painfully clear, his thoughts fearfully lucid.

The stewardess came round to check that seatbelts were fastened, chairs in the upright position, and spotted the white knuckles as they gripped the arm rest.

'First time flier?' she asked with a professional smile and an English accent. 'Nothing to worry about, sir. Safer than crossing the road.'

He was grateful for her assumption that it was flying that terrified him.

As the plane rose high over the Irish Sea, he looked down on the Harland and Wolff shipyard, on the docks where his grandfather had helped to build the *Titanic* more than eighty years before.

Somehow, that was oddly reassuring.

★ ★ ★

Safely airborne, Malcolm took from his hand luggage the bundle of Robyn's letters. He'd kept them — six-years' worth — but he concentrated now on the latest batch, the ones that had come over the last year on squared exercise paper with an Albi postmark.

She was a good correspondent. Her unstructured letters made him laugh, meandering about from ideas to events and back again as they were recalled to her. *We went to the pictures last night at the hypermarket*, she would say, *and there was a woman reminded me of Mrs Meaney who had the corner shop when I was little. I wore my new suede jeans which cost a bomb but, boy, were they worth every centime.*

She drew pictures of people, places, animals in the margins of her written

16

thoughts: Mrs Meaney weighing out boiled sweets, belying her name by adding a couple extra for the greedy child. She was no artist and the pensive cat might seem to have one leg much shorter than the others — an illusion of perspective, she insisted — or a chicken be endowed with an improbably large head.

Pictures would, as often as not, be abandoned altogether with crossings out, exclamation marks and scribbled '*yeuks*!' An account of some steak tartare, injudiciously eaten in a cheap restaurant on a hot summer's evening, was accompanied by a sketch of herself with her head over the lavatory bowl, a full moon laughing down at her.

Her job excited her into exuberance. It gave her all she wanted out of life at her young age: travel, the romance of history unearthed, a feeling of usefulness. Professor Clements and his team of six were excavating the long-lost hill town of Montprimeur which had been, Robyn explained to her uncomprehending father, destroyed in the spring of 1211 by the Catholic crusaders who saw it as a hotbed of the Cathar heresy.

Everyone in the town had been slaughtered, even the babes in arms: put to the sword if they were lucky, or burnt alive on mass pyres of roasting flesh if they were not. The site had been left derelict, never to be rebuilt, since the

17

local people believed the place accursed.

It was a slow business, she said, but a rewarding one: pottery had been unearthed intact, some rudimentary silver coins — rare in a civilisation where barter was the main commerce — a ring made for a dainty finger, too small for modern hands, even hers.

Montprimeur was unique in that life in the town before the tragedy had been documented by a young noblewoman, Louise d'Ambriers, whose family lived nearby. Louise had been a poet in the *Langue d'Oc* and a diarist and her memories of everyday life in these hills had been meticulous.

The stewardess offered Malcolm a tray and he took it absently, unwrapped clingfilm and ate, mostly with his fingers; he couldn't have said a few minutes later what the meal consisted of. He read on. As on only child, Robyn had had imaginary friends, fantasy companions. It seemed the habit had resurfaced.

I'm coming to feel I know these people, Dad, as if they were my neighbours: Father Hugues, nominally the parish priest, but really a 'Perfect' — an initiate of the new faith; Bruno the cobbler, and Jehane his wife who was the village midwife and herbalist. Then there was Dias the laundress with her bastard son, Pietre, whose father she refused to name . . .

She'd drawn sketch portraits of these new friends for her father: Hugues, large in his soutane, black-bearded, bare-footed in the dust, his skirts hitched up above his knees, muscular and tough; Jehane, plain and pock-marked in her dirty blue gown; Dias, the village flirt, pretty and slender in an apron and clogs, banging at the linen with a stone and a good will, her slant-eyed baby in a sling on her back.

With the bundle of letters he had a photograph; we would need it to show to people, to ask if they'd seen this girl. He'd taken it himself at her graduation ceremony with the Olympus camera he'd bought as a Christmas present to himself that year; it was a good one and it seemed impossible to take bad photos with it. She was serious, unsmiling in her cap and gown as befitted the solemnity of the occasion. 'Honestly, Dad,' she'd complained. 'Anyone would think this afternoon's play-acting was what three years at university was about, like the late-night swotting and the discoing and the hangovers didn't count at all.'

He examined her image as dispassionately as he could. He thought she looked nice, the sort of young girl he'd like to meet, the kind that was worth preserving. The happy and co-operative child had grown into a good-natured and handsome woman. She hadn't changed in those three years. She was of medium height and boyish build; flat-chested, small hipped like her mother. Her straight and glossy black hair was cajoled into the pageboy cut she'd worn since the age of twelve and which suited and framed her delicate features. Her skin tanned easily and she wore no make-up.

'Best to save that muck for middle age,' she would say. 'Otherwise there's nothing to look forward to.'

He felt a distinct movement in his chest, where he imagined his heart to be, similar to the lurch it had given the day he'd opened his front door to the pair of constables who'd come to break the news of Ann's death to him. He felt sick.

Dear God, he prayed, let her have a middle age to look forward to.

★ ★ ★

The airport bus dropped Malcolm outside Toulouse station shortly after seven that evening. The second flight had been late leaving Gatwick and had landed just before six. His nerve had failed at the car-hire place and he'd been told in excellent English at the information desk that he could catch a train to Albi from Toulouse. From there, he supposed, a bus or taxi could be found to take him to Montprimeur.

He'd never been much of a traveller and the bustle of the station with its numerous platforms, its signs in French, its timetables in the twenty-four-hour clock sank his heart. French people, he found, were not patient with bewildered anglophones, turning away with a wave of the hands, an exasperated noise like 'Pah!' To be fair, he doubted that a Frenchman would have fared better in Belfast, or as well.

He put his bag down on the floor, squeezed it between his feet for safe keeping, and traced a finger down the lines of timetable until he found Albi. He'd assumed that the railways would operate as they did at home — that there would be regular train services from the big regional capital of Toulouse to the small market town of Albi — but he found to his dismay that the last train for Albi had departed more than an hour earlier and that the next one was not until seven-thirty in the morning.

Nineteen hours had gone by since the telephone call; almost a day. The chances were that Robyn had turned up safe and well and that his mad, adrenaline-led flight had been pointless. She was probably now frantic about *him*, ringing the house at half-hourly intervals and getting no reply, fearing he'd collapsed with the shock, trying to decide whether to call in the police or not.

He cursed himself that in the terror of the night he hadn't got a return telephone number from the professor.

He picked up his case and walked disconsolately out of the station. He'd never felt so alone or so desolate in his life. It wasn't just the alien landscape, the gibbering people; the loneliness came from within. The day was warm and the street dusty, as he'd expected, despite the presence of a canal a few yards in front of him.

As he dithered over which direction to take, a young woman stopped and looked him up and down. He soon realised she wasn't exactly young, although her crude yellow hair falling long down her back, the blue eye-shadow daubed around her lids, the halter neck which left her midriff exposed, and the plucked bare legs between skimpy shorts and impossibly high-heeled boots, were designed to give that illusion.

She said something to him, a question of some sort by its intonation, but he shrugged helplessly, saying, 'I'm afraid I don't understand.'

'Two h-hondot francs only, baby,' she said, breathing out the unfamiliar aspirate, holding up two fingers to count them off.

'Ah, I see. No . . . Thank you very much all the same.'

'*Non*?' She laughed and walked away, her shoulder bag banging cheerfully against her prominent rump.

A prostitute, then, a scarlet woman, rather than the Good Samaritan he might have hoped for, although there was no reason the one shouldn't also be the other. He wasn't shocked by her appearance, or by her trade, only saddened that men — men such as himself, apparently — should feel the need for her services.

He crossed the road, tossed a mental coin and turned left along the canal. After a few minutes he reached a busy street and turned right this time. The words 'Centre Ville' on a signpost weren't beyond him and that seemed the best place to look for a cheap hotel.

He found himself in a broad, tree-lined avenue with cars parked at an angle to the highway on either side. He stopped to get his bearings, fingering obsessively at the inside pocket of his jacket which contained his passport and about five hundred pounds in English and French currency. It was a gesture that would speak volumes, he knew, to any passing pickpocket, but which he couldn't seem to stop.

A car horn made him swing round in fear and guilt. A car was attempting to back out of the space he was blocking. A young woman leaned out of the driver's window and said something to him in French. It didn't sound especially rude or angry, merely neutrally asking him to move.

He started to back out of the way when it dawned on him that the head was poking out of the right-hand window — the driver's window — which meant that the car was, therefore, probably English. The number plate and prominent GB sticker confirmed this. It was an ancient, battered Reliant Robin in a shade somewhere between pink and grey, like the skin of an office worker caught out by the first sunray of summer.

'Excuse me!' he called out. The car came to a halt, half in and half out of the parking space and the head reappeared. 'Can you tell me the way to a cheap hotel?' Malcolm asked. 'I'd be awfully grateful.' The driver sighed, put the car into forward gear and reclaimed her slot. A Citroën, which had been waiting for the space, hooted long and hard; the male driver shouted something at them both that didn't sound at all neutral, and drove off.

The girl got out of the car. She was about twenty, he guessed — although he wasn't good at ages — small of stature and verging on plumpness. Her cap of hair was black, smooth and shiny and her skin the pale olive he normally associated with Latin countries. She had a large nose and a full mouth and dark eyes. He wouldn't, on the face of it, have taken her for English, but perhaps Spanish or Portuguese.

She wore jeans, raggedly cut off below the knee, and a tee shirt with something written on it in French, the wording distorted by her full breasts. Her feet were bare and not clean and she arched them as she stood on the warm pavement, her hands on her hips, expectant.

Another car, a large Renault, pulled up at the kerb and its driver shouted something before moving on. The girl called 'Wanker' after him and made a gesture in which her right hand gripped her left elbow on the inside and her left forearm shot up aggressively.

Malcolm looked at her in surprise. It didn't look much as if this was his Good Samaritan either. 'What did he say?' he asked.

'Oh, he said three-wheeled cars were illegal in France and I ought to be arrested,' the girl said in an accent he'd heard described as Estuary English — a bastardised cockney fashionable among all levels of society. 'It's comple'ely untrue,' she went on, 'but I get it all the time. Now, what was it?'

'A hotel,' he said hopefully. 'Something cheap and . . . er . . . ' The pavement was no longer flat and still beneath his feet but moving like the deck of a ship. His bag dropped from his hand which would suddenly not respond to his automatic commands. The dark girl's face went rapidly out of focus and back in again as she peered at him in alarm.

'Hey!' She had him by the arm now. 'You can't faint here. This is a no-fainting zone between the hours of six and eight p.m. when there's an 'R' in the month.' She more or less manhandled him round the car and into the passenger seat.

'My bag,' Malcolm protested feebly. She went back for it, threw it into the boot and got into the driver's seat beside him. She produced a plastic carrier bag from the back seat and rummaged in it, sending a shower of greasy sandwich wrappers, chocolate papers and an apple core onto his knees and thence the floor.

'Got some diet Coke here somewhere,' she explained as he flinched under the onslaught. 'Yeah. Here it is.'

He'd never drunk Coke. It was warm and flat and much too cloying, with the chemical aftertaste of artificial sweetener. He thought it perhaps the nastiest thing he'd ever tasted, but he felt a little better.

The girl looked at him without enthusiasm. 'The trouble with helping someone,' she said, 'is that you're then responsible for them. The Chinese believe that if you save someone's life, you have to look out for them as long as they live.'

'We're not Chinese,' Malcolm pointed out, 'thankfully, and my situation wasn't desperate. I'm grateful for your kindness and if you'll point me in the direction of a hotel I'll get out of your way.'

'Hold on. You don't look too well to me. Have you not eaten today, or something?'

'I'm fairly sure I had something on the plane from Gatwick.' A meal, something between tea and dinner, indistinguishable from the one — breakfast? lunch? — he'd eaten on the plane from Belfast.

'You're not a vagrant then?'

'No,' he said with dignity. 'I'm nothing of the sort.'

'Have a boiled sweet.' She rustled a bag out

of the glove compartment and he obediently unwrapped a Murray Mint and began to suck it. It took away the taste of the Coke.

'I laid in a store at Christmas,' she said. 'I like them for long car journeys. My name's Janey Silverman. What's yours?'

'Malcolm Dawson.'

'Here on holiday?'

'No,' he said.

'I live here,' she went on, when it became clear that he wasn't going to elucidate further. 'Pro tem. I teach English to ungrateful little buggers at a grammar school at Muret, which is an ugly market town a few miles out of Toulouse. Well, I say market town; industrial dormitory town would be more like it. Part of my university course, you see.'

'Yes. I do see.'

Robyn had done something similar as part of her course at Durham. She'd been away in Paris from September to May in her twenty-first year and had come back looking, even to Malcolm's time-warped eyes, like a real, grown-up lady with an invisible coating — like a varnish — of style. He remembered thinking: if only her mother could see her now, how proud she would be.

He began to cry. The boiled sweet slobbered from his mouth and joined the rest of the debris on the floor. He wiped his eyes with the cuff of his shirt. He didn't feel up to apologising. Things had to be bad, he thought, when an Ulsterman shed tears publicly and without shame. He'd not been able to cry when Ann had died; somewhere along the ensuing sixteen years he'd learned how.

'I think you'd better tell me about it,' Janey said.

He did so in a few short sentences, without elaboration. He didn't expound on his terror — she could see that for herself as his face twisted to stall the tears — he just recounted the facts of the last twenty-four hours. 'And now I don't know how to get to Albi,' he concluded, 'let alone to this hill town place, or what to do when I get there.'

'Do your seatbelt up.' Janey started the car engine. She rummaged on the back seat again and surfaced with a map this time. She unfolded it and he watched as her brown finger with its nibbled nail traced a route to Montprimeur. 'We'll be there in less than an hour,' she stated.

'You can't drive me there,' he said.

'Why not?'

'You don't know me.'

'Let's pretend,' Janey Silverman told him, 'for the time being at least, that we are both Chinese.'

Malcolm fastened his seatbelt as ordered but continued to protest as she backed the car out, turned towards the town centre for a moment, then did a U-turn through a gap in the central reservation, taking them back towards the station. She turned along the canal and in twenty minutes they were clear of the conurbation and travelling east.

Janey flung the map across, onto his lap. 'Shut up and navigate. I'm doing this for me, okay, not for you. I love a good mystery and I won't rest till it's solved. If we find your Robyn at Montprimeur happily having a nice drink with her mates, well then you can pay me for the petrol.'

Malcolm didn't like to be beholden to the generosity of strangers. Family was different: that was what family was for, to be there when you needed them. Blood was thicker than water. He asked neighbours for help only in extremis — as when Ann had died — and felt uncomfortable until the debt was repaid.

On his tombstone they would put: He Was No Trouble. It would be a compliment.

He was embarrassed too, embarrassed to be seen crying in public, to be spilling out his problems to this young girl — unknown, another race, another gender, another generation — with her glottal stops and her dirty feet and her bitten nails; the most unlikely travelling companion he could envisage.

He found young people difficult — except for Robyn, of course. He didn't understand or like their music, their dress, their morals. When they were first married Ann used to laugh at him sometimes and say he'd been born middle-aged.

He shrivelled in his seat, diminished in his own eyes. The road was straight and tree-lined and empty. The odd petrol station skidded past at speed; here and there, more a hamlet than a village; or a lone house on a sparsely-grassed hillside amid uninterested sheep. Malcolm wasn't comfortable sitting in the passenger seat but in the middle of the road. Every time an oversized lorry passed them going the other way he flinched and had to fight the urge to yell that she was on the wrong side.

'What about your work?' he asked hopefully. 'Surely they're expecting you back at your school?'

'It's the Easter hols,' she said. 'No one will be looking for me for at least a week.'

'You didn't go home for Easter?'

'Where's home? My mother and my

latest stepfather in stockbroker-belt Surrey? No thanks. I've been touring around: Carcassonne, Narbonne, Marseille, Avignon. I was going to head south-west next to Lourdes, but that'll keep.'

He swallowed, not wanting personal revelations from her of mothers and step-fathers, and said, 'Lourdes? The shrine?'

'Sure. Why not? I wanted to see what it was like — the site of some sort of mass hallucination. Then I was going to go up into the mountains, maybe into Spain, through the pass at Roncesvalles where Roland died.'

Malcolm didn't ask who Roland was since he didn't want to incur her scorn. Some pop star, he supposed, high on drugs, giddy with new-found wealth, taking a mountain bend too fast in his white Lotus or on his black Harley Davidson. He saw the car turn over and over as it bounced down to the rocks, like in the films on TV, exploding as it hit the bottom, without hope of survival.

He realised that Janey was speaking again. 'I'm sorry?' he said.

She repeated her question. 'You Scottish?'

'Northern Irish.'

'Oh, sorry. It sounds the same. To me, anyway.'

'It's a common mistake. I live in Belfast.'

'Does your daughter sound like you?'

'Not really, not any more.'

It had been noticeable on her first Christmas home from Durham, although he'd never mentioned it and nor had she. It made her seem, for the first few minutes until he got used to it, like another person, a stranger. He assumed she'd been mocked and mimicked out of it by her new English friends.

'And what do you do there?' Janey asked. 'In Belfast?'

'I'm retired now.'

She glanced sideways at him. 'You don't look old enough.'

'I'm fifty-eight. I took early retirement.'

With his wife dead and Robyn grown up and independent, the reduced pension on offer had been more than adequate to his needs.

'From what?' she persisted.

She asked too many questions, he thought, of such a private man, but he could hardly tell her to mind her own business in the circumstances. He wished she would concentrate on the road; the speed of this joke car surprised him. 'Oh, office work,' he said. 'I did clerical work for Belfast City Council.' He realised that he sounded deliberately evasive but the truth was that the job had been no more, and no less, than that.

His parents had been pleased to see one of the family go into white-collar work with a handful of exam passes, instead of into the docks like his forebears. Malcolm himself had looked wistfully at the distant derricks, the two giant yellow gantries, as he ate his sandwiches each lunchtime, envying the camaraderie of the dockers, their fine muscles that scorned suits and thick necks that abhorred ties, wanting to be one of them and knowing himself too weedy.

His grandfather McCreedy had been one of the Black Squad, entrusted with the hardest and dirtiest work, the proudest work. 'My grandda built the *Titanic*,' he said with a smile. 'Well, him and one or two other blokes.'

'Fancy that,' Janey said, after a pause. 'The one that got away.'

The *Titanic* had been hailed a lucky ship: only two men had died in the building of her, well below the average for a vessel of that size. Grandda had frightened him as a boy with tales of ghostly tappings from the men trapped in the hull by the speed of construction. He'd gone deaf in middle age from the years of incessant hammering. In old age he'd become crude

34

and aggressive and not clean, not proud of his only grandson whom he referred to as 'the office boy'.

And then he'd died.

★ ★ ★

'So she's interested in the Albigensians, your daughter?' Janey said.

'The Cathars. Is that the same thing?' She nodded. 'I don't understand any of it.'

'A Christian heretic sect,' she said. 'More popular than the regular religion here by the twelfth century, crushed by a Papal crusade led by an Englishman called Simon de Montfort.'

'That name seems familiar.'

'You're thinking of his son, Simon junior, the father of English democracy. Ironic. Anyway, that was the beginnings of the Inquisition.'

'You know about it?'

She shrugged. 'You can't live round here for any length of time and not know. The locals will tell you that the Languedoc was once the greatest civilisation of western Europe — a non-stop feast of music and poetry, art and gracious living; a centre of international commerce — with Toulouse as its red-gold capital. Until de Montfort came.'

35

The signposts to Albi flashed ever diminishing distances as they passed through the villages of Verfeil, Lavaur and St Paul. Shortly after this Malcolm said, 'Next left, I think.'

Janey signalled and turned the Reliant onto a single-track road which crossed a stream via an old stone bridge before winding gradually uphill to the increasing complaints of the engine. Cattle grazed in the surrounding fields, the soil too poor for grain. They rattled over some potholes. 'Shit! My suspension.'

They passed a couple of school-aged children who stared at the car in disbelief, giggling and pointing, nudging each other. Janey stuck her tongue out at them.

As they rounded a corner five minutes later a lone hill came into view, perhaps half a mile ahead. It was high, wedge shaped, its flat top a mass of ruins with stones piled higgledy-piggledy where once had been embracing walls. On the south side the slope was fairly gentle and they could make out a well-worn path zigzagging up to the top; the other visible faces were sheer and forbidding with the north slope in particular a succession of ragged rock, each sharper than the last, like black icebergs.

It was dusk, the sun only just above the

horizon. A few small but determined clouds hung about the summit, reflecting red in the last minutes of the day, casting a ghostly haze like washed blood on the ruins.

'Creepy,' Janey said, but as though creepy was good.

'Montprimeur,' Malcolm stated.

★ ★ ★

The whole site was surrounded by a wire fence perhaps twelve feet high and in good repair. Janey drove through an open gate with a large sign on it that said *Privé. Défense d'entrer.*

'What does that sign say?' Malcolm asked, guessing at the first bit.

'Private. Keep out.' She added smoothly, 'I'm sure they don't mean us.'

She pulled the three-wheeler up neatly between a Renault minibus and an old but lovingly-maintained racing-green sports car.

There were signs of activity at the foot of the hill: a group of six people — four men and two women — engaged in packing things away for the day, stopped to look in their direction. Two of the men conferred briefly together then the younger of the two disengaged himself from the group and came towards them with a quick, light step.

'He doesn't look exactly thrilled to see us,' Janey remarked, 'and will probably be considerably less thrilled when he finds out who we are.' She switched off the engine and sought once more in the goldmine of the back seat, to emerge this time with a pair of black leather sandals which she hooked on her hard and dusty feet. 'Any sign of your Robyn?' she asked.

'No.' Malcolm's eyes had been searching eagerly but in vain.

Janey got out of the car. He could see no course but to follow her. The other man was by now in earshot.

'I'm afraid this is private property,' he said in English, having presumably noted their number plate. 'This is a precious archaeological site and I shall have to ask you to leave at once. Really . . . ' he added, but only to himself, 'idle sightseers are all we need just now.'

'Like something out of Burton's window,' Janey muttered. 'If short of sleep.'

The man was in his late thirties, Malcolm surmised, good-looking and probably well aware of it: short brown hair with no trace of grey, brown eyes, regular features, a firm chin, a well-toned body. He looked like any one of a hundred bit-part actors looking for the big break, although his eyes, as Janey

38

had suggested, were smudged with fatigue.

He'd reached them by now and loomed over the girl, unsmiling, displaying the lack of interest with which a handsome man disdains a woman who isn't fair of face. His clothes had been good, though now shabby: jeans, a cotton checked shirt unbuttoned too far to reveal a taut, smooth chest, leather lace-up shoes with scuffed tips. He stood with his thumbs thrust into his belt loops, awaiting their compliance.

'I'm Malcolm Dawson,' Malcolm said over Janey's bristling head. 'Robyn's father. Are you Professor Clements?'

'Oh my God!' The shop-window dummy turned suddenly human and ran a dirty hand across his face in agitation, leaving a streak. He raised his voice towards his colleagues. 'James! Come here, quickly.' He turned back to Malcolm. 'I'm Dr Simon Guzman, Professor Clements's second-in-command. We had no idea . . . You should have let us know . . . '

He held out a hand for Malcolm to shake, thought better of it, wiped it down the back of his jeans and offered it again. Malcolm shook it dumbly.

They were joined at that moment by an older man who said, 'What, um, is it, Simon?' Malcolm recognised his voice from the telephone, with its bones of a long-dead northern childhood, the polite hesitancy of tone which betrayed no true lack of confidence. He wasn't Malcolm's image of a professor, being a tall man somewhere in his middle fifties, heavy of build, though not fat, with no trace of a bookish stoop. A man of action, this, rather than a scholar. He was deeply tanned in a way that spoke of years, if not decades, spent digging in the open air, his face overly-wrinkled from the sun's drying rays. He removed a straw hat to reveal a tousle of thick black hair, greyed only round the edges. His dark eyes flashed irritated enquiry at his colleague.

'It's Robyn's father,' Dr Guzman said in a low — warning — voice. 'Mr Dawson, this is Professor Clements; James, Mr Dawson and . . . '

'Miss Janey Silverman,' Janey said. 'I'm a friend of the family.'

Malcolm stared at her hard for a few seconds while shaking hands with the professor. Grateful as he was to Janey Silverman, he didn't want her to take too much for granted.

'We've been trying to ring you,' Clements said, using his hat as a makeshift fan. 'All day, but there was no reply, no ansaphone.' He made the lack of an answering machine sound like a deliberate social dereliction.

'She's turned up.' Malcolm felt faint with relief. He looked round, half laughing. 'Where is she?' He called out, 'Robyn!'

'Well, no,' Clements said with a grimace. 'It's not actually that she's turned up, it's just that, well, this morning we instituted yet another search and we realised that her overnight bag is missing too, and a few of her things. You know, a change of clothes, um, toothbrush, that sort of thing, so it seems clear that she's taken off for a few days and there's nothing sinister about it after all.'

Malcolm could think of nothing to say to this, his heart crushed by the weight of disappointment. It was Janey who asked, 'And she said nothing to anyone?'

'Well, no.'

'And did she have some leave due?'

' . . . Not exactly.'

'What exactly?' Janey asked sharply.

'We're flexible.'

'And has she ever gone off like this before without saying a word to anyone?' Janey sounded, Malcolm thought, like a policeman on TV: brusque, grave, cutting through to the heart of the matter with a machete, not minding if people liked her or not, the way Malcolm did. He looked at her with renewed respect; she seemed like a friend the family could do with after all.

Clements and Guzman exchanged unhappy glances. 'No,' Clements said finally. 'Not without saying.'

'So it was out of character.'

'I suppose so.'

'And what did the police say when you called them?'

'That, um, she would be bound to turn up.'

Policemen, Malcolm reflected, were the same the world over: in Albi, as in Belfast, they relied on her just turning up.

'You got the *police judiciare* out from Albi, of course,' Janey went on. 'The CID?'

Clements shook his head. 'Just the local people from Castres, although it was a CID inspector I spoke to in the end. Seemed a capable fellow. What was his name, Simon?'

'Laroche.'

'Oh, yes. They don't take missing persons reports seriously until forty-eight hours have elapsed, you know, Miss, er . . . '

'Silverman. And when was Robyn last seen . . . last seen by anyone in your party?'

Last seen *alive*? Malcolm wondered. Was that the word Janey had so audibly omitted.

'Early yesterday afternoon,' Guzman said. 'We had a late lunch and most of us took a siesta in the shade afterwards. Robs was

42

restless, though, and wandered off, saying she was going to take a walk right round the hill before getting back to work up on the summit. It's a mile and a half, wouldn't take her half an hour. She's a good walker, you see.'

Malcolm found himself nodding, as if he needed this arrogant young man to tell him that his daughter was a good walker.

Robs, indeed!

'Then we got back to work,' Guzman continued, 'and no one realised that she hadn't returned until about six.'

'Isn't that odd?' Janey said. She glanced over at the small group of people who had now gathered at a respectful distance, watching with unconcealed interest and murmured speculation. 'You're not exactly a crowd, are you?'

'We're spread out,' Clements explained, 'working in ones and twos. Some on the summit, some down below. Everyone thought she was with someone else.'

'So you went to look for her when you finally realised she was missing?'

'Naturally, but there was no sign. Simon drove back to our hotel in Castres to see if she'd gone there but they hadn't seen her since breakfast. We formed a search party, spent something like two hours looking for

43

her. Then it was getting dark and we called the local police. When she hadn't turned up at the hotel by midnight,' he turned to Malcolm, 'I decided I must ring you.'

'And this overnight bag,' Janey said. 'Where was that?'

'At the hotel, naturally.' Guzman was looking at Janey with something like dislike. 'In . . . *her* room.'

'So she must have gone back there to collect it if she decided to take a few days off.'

'I suppose so.'

'But you said she hadn't been back there.'

'I said no one had *seen* her,' Clements objected. 'Which doesn't mean she wasn't there briefly. There's no one much about in the afternoons.'

'How far is it to Castres? Five, six, miles?'

'Eight, I should say.'

'How would she get back there? You would know if any of your vehicles were missing?' She pointed. 'Don't you come out here together in that minibus?'

'Yes.' Clements licked his lips. 'Except for Simon who brings his own car.' He indicated the sports car. 'She might have hitchhiked,' he suggested feebly.

'And you've come back to work today, as normal?'

44

'There seemed nothing else we could usefully do.'

'You could have driven around a bit, made enquiries.'

'With respect, Miss Silverman,' Dr Guzman said, 'that would have been an absurd waste of time. We got back to work, not because we think it's more important than Robyn's disappearance, but because it kept us occupied and stopped us from brooding too much.'

His tired, dark eyes were full of reproach and, perhaps, something like pain. Janey looked at him for a moment, understanding.

She glanced at her watch. 'It's getting late,' she said, 'and getting dark. We'll follow you back to your hotel and see if we can get rooms for the night and you can tell us the rest there.'

'It'll take us a few minutes more to pack up,' the professor told her.

'I'll go ahead,' Guzman volunteered, 'and you can follow me.' He looked with contempt at her car. 'I'll drive slowly.'

★ ★ ★

'I wouldn't like to be given the third degree by you,' Malcolm hissed as they got back into the Reliant. 'Do you have to talk to

45

them as if they personally were to blame for her disappearance? The idea is that they're on our side . . . *My* side. *Our* side. Mine and Robyn's.'

'Well, what a pair of useless wankers. The story's so full of holes you could sift rocks with it. They're both scared shitless that it's their fault she's missing and indulging in a massive dose of wishful thinking that she's gone to whoop it up at the seaside for a day or two.'

Malcolm cleared his throat. 'I didn't take to that Simon,' he ventured. 'You don't think he and Robyn were having a . . . a relationship?' He looked at her intently, willing her to say No, she didn't think so, not at all. Impossible. Unthinkable. Ludicrous. How could you ask?

Robs.

'Almost certainly,' she said instead. 'I suspect we'll find back at the hotel that they were sharing a room.'

'Oh.'

'Which makes it doubly unlikely that she would take off without a word.'

'Unless they'd had a row,' he hoped.

'Mmm. Possible. But I think he'd have said, given the ruckus. There has to be some limit, even to the male ego. Even for men like him.'

Janey hadn't taken to him either.

'Oh God!' Malcolm buried his face in his hands.

'She's twenty-four,' Janey reminded him. 'You didn't think she was still saving it, did you, Malcolm?'

He wasn't used to young women who talked as straight as Janey, and who called people 'wanker' so often. 'Well not squandering it on men like him, at least,' he said bravely. 'He must be twenty years older than she is.' He added a good five years to Guzman's age, out of spite.

'Don't worry,' Janey said. 'He's one of those people who think they're special, but aren't; they waste their whole lives waiting for someone to notice their specialness, and they grow cynical. At the moment Robyn thinks he's the height of world-weary sophistication, but she'll soon see through him. You'll see.'

They fell silent, remembering that it might be too late for that. 'How do you come to have such an old head on such young shoulders?' Malcolm asked eventually.

'Dysfunctional parents.'

'Eh?'

'Never mind.'

★ ★ ★

47

Castres was a larger town than Janey had been expecting and she stuck close to Guzman's MG as they negotiated the town centre while night fell, finally following him to an ancient town house hidden down a side street. There was nothing to indicate that it was a hotel. There was a small car park and Janey tidied her car into a corner and switched off the engine.

Malcolm laid a hand on her arm to stop her as she made to get out. 'Thank you for your help, Miss Silverman,' he said. 'I can manage now. Professor Clements can give me transport and someone to interpret for me.'

'Malcolm,' she said, looking him straight in the eye. 'There is no way you can stop me staying at this hotel tonight if I choose to. It is, as they say, a free country.'

'I've dragged you all this way,' he protested. 'You haven't got any luggage.'

'Wrong!' she said in triumph. 'I told you I was on my way to Lourdes and Spain, remember. I have my case in the boot, next to yours.' Without further argument, she got out, removed both cases and entered the hotel through a small back door where she'd seen Guzman disappear a moment before. Malcolm scurried after her, not wanting a woman to carry his case but unable to catch her up long enough to wrest it from her. In the doorway she paused and he cannoned into her. 'Anyway, how would you know they were translating truthfully?'

She was right, he thought: she, a complete stranger, was the only person in this wretched country he could trust.

The door led through a winding and dimly-lit corridor to a small reception area where Dr Guzman was engaging a black-garbed, middle-aged woman in conversation, his French proficient, if lacking in some of the finer points of grammar. The woman was leafing through a book, nodding her head with its tight black bun, and saying that there were two single rooms to spare.

'That's great,' Janey said, not giving Guzman the opportunity to lie to them and say the hotel was full. She called over her shoulder. 'She's got rooms for us, Malcolm.'

'Oh . . . good.'

'I warn you, it's not the Ritz,' Simon said, confident that the old woman didn't understand him.

'If it's good enough for you, I dare say it'll be good enough for us,' Janey replied.

She spoke to the woman, who identified herself as Madame Monami, the owner, secured the rooms and filled in the necessary forms in a matter of minutes. Malcolm reluctantly surrendered his new passport. The minibus arrived in the meantime and the rest of the archaeologists silently claimed their keys and disappeared upstairs. Malcolm watched them almost dispassionately as they avoided his eye or gave him thin smiles of curiosity or pity.

A ruddy-faced man in his forties simply leaned over the counter and helped himself to his key, turning away without looking to left or right, speaking to no one. He brushed past a grey-haired woman who seemed too old for work and she moved courteously out of his way. A boy of perhaps twenty-two hung his head as he shuffled past. The professor sucked briefly on his keys as he hesitated, wanting perhaps to say something, before deciding to leave it to Simon.

Only a blonde woman, the younger of the two remaining female members of the dig, paused. She didn't speak but laid her hand briefly on Simon's shoulder, her supple fingers applying light pressure. His hand touched hers in acknowledgement and then released it. Unspoken support — even affection — had been offered and accepted.

Madame Monami called something into an inner room from which the sound of a television — some sporting event — erupted loudly. The noise of cheering and shouting was abruptly quenched and after a few seconds a young man came to the open door and looked questioningly at the black window. He was in his late teens, Janey guessed, but tall and sturdily built with pronounced features, heavy black eyebrows that almost met and a down-turned mouth. A check lumberjack shirt hung unbuttoned over shabby blue jeans; every visible part of his torso was covered with thick, curly, black hair.

'My son Joachim,' she explained. She said something to him under her breath and he did up a few buttons of the shirt with one hand. 'He will show you the way.' She pointed at the newcomers' suitcases and spoke slowly and clearly to the boy. 'Rooms six and seven, Joachim. Understand?'

The boy nodded and turned silently up the stairs, not looking to see if they were following.

'Which was Robyn's room?' Janey asked Simon.

He reddened and looked away, not meeting Malcolm's eye, folding his arms defensively across his chest. 'We're on the first floor at the front. Room two. Just across the landing from you, next to the bathroom.'

Malcolm's mouth tightened.

'Then we'll meet you there in ten minutes,' Janey said coolly, picking up her key and Malcolm's. 'Come along, Malcolm.'

They scurried after the sullen boy.

★ ★ ★

The chambermaid had closed the shutters of room two in the course of her morning cleaning, as was usual in France, and the double room at the front smelt humid and stale as Janey entered it after her soft tap on the door went unanswered. She crossed to the window and pushed it and the shutters open, filling the room with clean night air and allowing a shaft of moonlight to penetrate. 'Dr Guzman?'

'I'm here, Miss Silverman.'

'Jesus! Why were you sitting there in the dark?'

'Because,' Guzman said, 'I feel like a house that's been broken and entered, or perhaps a village that's been looted and pillaged, and I needed a moment alone in the dark and peace.'

Janey switched on the bedside lamp, throwing yellow light over the capacious double bed with its blue patchwork quilt and bolster pillow, its heavy wooden surround.

The mattress was an old one, the sag in the middle clearly visible, but it looked comfortable and intimate, the resting place of a couple long and successfully joined.

The Oustal Monami was an old-fashioned sort of hotel, the owners having felt no need to spoil the dimensions of their rooms by carving stifling, windowless shower cubicles into the corners. There were no TVs tuned to Sky One via rooftop satellite, no telephone on the desk.

Guzman sat on the bed holding a white cotton nightdress on his lap. He looked middle-aged and worn and not handsome at all. He gave her a weak smile. 'What a powerful personality you have, Miss Silverman. So exhausting.'

'Not for me. That's hers, I take it.'

'Well, it isn't mine.' He got up, folded the nightgown with care and smoothed it beneath the pillow on the side nearest the window. 'Whatever you may think of me, Miss Silverman, I care very much about Robyn. She's . . . she's the best thing that ever happened to me.'

'Oh, I can believe that!'

He said quietly, 'If anything bad has become of her, I shall go crazy.'

'Then that makes two of us!'

Malcolm stood in the doorway, his arrival

unnoticed by either of them. The two men looked at each other and a silent if uneasy truce was called. Hostilities could be resumed when Robyn was found safe and well.

'Three,' Janey said firmly. 'Who care about her, I mean. I'm not going crazy for anybody. This was her side of the bed, I take it?' Guzman merely nodded. She examined the bedside table: a box of tissues, a glass of water now warm and scummy, a paperback book — a racing thriller. She jerked open the drawer and held up a foil bubble pack. 'She wouldn't have gone away for a few days without these, would she, Simon?'

He looked startled. 'No. I suppose not. I hadn't thought to look . . .'

'What are they?' Malcolm asked.

'Contraceptive pills.'

'Oh . . . Mightn't she have a spare packet?'

Janey shook her head. 'You use the same one to keep track.' She read the days in black letters on the foil. 'Sunday is the last one she took and today is Tuesday. Yesterday she went missing, ostensibly taking her overnight bag and toiletries with her, but without her pills. I think not.'

'The bag is gone, though,' Guzman said, 'there's no doubt of that, and her toothbrush and flannel, everything from the sink.' He nodded at the corner where there was a white

54

porcelain washbasin scattered with his toilet things.

'What time was it when you got back to the hotel last night?'

'I drove back here at about six-thirty after we discovered she was missing, but I checked with Madame Monami downstairs that she hadn't seen her and glanced in here to make sure she wasn't asleep, or ill or something. I went straight back to the dig then and it was ten by the time we got back here again.'

'Did you notice if any of her things were on the sink at six-thirty?'

Guzman covered his eyes with his hand, trying to remember. Finally he shrugged. 'I can't say. Sorry.'

'But by ten, her bag was gone.'

'I realised that only later, after James had rung you.' He nodded to Malcolm. 'Only this morning, in fact. I couldn't think that she would wander off without saying anything to me, you see, so it didn't occur to me to look.'

'You hadn't had some sort of row?' Malcolm asked.

'Not at all. I swear. Robs is . . . unargumentative.'

Malcolm nodded.

'You mean she does what you tell her,' Janey said.

'I didn't say that!'

'Oh, no,' Malcolm said to both their surprise, 'not my Robyn. She's never been one for doing as she's told.'

'What was she wearing,' Janey asked, 'the last time you saw her?'

'Let me think. Those brown suede jeans she was so thrilled with, the ones she bought in Toulouse a couple of months ago. I told her they were too good for the dig, considering what they cost, but she wouldn't be parted from them.'

Malcolm nodded. 'She mentioned them in her letters — which is more than she did about you, I might add. What else?'

'A white shirt, cotton — soft, thin, cool cotton — long sleeves, granddad-style neck. She had a jerkin, too, though I think she might have taken that off during lunch, a sleeveless tunic thing in black velvet, black suede ankle boots, the sort you pull on. That's all.'

'It's time to call in the police again,' Malcolm said with a sigh. 'It's been over a day now. We must make them take notice.'

'They'll ask the same questions we've been asking,' Janey objected. 'And ask them more slowly. Then they'll file some tedious report and keep us hanging around making statements. You've no idea what French

56

bureaucracy is like, Malcolm.'

'Then what do you suggest?' Guzman asked.

'Let's go and get some dinner, and talk some more,' Janey said. 'I'm starving.'

'May I come with you?' They turned to see Professor Clements standing in the doorway. He moved quietly, Janey thought, for such a large man. 'We need to talk,' he continued. 'Perhaps between us, we can thrash out what has happened to Robyn.'

2

'La nueg ven, pois lo jorn renais
E no s'pot meillora mon dol,
Car es de mon cor lo trandol
Tal que no pot tornar gais.'

Dias de Muret

'Father Hugues is the best man I have ever met — not merely priest but friend, counsellor, a literal father. The people of Montprimeur are truly blessed in his presence. In better times he and I would walk in the countryside and discuss the great questions of life, often for hours at a time. He was a welcome guest in our home, when he could be spared from his duties.'

Diaries of Louise d'Ambriers, Scholar and Matriarch

Ed/Trans Arpaïs de Chambertin
Editions du Languedoc, Toulouse 1898.

Robyn had never been so uncomfortable. Not only did her head hurt as though someone had pounded a rock into it with enthusiasm, but this was the hardest bed she'd ever lain on, harder than the floors of university friends, harder by far than the college lawn where she'd once dozed off under a tree. She moved a finger of her right hand carefully over the surface beneath her and winced as she felt a splinter nudge into it. Rough wood and — what was this on top of it? — a few scraps of scratchy straw wrapped in a rough material like sacking.

She lay on her back, her eyes closed, becoming aware of the background of voices, tuning her mind into them as she would tune into a channel on her radio, seeking out the elusive World Service last thing at night against a cacophony of intervening stations. There were two people in the room, or two who were speaking; one voice was certainly gruffly male and the other, while much higher and lighter, was also, she quickly concluded, that of a man, the elder, or at least the more important of the two, since the gruff man spoke to him with a certain humouring deference.

At first she thought they were speaking Spanish, a language of which she knew enough to understand and make herself understood; then that it was French with the local accent more exaggerated than usual. Then she knew that it was Occitan, the old *Langue d'Oc*, crushed and bullied almost out of existence, reduced to the status of a dialect by French, the only language recognised by the state.

'He's clearly been attacked and robbed,' the senior man was saying. 'You have only to look in his purse.'

Who had? Robyn half opened one eye. The room was dark although it was full daylight outside as she could see through an open door. Such light as there was came from a blazing fire that rendered the room uncomfortably hot. She could just make out that one of the men was swinging her leather belt-bag from his hand.

'Nothing,' the speaker went on, 'but some useless, if gaudy, bits of parchment.' He pulled a roll of hundred-franc notes from the purse and tossed them to one side on a trestle table.

'There are coins too,' the rougher man said. 'Gold coins. No cut-purse worth his salt would leave those.'

The first man raised a ten franc coin to his mouth and bit into it. 'Base metal,' he said in disgust. 'Far too hard for gold. Worthless medallions, if curiously well crafted.'

He walked over to the door and held the coin up to the light, turning it as he read the words around the brim. ' '*Fraternité-Liberté-Egalité*.' ' He palmed it again to read the front. ' '*République Française — respublica —* ' Latin — the business of the people. There was such a concept in ancient times when the Romans disposed of their kings and replaced them with elected officials.'

'Did they? Good luck to them. What a lot you know, Hugues, and all of it useless.'

'Thank you, my friend. This is in the *Langue d'Oïl*. Some sort of motto? A device from a coat of arms? But they are usually in Latin. I haven't heard it before. Have you?'

The other man didn't bother to answer but said, 'Could he be a forger? Sent to disseminate false coin among us and undermine our economy?'

Robyn could make out the gist of this conversation or thought she could, although what she understood made little sense. She'd studied the language to read documents, the primary sources the importance of which James Clements was forever urging on her.

She'd heard it once also in a bar in Toulouse where bearded young men warbled songs of love and loss to the strumming of an acoustic guitar. She'd persuaded Simon to take her there and he'd laughed all the way through. He'd made her feel young and unsophisticated but she'd stood her ground and wouldn't let him leave.

61

'I never heard anything so ersatz in my life,' he'd said afterwards. 'If a troubadour came to my castle singing that rubbish, I'd have him whipped and thrown out into the snow.' But to Robyn it had been almost unbearably poignant: a language steeped in sadness and mourning, all that was left of a culture — a civilisation — crushed into splinters eight hundred years ago.

Splinters: she raised her right forefinger to her mouth and gripped the protruding sliver carefully with her teeth, pulling. It came free, leaving a smarting red hole. She spat it out discreetly, away onto the floor.

'Our guest is stirring!' the gruffer of the two voices exclaimed. 'Perhaps now we shall have an answer to our questions.'

She heard the rustling of loose garments and a creaking as someone sat on the rough pallet beside her and laid a hand as kindly as a mother's to her hot forehead. She opened her eyes again, squinting into the darkness, wondering why no one would put on the light. A face was close to her own. It was a bony face, yellow in the firelight, with the hollowed cheeks of a starving man. This was the strangest hospital she'd ever known, this the oddest doctor. 'How are you feeling, my son?' the face asked.

As her eyes grew accustomed to the

greyness, she saw that he was a short man and slight of build. His concerned face was sallow, with a scrap of fair beard — as if he hadn't the strength to manage more — growing wispily round the edge of his chin, leaving a bald spot in the middle under his thin-lipped mouth. He wore a black woollen robe belted at the waist with leather from which hung scraps of parchment. She thought he must be hot in the stifling heat from the fire. He smelled of sweat long-dried into unwashed garments. He was bare-headed, the hood of his robe thrown back, and his limp brown hair grew unkempt in all directions, a fringe floppy over hazel eyes.

She didn't answer him. She didn't dare to ask the age-old question — Where am I?; wasn't sure she wanted to know. She wanted to laugh instead, and rub her sore head and say 'Hey, guys, that must have been quite a party! Did you boys think it was fancy dress?'

'That was a bad blow he took on the back of the head, Hugues,' the other man said in a more kindly tone than before. He leaned over her in his turn and she moved her head aside to mitigate the blast of his breath through sparse and tawny teeth as his tangle of black hair tickled her cheek.

'He's a young nobleman, to be sure,' the man went on. 'You have only to look at his clothes.' A rough hand fingered her suede jeans above the knee where the material was loser. 'See the soft buckskin of his hose, the unnatural evenness of the stitching, the white lawn of his shirt. I never saw anything so fine.'

The priest nodded. 'And look at his face, Bruno, his smooth, beardless face. That's a face that has known neither famine nor fear.'

'If he's known no fear,' Bruno replied with a growl, 'then he's a fool.'

If she'd never known fear, Robyn thought, she was making up for it now. Could this really be happening? Had fate actually spun her back in time? It was at the same time both terrifying and exhilarating.

'They didn't take his ring,' Bruno said, pointing. 'The silver ring on his finger. Strange sort of robber to leave a valuable object like that.'

'Perhaps they were disturbed,' the priest said, 'or couldn't get it off.'

Bruno spat into the fireplace, making it hiss. 'Then they'd have cut his finger off!'

Robyn slid her left hand automatically over the right, shielding the silver ring Simon had bought her in a back street in Albi a few weeks ago. She hadn't liked to put it on her ring finger in case that seemed presumptuous, so wore it on the corresponding finger of her right hand.

'It's all right,' the older man said, 'we won't steal your ring, my son. Pass me his belt, Bruno. Let us give him back his purse before he takes *us* for footpads.'

Bruno complied, dropping the bag at her side, then spoke slowly, enunciating every word as if he thought her slow-witted. 'Can you understand me, boy? Do — you — speak — our — language?'

She found her voice, not answering him but turning to the priest, half sitting up in her eagerness, speaking in French, her curiosity overcoming her fear. 'You are Hugues? Father Hugues of Montprimeur?' He wasn't as she'd pictured him in her simplicity, confused by his name: Father Huge.

'A northerner,' Bruno said. 'A Frenchman, as I thought.'

As her eyes grew accustomed to the dark, she could see that the man Bruno was a peasant in his dress as in his voice. He stood six feet tall and sturdily built, his beard bushily dark about thick red lips, topped by a large nose and heavy-lidded black eyes. He wore stout boots on his big feet — good boots as befitted a cobbler — loose hose and an undyed shirt in coarse linen topped with a none-too-clean green tunic belted low on the hips. Robyn could make out his own leather purse hanging from the belt and, placed carefully for his right hand, a knife.

'His dialect is strange to me,' Hugues mused. 'I travelled a great deal in the kingdom of France in my youth, as you know, but this accent — where are you from, lad?'

'Britain.'

'Brittany?'

' . . . England.'

She couldn't say Ireland, which Hugues would know, if at all, as a wild barbarian land — Hibernia — where warriors rode bareback and half naked, armed only with axes long as quarterstaffs. A land where they killed strangers first and asked questions later.

'Ah!' Hugues looked pleased.

'What's he saying?' Bruno asked impatiently.

Hugues explained. 'King John's man, Bruno. I've never been in England. That explains the strangeness of his speech. I am Hugues,' he answered her at last. 'Why? Have you a message for me?'

'A message. I . . . no.' She sank back. 'No.'

Yes. Leave this place. Now. While you still can.

'What's your name, son?'

'Rob . . . Robert,' she said. 'Robert of Durham.'

'Where's that?' the man called Bruno asked the priest.

Hugues shrugged. 'Somewhere in England, obviously.'

'De Montfort is an Englishman — the Earl of Le-cesseterre.' He mispronounced the words with a sneer.

'Perhaps,' Hugues said. 'Common sense calls him a Frenchman.'

'I told you. The boy is a spy.'

'King John is no friend to Pope Innocent,' Hugues pointed out, 'not with England under papal interdict these five years or more.'

'Which makes John of Anjou the more anxious to regain the Pope's favour by supporting the crusade,' Bruno insisted. 'We should get rid of him, fast. Throw him off the northern cliffs and let the vultures have him.'

'Enough.' Hugues held up his hand to silence his friend. 'Those are the ways of de Montfort and his murdering mercenaries. It's not our way.'

'We must fight fire with fire,' Bruno said. 'An eye for an eye and a tooth for a tooth.

67

That's what my father always said.'

Hugues's voice was patience itself. 'Those old scriptures are the work of the devil, Bruno, you know that. It's only in God's gospel, the testaments of the evangelists, that we find truth.'

'It's all right for you. You may long for death to release you from the body and into the world of the spirit, but I still have a lot of living to do.'

Father Hugues smiled at him, shaking his head indulgently before turning back to Robyn. 'Don't be afraid, Robert,' he said. 'Bruno may bluster, but to us Christians life is sacred.'

'You are Cathars?'

'Yes. Christians, we call ourselves.'

She pulled herself up again. It was so hot, the sweat on her body like an extra shirt. Medieval homes, she knew, kept the fire going day and night, summer and winter, to heat their water and cook their food and she wondered how they could bear it. She felt for the back of her head. Her hair was damp, sticky as hair gel, tender.

'What happened?'

'We were hoping you would tell us.'

'I can't remember anything.' Nothing since getting up that morning — or *a* morning — and breakfasting with Simon in the hotel courtyard as usual: coffee and rolls with the inevitable apricot jam. The ride to the dig in Simon's car? Perhaps, dimly, although the memory might belong to any one of a hundred days. Then nothing.

'You were found staggering along the street by the market square shortly after dawn this morning,' Hugues said, 'then you collapsed unconscious. At first the householder who found you thought you were drunk, but then he saw the wound on your head and brought you to me and I sent for Bruno.'

'It's strange that no one remembers seeing him come in at the gate,' Bruno said.

'They're not as vigilant as they might be,' Hugues replied.

'Especially first thing in the morning, to talk of people being drunk!'

Hugues continued with the story. 'Bruno and I went down as far as the river bank to see if we could find your horse but there was no sign of it.'

'My horse,' she repeated stupidly. 'Yes, of course. My horse.'

'It must have been taken by the footpads who robbed you.'

'Footpads?'

'What else could it have been since your sword is also gone, along with your travelling cloak. And everything of value is missing from your purse, I'm afraid.'

'Where were you headed?' Bruno asked. 'Where had you come from?'

'I . . . I don't remember.'

'You ask too many questions,' the priest chided his friend.

'It's not much to ask a traveller!'

'This is Montprimeur?' She wanted it confirmed as if there was doubt.

The priest nodded. 'Was your business here? With us? Or at the Château d'Ambriers, perhaps, with the Comte or the Lady Louise?'

'I don't remember. How long have I been unconscious?'

'It's a few hours since we found you. I suppose you were attacked some time in the night.'

'What day is it?'

'Saturday.'

'But what date, what month? What year?'

'You have got a bad head. I told you, you've been out only a few hours. It's still the beginning of May. Today is the feast of St Philip and St James, although the people seem more inclined to celebrate the pagan rites of May Day. The year 1211.'

Montprimeur, 1 May 1211. A matter of days before the massacre, and she, Robyn, somehow, right in the middle of it. Her brain, unable to cope with this thought, took refuge in unconsciousness once more.

* * *

'We're on the same side,' Simon pointed out as they slid into a booth at a restaurant not five minutes walk from the hotel. 'We want Robyn found safe and well. Please stop treating me like the enemy, Miss Silverman.'

'Janey,' she conceded. She found herself sitting opposite the professor with Malcolm on her outside, face to face with Simon. The booth was a tight squeeze for four and she was aware of Malcolm's tense bewilderment beside her.

'This meal is on me, by the way,' Professor Clements said, in his quiet-spoken way.

Malcolm opened his mouth to protest that he'd pay his own way but the offer had been made as a simple statement of fact and Janey had already acquiesced with a smile. It wasn't as if he had much cash to spare. On the one hand he had unlimited travelling expenses to pay and, on the other, only five hundred pounds and an open return ticket to Belfast. It wasn't much of a contest. The waitress came promptly and the professor ordered cassoulet for them all, although Janey would have settled for something more familiar and less challenging for Malcolm.

Sitting directly opposite the professor, she was able to look him over without being too obvious about it. If she'd passed him on the street she might have taken him for a politician, she thought, or the more hearty sort of bank manager, or even a well-to-do farmer; not an academic, anyway. He didn't wear glasses and she had a clear view of his brown eyes with their sparse lashes. His nose was prominent, straight but long, winged by two deep furrows curving down to the corners of his mouth. His lips were full and sensual and he opened them now to speak.

'She's such a *sensible* young woman,' he said, distantly, as if discussing an abstract concept. 'So throughly mature. I can't believe that anything untoward has happened to her, that she would *let* anything . . . ' He looked hard at his hands spread out on the table before him. They were big hands, Janey noticed, bare and powerful, with wizened great knuckles that no ring, surely, could ever slip over. 'I was swamped with people wanting to come on this dig,' he explained to the hands. 'I wasn't going to consider Robyn, with her being so young and inexperienced, but her references were so glowing, both academic and personal, that I decided at least to talk to her, maybe give her a bit of encouragement.'

'I remember how excited she was to get an interview,' Malcolm said.

'I was so impressed with her, her skills, her enthusiasm, her ease of manner, her sense of humour, her confidence and maturity, that I found myself offering her a job on the spot. Young people today . . . most of my students are lazy and slapdash, lacking in commitment. Robyn was special. She was like . . . ' He looked up at last and Malcolm thought for a moment he was going to say 'like a daughter to me', but he didn't. 'Like a breath of fresh air,' he concluded, without much originality.

'Have you got children?' Malcolm asked this man who was of his own generation and ought, therefore, to have something in common with him.

As if the answer should be obvious Professor Clements said, 'Me? No. I've never married.'

Janey wasn't surprised by his reply. She'd met plenty of his type at Oxford: men — occasionally women — who were simply, naively, baffled that anyone thought anything more important than sterile academic study. James Clements was clearly not gay — his presence across the table from her over-whelmingly masculine — but work was wife

73

and mistress and child to him. Working class, she thought, brilliant grammar school boy from some northern industrial town, a complete mystery to his long-suffering parents. She was sure that it had been decades since anyone had called him Jim.

The people who mattered most in the world to James were people who had lived centuries ago, who'd been born, worked, suffered, loved, laughed and died unrecorded by history, whose names he didn't know. The exact layout of a medieval hovel, a few shards of crude pottery, fragments of rotten clothing accidentally preserved in limey soil: these were his excitement, his passion, his reality.

It was a simple life in many ways and, although Clements was clearly worried about his young colleague, he gave off the overall aura of a man with few cares, drifting through life unencumbered by baggage.

The waitress arrived and he jerked back, folding his hands into his lap to make room for the steaming plates. 'Some wine, I think,' he said. 'Quite a lot of wine, perhaps. *Deux bouteilles du vin rouge de la maison, s'il vous plaît, madame.*'

His French was fluent enough but his accent comically English. The woman understood, however, and said briskly, '*Très bien.*'

She went off to fulfil his order, returning two minutes later to deposit two open and unlabelled bottles on the unpolished table top. Clements poured wine for everyone without asking them, then sipped steadily at his own glass throughout the meal.

'What on earth is this?' Malcolm asked, stirring his cassoulet with his fork in wonderment. He'd thought French food to be smooth, clever sauces; this stuff made Irish stew look sophisticated.

'It's cassoulet,' Simon said. 'A local speciality.'

'It's pork with fat goose,' Janey elucidated as Malcolm continued to look bemused. 'Garlic sausage, haricot beans, vegetables, stock. It takes a bit of getting used to, but it's okay.'

'And what is *this* with it?'

'Sauerkraut,' Simon said, with an apologetic note in his voice.

Malcolm shrugged and ate some. Janey was right: it tasted okay. Professor Clements had cleared half his plate.

'Has Robyn been behaving unusual lately?' Janey asked as they ate. Malcolm helped himself to a lump of baguette from the basket and chewed on that, finding it a little spongy. He was tired to the bone and willing for the moment to let Janey do the talking.

Simon shook his head. 'She was mad keen, keenest of all of us. But then,' he smiled indulgently, 'this was her first time. I guess we all feel like that on our first dig.' Clements grunted assent. 'She was doing a lot of background reading in her spare time,' Simon went on, 'social history and so on. Come to think of it she'd been a bit . . . excited this last couple of days, like she'd got a secret, but then she wasn't the most open of people at the best of times. Well, you'd know that.'

'No,' Janey said, 'I never met her.'

Simon said in surprise, 'Oh.'

She wished she'd said '*I've* never met her' but Malcolm didn't seem to notice the slip of tense. 'She was a totally honest and candid child,' he said frostily.

'She wrote to you often, didn't she, Mr Dawson? She was always going off, saying 'Time for the letter home'. Not that it was a chore,' he added hastily. 'She enjoyed it.'

'Every week, more or less.'

'But she didn't tell you about me — you said as much earlier.'

' . . . No. Not a word.'

'You see.'

Malcolm frowned. 'If she had a secret, it wouldn't have been anything sinister.'

'I didn't say it was,' Simon protested.

'People have all sorts of secrets, if only what they're getting you for Christmas.'

'If she's met with an accident — ' Malcolm began.

'Whoa!' Janey Silverman spat out a mouthful of pork in her hurry to interrupt him. 'Let's forget about accidents, shall we? Or are we assuming that Robyn's bag packed itself and took itself off for a fortnight on the Costa del Sol?'

'Shit!' Simon said. ' . . . But any alternative is absurd. Everybody liked — *likes* — Robyn.'

'Does anyone have access to the dig?' Janey asked. 'Other than your people?'

'The site has been deserted for more than seven hundred years,' Professor Clements said. 'It has a reputation for being haunted, in fact. Not, obviously, that I believe in that sort of thing. It's off the beaten track, as you've seen, and it's also private land which has belonged to the Ministry of Defence since the last war. For years they used it for manoeuvres, or whatever it is these soldier types do.'

'It's only since the Cold War ended and the Berlin Wall came down that they've no further use for it,' Simon explained.

James nodded. 'We have permission to be there and no one else, which was why Simon asked you to leave when you turned up all of a sudden, before we realised who you were, of course. The Ministry were firm about that. Quite adamant.'

'We saw some school children as we turned off the main road,' Malcolm said.

'Children from St Paul, I expect, but they don't come inside the perimeter fence. Besides, why would they want to hurt Robyn?'

It was the first time anyone had used the word *hurt* in this context. Malcolm pushed his plate away unfinished and gulped some wine from his glass, although he didn't usually drink wine and thought that he didn't like red. Professor Clements reverted to the study of his hands.

Janey and Simon exchanged glances. Allegiances were shifting. From a position of mutual distrust, they were now joining forces to protect the older man, the bereft father. Malcolm, aware of the silence, made a valiant effort to pull himself together. He didn't want their pity, and he didn't want his own. That couldn't be why he'd come. 'I don't get what it was you were excavating,' he said, 'although Robyn tried to explain it to me in her letters.'

'Montprimeur was a Cathar stronghold in the twelfth and early thirteenth centuries,' Simon said. 'There weren't many this far north and the crusaders left them alone until 1211 when they arrived at the beginning of May and besieged the town.' Once the concept of a siege would have seemed alien to Malcolm, but now he remembered television news reports of the war in Bosnia, of the wholesale brutalisation of towns where, a few years earlier, tourists had stood and marvelled at their beauty. It seemed that nothing changed. 'In principle,' Simon went on, 'the townspeople should have been able to withstand a siege easily. As you saw, the northern, eastern and western faces of the hill are unscaleable and the south face, where the zigzag cart track is, would have been easily defended by a few archers on the watchtower over the gate. Also, the hill is too high for the siege machine to have been used with any precision.'

'Siege machine?' Malcolm queried, baffled.

'This was in the days before cannon, of course. Trebuchets, mostly, like a huge catapult, hurling boulders at the walls and watchtowers to break through the defences. Boulders weighing more than a hundred pounds, I might add. And then there were ballistas which were giant crossbows wound back with winches to fire long bolts into the town, or flaming brands.'

'Crude,' Janey said.

'Unsophisticated, maybe, but very effective as a rule.'

'But not at Montprimeur?'

'As I say, the angle was too steep, the distance too great. They would have had to fire almost straight up into the air and then it was just as likely that their boulder would fall back down on them. Or land halfway up the hill and *roll* back down on them.'

'Serve them right!'

'The townspeople had fair warning that de Montfort was on his way and knew what he was capable of in the way of cruelty and murder, so they laid in enough stores to last at least three months.'

'Would a siege of three months have presented any real problem to de Montfort, though?' Janey asked.

'Most certainly!' Professor Clements broke in. 'He had his previous conquests to defend, and a lot of his knights were doing feudal duty lasting four to six weeks at most and would pack up and go home after that. He'd just spent two whole months laying siege to Lavaur and the fall of that town would have been the obvious time for mass defections, even among the mercenaries.'

'They did their big pushes forward in the spring,' Simon added. 'De Montfort lost half the towns and castles he'd taken again each winter. Two steps forward, one back.'

'Which gets you there eventually,' Janey pointed out.

'And perhaps we should remember,' Simon continued, 'that the locals also committed the most appalling atrocities when they took back lands and castles in their turn.'

'More understandable, though,' Janey said. 'I mean, if you're just taking reprisals — '

'But then there's no end to it,' Malcolm butted in. 'Each side taking revenge in its turn — that way it goes on forever.' He blushed slightly, not used to interrupting, to having everyone listen to him, but Janey turned to him and nodded thoughtful agreement, which emboldened him. 'There has to come a time,' he concluded, 'when somebody has the courage to say, enough. To forgive and move forward.'

'It was all-out assault with a view to a quick surrender,' Professor Clements said, 'but, and this is the point — the great unsolved mystery of Montprimeur — the town collapsed with hardly an arrow being exchanged.'

'How come?' Janey asked.

It was Simon who answered her. 'The crusaders came up a secret path on the western slope and poured in through a small gate at the back on the first night. They put the whole town to the sword — man, woman and child, Cathar and Catholic — except for the ones they dragged out to burn alive as a terrible warning to all heretics. Then they torched the town more or less to the ground.'

'They were betrayed!' Janey exclaimed. 'By someone inside the town.'

'It would seem so. As James said, the local people have concluded ever since that the hill has a curse on it and never attempted to rebuild the stronghold. What with that and the military annexation, it's remained one of the most unspoilt sites in the region and a goldmine for archaeologists for that reason.'

'I spent years getting access,' James told them, 'filling in forms, locking horns with the sort of staggering bureaucracy that only the French know how to devise. There's work there to keep us occupied for many years, perhaps the rest of our lives. As yet, we can't conjecture as to the location of the secret path, or where it entered the town.' He mused. 'Fascinating people.'

'Narrow, superstitious peasants.' Janey had no time for the school of thought that said that life was simpler, more *real* in the Middle Ages, that the people were in touch with Nature and the land, with themselves.

But Clements was shaking his head. 'They

were not narrow. It's true that they couldn't jump into a jet aircraft and be in Australia twenty hours later, or spend hours every night squinting at a cathode-ray tube and calling it leisure, but itinerant shepherds travelled hundreds of miles with their flocks each year, bringing the news, the gossip — the latest fashions, even. Merchants covered most of the south-west in their mule trains, huddled together on dirt roads for fear of footpads, it's true, but venturing as far north as Scandinavia.'

Malcolm listened tiredly. He didn't like the pink-fleshed melon he was now eating; to him it smelt of putrescence.

'They traded all over the Mediterranean,' the professor said, 'even into North Africa. They were a civilised and tolerant people, far ahead of their neighbours when it came to art and literature. And then there were the courts — the castles of the great nobles: Count Raymond of Toulouse, the Comtes of Foix and the Trencavals of Carcassonne — with their laughter and dancing, their painters, musicians, writers and singers, their jousts, beautiful women and brave knights.' He looked at Janey over the table, his face austere, handsome in its solemnity. 'One of the greatest civilisations of medieval Europe was destroyed in these lands in a few short years — crushed, and for what? Superstition and dogma. One pointless set of beliefs ranged against another, to the death.'

They ate in silence for a few minutes, then Malcolm said, 'I don't understand where these crusaders came from.'

Simon answered him. 'All over, but France mostly.'

'But this *is* France.' With unaccustomed wine in him Malcolm was starting to sound tetchy.

'It wasn't then,' Simon explained, like a patient lecturer. 'People think the modern boundaries of a country are somehow right and natural, that the south-west was just waiting to become part of France, instead of being a perfectly viable country in its own right. Okay, in theory the Count of Toulouse was the King of France's vassal, but that was more honoured in the breach than in the observance, since Paris was a long way away.'

'You must know, surely,' James cut in, 'that Germany and Italy, for example, weren't autonomous, unified countries until a hundred years ago.' His words were gentle — not a chiding of ignorance, but the good father imparting knowledge.

'Yes,' Malcolm admitted. 'I suppose they

did tell me that at school, come to think of it.'

'And now we see geographical areas we have long thought of as unified countries breaking up again. Czechoslovakia, for instance, the Soviet Union and, most painfully, Yugoslavia.'

'The Massif Central is every bit as impenetrable a natural border as the Pyrenees,' Simon added.

'More,' Janey put in. 'I had a job to get my car up some of the roads there last half-term. At least there are passes in the Pyrenees.'

'I'm surprised you can get your car up a molehill,' Simon said wryly.

★ ★ ★

'Jehane knows the properties of plants and herbs better than any town doctor who has studied at the university. She gives me an infusion of lemon balm and rosemary for my frequent headaches which does more good than any remedy I have tried in my life. She made a phial of lavender oil too, for me to rub into my temples if the pain persists.

Each month she cures my women's troubles with chamomile and fennel and when my father sprained his ankle she walked five miles to the castle to put a cold compress of witch-hazel and burdock on it with her own hands, trusting no one else to the task.

Strange, though, she seems to take no pleasure in her dosing of us but frowns at us throughout as if we alone were to blame for our ailments.

There must be a herb somewhere against ill-humour!'

Diaries of Louise d'Ambriers, Scholar and Matriarch.

ibid.

* * *

When Robyn came round again the light outside told her that it was evening, presumably of the same day. Her head was throbbing a little less but her throat felt dry and she realised she'd had nothing to drink for many hours. It was like when you sobbed a lot, until there were no sobs left, and something in your throat swelled until you could hardly breathe.

A woman was bending over her with curiosity but without anxiety. Robyn could see that she was about thirty-five, although slightly hunched, like an older woman, as if age might lend authority. She was bony in the way that comes from Nature and not from hunger, voluntary or otherwise. She wore a brown woollen tunic with long sleeves laced from wrist to elbow. A chemise was visible beneath it at the neck, cuffs and hem and she had loose-made leather shoes like moccasins.

Her grey-streaked brown hair was parted in the middle, plaited into two thick ropes and topped with a white linen wimple. A bunch of keys jangled at her belt. Her lips turned resolutely down as if she seldom smiled, wasn't sure how, and her pores, as she leaned close over Robyn, were open and not altogether clean. Nevertheless, she was a handsome woman and Robyn wondered why Louise d'Ambriers had never mentioned that fact.

'You must be Jehane,' she croaked. 'Bruno's wife.'

The woman looked startled and shrank back. 'Who told you that?'

She moved to cross herself, suspecting witchcraft, but the instinctive movement was halted before it began. Cathars didn't venerate the cross. All matter, including the human body, was the work of the devil. Christ had come to earth, the greatest of angels and prophets, with only the *appearance* of corporeality — a sort of hologram.

'I don't know. Nobody. I was guessing.'
The woman looked unconvinced. Robyn
took refuge in the sketchiness of her Occitan.
'I must did heard . . . when half asleep.'

Jehane frowned. She was holding a crude
pottery bowl with a small amount of clear
frothy liquid in it. 'Sit up!' she instructed,
unlacing her right sleeve and pushing it back
up her arm. Robyn obeyed and Jehane's
fingers sought the sore place at the back
of her head with unexpected delicacy. Then
she dipped her hand in the bowl and began
to smear the liquid in a thin layer on the
wound. It felt cold and sticky.

'Whatever is it?' Robyn asked, in some
alarm, imagining potions of evil herbs and
cow dung.

'It's only egg white, my young lord.'
She answered shortly as if she resented the
question. No doubt she liked to keep her
recipes to herself. 'Mostly,' she added.

'Egg white?' Surely she'd misunderstood.

'It will dry on the hurt place to stop further
bleeding,' the woman explained with grudge
in her voice. 'Then it will not go putrid.'

It could have been worse, Robyn thought:
it could have been a spider's web. It made
a certain sense: the forming of a membrane
over the gash to prevent infection. 'Thank
you,' she said. 'You're very kind.'

Jehane unbent a little at this courtesy, although Bruno had clearly conveyed to his wife his misgivings at this inopportune guest. 'Some swear by wine to clean a wound, but nothing beats egg white to my mind.' She got up. 'I'll look in again later tonight if I can but Dias is near her time.'

'Dias?'

'The laundress. Her time will come tonight, if I'm not much mistaken, but that's women's business and not for you to fret on.'

Jehane, Robyn remembered, was the town midwife as well as its wise woman. Dias's little by-blow must be due tonight.

'Please,' she said. 'I'm thirsty.'

'Wait.' Jehane went out and didn't come back for so long that Robyn thought she'd either forgotten or been sidetracked by the breaking of Dias's waters. Then the door opened again and the midwife reappeared holding a metal goblet, simple and unadorned. 'Drink this, boy,' she said, resuming her seat and handing the overfilled cup to her patient. Robyn took it gratefully but her action startled her companion. 'You're left-handed!' Jehane's voice was as sharp as a flint. Robyn cursed herself silently: no medieval child was allowed to grow up left-handed, if it had to be beaten out of him. It was unnatural.

'What's the matter, Jehane?' Robyn was glad to hear Hugues's voice in the doorway.

The woman turned on him. 'He favours his left hand, your little foundling in his princeling's clothes. Not only is he a spy from the King of France, he's a spawn of the devil too.'

Hugues didn't bother to answer her. 'I've come from Dias,' he said instead. 'The child is coming. Go to her. She's calling for you. Loudly!'

'Better if the fatherless mite dies, if you ask me.' But her actions gave the lie to her words as she jumped to her feet and picked up her skirts. There was a look on her face like that of the master craftsman setting about his work. Neither Dias nor her baby was going to die if Jehane knew anything about it.

'All flesh is sin and even the marriage bed is accursed,' Hugues said. 'Better that none of us should procreate. You know that.'

Jehane snorted and left the room without another word.

'She's superstitious,' Hugues said with a sigh. He spoke in French which Robyn found much easier to follow, even the medieval variety. 'They all are. It's the greatest battle for the civilised man, the educated man, in modern times. Drink your water, my son.

90

You must be in need of it.'

Robyn looked timidly at the well-water in the goblet. It looked clear, clean, but she knew it couldn't be — that it was teeming with lethal microbes, invisible to the naked eye, against which she, of all the people in the town, had least natural immunity, never having been exposed to them, not having suckled such protection from her mother's milk.

Words filled her head: typhoid, dysentery, cholera — or had that come only later? That was the trouble with the sort of history they taught you in school: what was the use of knowing the dates of famous battles and the reigns of kings and popes if you knew nothing about how simple people lived and how they died?

She sipped; she had no choice. One tiny sip, little more than a moistening of her dry lips, although logic told her that the amount could make no real difference. It was like no other water she'd ever tasted, but not unpleasant. There was none of the staleness, the brackishness she'd anticipated from well-water; on the contrary. No chemicals, she thought, no chloride, no fluoride. It was what water might have been before the fall.

'Drink up,' Hugues urged her. 'You must be parched.' Without further demur, she drained the cup. She didn't want to think about the next thing but she was going to have to and a good deal sooner than later. Her bladder was full to bursting. She cleared her throat. 'The necessarium?'

He laughed. 'Why so coy? I suppose you're used to a fine private garderobe where you come from, with drainage down to the ditch?'

'I suppose I am,' she agreed with a wry smile.

'We're not so luxurious here but there's no shame to ask for what we all must need. If it's making water I can bring you a pail.' She intimated that that wouldn't be enough and he asked, 'Can you stand?'

'If you will help me.' He gave her his arm and she eased herself off the rudimentary bed. He gave good support for so small a man and she leaned gratefully against him, feeling the rough cloth of his cassock, stiff with his sweat. They left the house and crossed the street, following an alleyway for a few yards into a small wooden hut which leaned against the town walls.

Robyn took a deep breath before entering but it wasn't as bad as she'd feared. There were three holes in the floor and a few flies but it didn't smell much worse than the public lavatories in the Place du Capitole in Toulouse. Little heaps of straw and limey soil stood around to sprinkle into the holes after use. 'It gives out on the hillside,' the priest explained. 'Not as good as a ditch but better than the streets. It comes in handy for repelling invaders!'

'You may need that.' She was standing without his aid now and waiting desperately for him to go but he showed no inclination to do so, seemingly prepared to stand and chat while she relieved herself.

'You may be right,' he said seriously, 'but we can withstand a siege longer than the Sire de Montfort can pursue one. We can outwait him.'

'Would you mind . . . ' She gestured at the door.

He understood at last and laughed. 'You're a fastidious young sir. Shall I stand guard outside for you in case anyone comes?'

He was joking but she said, 'Please.'

He shrugged and went out.

Thank God!

★ ★ ★

It was dusk as she came out a few minutes later and a bell was ringing nearby to warn that the main gate was about to close. The streets were busy and Robyn was surprised to see people settling down for the night to sleep in snug corners under the wall. They looked undersized to Robyn's twentieth-century eye, skinny and ill-nourished. Some were pock-marked. Some had twisted limbs from fractures that hadn't healed straight.

A shrivelled old woman brushed past her, peering suspiciously up at her, and she realised with a jolt that the face that braved her was no more than forty-five years old. In a time when the average life expectancy, even in peacetime, was perhaps forty, Hugues and Bruno, both the same age as Simon, were elder statesmen. It was as if all mankind were prey to progeria.

There were children among the crowd and most of them had livestock of some kind: goats, poultry, even a skinny cow in one case. A boy of five was fast asleep with his head pillowed on the panting sides of a white nanny goat, his thumb peacefully in his mouth.

'People are coming into town from the countryside around,' Hugues explained, following her glance. 'They're leaving their homes, their crops, and most of their cattle for de Montfort to burn and steal, bringing with them little but their lives. We can't give them all beds but we can give them the protection of our stout walls. The church is full and there must be a hundred more yet to come.'

'You let them sleep in the church? Isn't that . . . ?'

'We don't use it for worship any more,' he explained, 'so we may as well make practical use of it. We have no need of fine buildings to talk to our God. When I was young and wandered the world I saw many great churches raised to the glory of God, buildings that cost good workmen their lives. While all the time people slept in their shadows with no roof to their heads and no food in their bellies and no shelter from the northern winds. We Christians meet in a small, plain room. You can come tomorrow, see for yourself.'

'I will.' Robyn, feeling stronger with exercise, crossed the narrow street and climbed a series of steps rough-hewn in the wall onto the walkway. Hugues came up after her and they stood looking in the direction the crusaders must come. As far as the eye could see was pastureland and a few fields of wheat and barley, growing much lower than modern crops since the soil was poor and they had only natural fertilisers and pesticides. There was also, she noted, far more woodland than in the twentieth century, acres of dense oak where discount furniture warehouses, multi-screen cinemas and hypermarkets would one day flourish in their stead.

'We should be weeding in the fields,' Hugues said, 'but there seems no point. There will be no harvest this autumn.'

'When will they arrive?' she asked.

'We had a harsh winter with the trails impassable with snow, but then the spring came and de Montfort laid siege to Lavaur. He's been there now for two months and I fear the town can't hold out much longer . . . it may be weeks, it may be only days. One thing is sure: come they will.' The lapsed priest shook his head in wonderment. 'We ask only to be left in peace with our beliefs, Robert. We trouble no one. We seek no converts, although converts come to us daily of their own accord. We don't want to stop the Catholics from following their rituals and beliefs — why should we?'

'Perhaps it would have been better not to murder the papal legate if you wanted to be left in peace,' she suggested.

'Is that what you think? Is that what they say where you come from? No one here believes that tale. A lone horseman emerging out of the dawn to strike de Castelnau down with a single blow from his lance before disappearing back into the

January mist? Doesn't that sound very much like a tale to you?'

'Then what?'

'Innocent had been urging Christendom for years to take up arms against us but they wouldn't, didn't think it worth the expense and the loss of life they could expect from it. De Castelnau's death changed that. King Philip could no longer turn a deaf ear and the crusades were mustered within a month. It's obvious that the legate was murdered by his own entourage, on the orders of the Pope.'

'Are you serious?'

'Why else did they weep and wail him so desolately to his grave?'

'A conspiracy theory?' Robyn raised her eyebrows.

'Conspiracy theory.' Hugues liked the phrase and rolled it round his tongue. 'Conspiracy theory. What a facility you have with words, my friend.'

'I suppose it's possible. What will happen when the crusaders come?'

'We have large stores of grain. The harvest was good last autumn. We have chickens and geese, goats to give milk and meat. We can last out the summer and de Montfort will give up and go away long before that in search of easier targets.'

'But he'll come back again.'

Hugues smiled a sad, sweet smile. 'He won't give up but we have the advantage — we, the besieged. He can't bring his men up the steep sides of the hill and the path to the main gate is easy to guard. Even crusaders, with promises of papal indulgences ringing in their ears, don't take kindly to kettles of boiling water on their heads and arrows through their chests.'

'And is there no other way into the town?'

He looked at her with suspicious curiosity. 'A strange question, Robert of Durham. You surely can't expect me to answer it.'

'I'm sorry. I wanted to be sure . . . that you would be safe.'

She bit her lip, vexed at her own stupidity, turning away to stare as the darkness spread across the land. She'd stood in this same place at dusk many times during the dig, watching the gradual illumination of the valley — streetlamps, house lights, the neon of petrol stations in St Paul and Vielmur. This was a darkness such as she'd never seen.

'Are Bruno and Jehane right?' Hugues asked gently. 'Are you a spy?'

'No. I swear to you — '

He held up his hand to stop her. 'Don't, of your charity. Or not in my presence.'

' . . . I am a prisoner in this place.' She felt tears bubbling into her eyes and was glad that no one could see.

'We're not holding you prisoner, lad! You can leave here whenever you wish, although I would advise you to build up your strength a little first.'

'You don't understand.' Her voice sounded strange to herself, choked with misery. 'I can never go home.'

She felt Hugues's hand fall on her shoulder. 'Have you committed some crime in England, Robert? Something you must answer for with your life if you return? Don't be afraid to confide in me.'

She shook her head, her hair brushing against the friendly hand. 'Nothing like that. I promise you.'

'You need make no promises to me; only to God who knows the secrets of all hearts. Well, if you're a spy, you're not a very good one. A good spy doesn't turn up with a cracked head and a foreign dialect asking nosy questions and making us suspicious; he'd be one of us — someone we'd never suspect of treachery if we thought on it till the Day of Judgement.'

Somewhere below they heard the bellow of a woman in torment. The intensity made Robyn wince. It was the sort of scream a man might give if you lopped off his leg without anaesthetic. It was barely human. She put her hands over her ears.

'Dias,' Hugues said matter-of-factly, starting down the steps. 'Her time is near now. Come. You must eat.'

★ ★ ★

As the four of them left the restaurant the professor had his hand in the small of Janey's back, guiding her through the crowd. There was nothing sexual or even sensual about it, only protective, as if he was belatedly trying to shield Robyn from danger. A form of transference, Janey thought.

She missed her footing as they walked along the street, jostling a young man with a short haircut wearing a blue tee shirt with a gold fleur-de-lys on the front, one of a group of four who were crossing from the opposite pavement. 'Oh, pardon!' she said promptly.

He hissed, '*Juive!*' in her face, his breath full of beer and hatred. She felt his spittle like fine mist on her cheeks. She would have answered him, but the professor kept a firm grip on her and hauled her unceremoniously away. The men whooped victory and walked on singing some lines from the *Marseillaise*.

100

Marchons, Marchons,
qu'un sang impur
abreuve nos sillons.

'What did he say?' Malcolm asked, when no one else spoke.

'He called me a Jew,' Janey said. 'He didn't mean it as a compliment.'

'One of the *Enfants de France*,' Professor Clements remarked. 'Like the National Front. They get everywhere.'

★ ★ ★

Hugues's house, Robyn now saw clearly for the first time, was two storeys in height. The lower floor was built of stone with a smaller wooden structure topping it. A rudimentary ladder gave access to the upper floor on the outside. The room in which she'd been recuperating must be the solar or living-room with a bedroom for the priest upstairs.

'It's a big house for one man,' he said, misunderstanding her scrutiny. 'I would have taken in some refugees but now I have you as my guest.' He sighed. 'I've been here too long. It's the role of the Perfect to be an itinerant preacher, taking the message out into the fields and byways, not to settle in such comfort.'

Some comfort, Robyn thought. 'The people here need you,' she replied.

She followed him into the dark room and he took a taper from the fire and lit a candle. 'Do you play chess?' he asked.

'A little.'

'We must play one evening. There's no one here who knows the game and none who wants to learn. Here — ' he stirred a pot that hung over the fire. 'Jehane left you some porray.' She thought he'd said porridge and was surprised and not sorry when the bowl he handed her turned out to contain a savoury mixture — more than a soup but less than a stew — made of leeks, onions, milk, good thick lumps of ham and breadcrumbs. She began to spoon it greedily into her mouth, realising how hungry she was.

Hugues took a hunk of black bread and made a strange circular gesture over it before breaking it. She bowed her head, embarrassed, as he intoned the Lord's Prayer, a guest who hadn't waited for grace. He gave her half the bread and she wiped the empty bowl with it and swallowed it. She drank a glass of red wine, so much safer, she thought, than water, the pain in her head diminishing with every moment.

The priest himself, she noticed, ate only bread and drank only water. 'You're giving

102

up your food to me?' She felt guilty and doubly so in that she hadn't mentioned it until her bowl was empty.

But he denied it. 'I fast on bread and water three days of each week and I never eat meat or any animal product since a beast may house a fallen soul, so that porray with its ham and milk is not for me. Eat it and enjoy. If we live through a long siege you will think of it with nostalgia in the days to come.' She'd thought briefly and regretfully of the good things that weren't to be had here — tea, coffee, chocolate, even potatoes — but it hadn't dawned on her that she might actually go hungry. It didn't seem to occur to the priest to offer her another bowlful.

Hugues finished his bread and got up. 'I must see how Dias does, although I dare say we shall hear the baby's cry clearly enough from here.' He grinned. 'Jehane believes in giving newborn babes a good hard wallop on the behind to make them cry and drive out the devil.'

★ ★ ★

Yes, Robyn thought, settling back on her makeshift bed that was now coming to seem almost comfortable, the traitor must have been one of them, someone they trusted completely. She had perhaps a week to get out of here before the massacre. Albi was no more than a day's walk and she was a good walker. But what then? What would she do in Albi, she who had no right there, no right anywhere, not in this time? She would be no safer in Albi, nor in Paris, nor in Belfast.

She must stay in Montprimeur. The decision was made before it had entered her mind. There could be no appeal. If she died in the massacre, surely that was better than being stuck in a time where those she loved were not yet born, living out a span of perhaps thirty more years in a hostile and dangerous world where she didn't know the rules.

No, if she was here it must be for a reason. But why me, she thought, the tears welling in her eyes once more, why pick on me? She rubbed the cuff of her shirt across her eyes, sniffled away the wetness in her nose. If only she could remember how she'd got here.

★ ★ ★

Hugues was chuckling to himself as he returned, leaving the door open behind him. 'Jehane has ordered every door and cupboard in the town to be opened,' he explained, 'and every knot untied. She believes this is magic which will ease Dias's labour.'

'And you allow that?'

'I don't care sufficiently to argue. Besides, if Dias believes it then who knows but that it will help.' Psychosomatic healing when he put it like that: was it so different from Jehane's sympathetic magic? 'What she really wants, of course, is a bowl of water in which a murderer has washed his hands, which is, it seems, the most sovereign remedy against this pain, but no one is prepared to volunteer such a commodity. Perhaps we should send and ask de Montfort?' He smiled at his own little joke, sat down and poked at the fire with a stick, making it burn a little brighter.

'You're not as I imagined, Father,' Robyn blurted out.

He frowned. 'Call me simply Hugues, not Father. I'm not something from your imagination, my boy, like a unicorn or Ysengrin the wolf. What can you mean?'

'Only that someone talked of you to me and I thought from that . . . that you would be different.'

'And who was your informant?' She couldn't answer him, couldn't claim acquaintance with Louise d'Ambriers only to have the young woman deny it to her face. When he got no reply, Hugues didn't press her but continued, 'How different?'

'I didn't expect your sense of humour, your lack of self-importance.'

'Is that all? There's enough of that among the Catholic clergy. I should know, I was one for many years. The clergy is corrupt, greedy, venial and lustful; why do you think the people embraced Catharism so readily?'

'They see that you're a good man,' Robyn said warmly, 'a godly man.'

Hugues looked at his guest for a moment. 'Why do I keep getting the impression that you aren't what you seem?'

'I'm no spy.'

'No, not that. That's not what I meant. Never mind. In God's good time all secrets are revealed and I'm a patient man. How are you feeling, Robert?'

'A lot better, thanks.'

'You'll want to be on your way before de Montfort and his band of cut-throats arrive.'

'No,' Robyn said. 'If you'll keep me then I'll stay.'

Hugues considered this. 'You can shoot a bow and arrow, I take it.'

'Not exactly, no.'

He looked surprised. 'Don't Englishmen of any condition have to practise their archery regularly?'

'I don't know ... I mean, I'm sorry. Perhaps I can learn if you'll teach me.'

Hugues shook his head. 'There isn't time. It takes much skill and you'd waste our arrows.'

'Well, I'm strong and healthy,' Robyn said. 'I can read and write and do sums. You must be able to make use of me somehow. I don't eat much. Please, Hugues.'

'A healthy young man is always useful,' Hugues said after a pause for thought. 'You may stay, but on your head be it. Don't run away with the idea that they'll spare your life merely because you're not a Cathar.'

Robyn was under no such illusion. She knew by heart de Montfort's spine-chilling motto. *Kill them all; God will recognise his own.*

★ ★ ★

Back at the hotel, Janey saw Malcolm to his room. He was a little drunk and she suspected he wasn't used to it. 'I won't sleep,' he said.

'I bet you will. You look all in to me. You won't be able to help it.'

'The police. We must go to the police. Should have gone at once ... '

'I'll take you there first thing in the morning.'

He laid his suitcase on the bed and clicked it open. 'I'm going to reread her letters.'

'Looking for clues?'

'No, to . . . hear her voice. Perhaps I shall pray for a while. Do you pray?'

'Not really. I'm not a believer. I'm Jewish, as that charming young man noticed, technically, but . . . you know how it is.'

He smiled faintly. 'In Belfast they'd ask you are you a Catholic Jew or a Protestant Jew? But I shan't ask you to pray for her, in the circumstances. Who's the god of atheists? Mammon?'

'Reason. Goodnight, Malcolm.'

'Goodnight, Janey, and . . . thank you.'

★ ★ ★

The professor had disappeared into his own room and Janey knocked on Simon's door. She would have gone straight in without knocking but it occurred to her at the last moment that he might already be stripping for bed. But he was still fully clothed as he pulled the door open although he'd taken his shoes and socks off and his toes curled cold against the floorboards. He had his socks in his hand and was sniffing one to see if it

108

would do another day, which was endearing in its tackiness. Janey knew the horrors of living out of a suitcase.

'Well?' he said, wearily.

'I want to ask you a few more things.' Clearly sensing that resistance was useless, he stepped aside and motioned her in. The shutters were closed again and the bedside lamp gave the only light. She sat unbidden on the upright chair by the desk, her face in the shadows.

'Want a drink?' Simon lifted a bottle of scotch from his bedside table and showed it to her. It was almost empty. He already had a tumbler full of it on the nightstand and he picked it up now, letting the socks fall to the floor. His voice had the steadiness of a man who's drunk a little too much but believes that, if only he's careful, no one will notice.

'Why not?' Janey said. 'It's as good a god as any.'

'Better than most, I find. Tooth mug all right?'

'If that's the best you can do.'

He handed her a double measure of pale brown liquid and she topped it up with water from the tap and sipped. He sat down on the bed, cradling his own glass. His legs were apart, his head slightly bowed. He seemed calm, anaesthetised. He said quietly, as if to himself, 'I wish I'd asked her to marry me that evening in the dining-room, a couple of days before her disappearance. I was on the point of it but my nerve failed me. Then Joachim came in to lay the table and the moment passed.'

'I can't see what difference it would make now.'

'Don't you? As her declared fiancé, you see, I would have a defined role, a right to be terrified for her welfare. As it is, I'm nothing to her and her father hates me.'

'He doesn't hate you.' Janey softened at his obvious misery. 'It came as a bit of a shock because he didn't know she was shacked up with someone. Fathers are like that. Give him time to get used to the idea.'

'He does hate me. I saw his face. I saw the way his mouth went into a tight little line, the way hers does when she's pissed off at me about something.'

'Does that happen often?'

'I know it's irrational,' he said, not answering, 'but I feel as if my cowardice has somehow contributed to her loss. As though if we'd been shopping for a ring and complacently accepting the congratulations of our colleagues, then none of it would have happened.'

'Of course,' Janey pointed out, 'she might have said no.'

He laughed. As the laugh threatened to become a sob, he half choked on his whisky and wiped his arm across his eyes to clear the resultant flush of tears. 'So she might. I hadn't thought of that. How comforting! Thank you, Janey.'

'How many people are there on the dig altogether?' she asked.

'Apart from me and James and Robyn, there are four others, two men and two women, English, Scottish, French and American.'

'Who's the younger woman, the blonde?'

'That's Dr Meriel Richards, Merry to her friends. She's been with us on sabbatical from Edinburgh university for the past year. She's reader in archaeology there. She's due to go back in October.'

'And is she? Merry?'

Simon shrugged. 'As much and as little as anyone else. Are you?'

'And the older woman?'

'Madame Silvie de Chambertin — la *Comtesse* de Chambertin, if you're that way inclined. Her family have lived in this area for generations which is why she got a place on the dig, even though she's an amateur. She's pretty hot stuff actually and she works for nothing, so James got a good deal there. In fact, she claims descent from the d'Ambriers family, who were the local nobility at the time of the massacre.'

'Did they get 'orribly done in too?'

'They were safe in their castle at Lautrec, five miles away, by the time of the disaster, although Louise d'Ambriers was rumoured to be a Cathar.'

'One law for the rich and another for the rest of us?'

'You've got it.' He added snidely, 'I expect you know her poetry and stories?' Janey tried to look intelligent. 'One of the great songbirds of the *Langue d'Oc*, if you like that sort of thing.'

'Not much. Did Robyn?'

'Yes. She was young.'

'I'm young. Younger than she was . . . *is*.'

'Oh no, Janey Silverman. You were never young.' Simon leaned back against the headboard and folded his arms, then unfolded them again immediately to drink some more whisky. 'The middle-aged man with the gingery hair and the high blood-pressure is Dr Dexter Mooney, from Boston, Mass. Typical Irish American: more Irish than the Irish, in other words. Don't ask him to sing you any Republican songs. Please.'

'Middle-aged? He can't be more than a

112

year or two older than you, Simon.'

'Five or six years, thank you.'

'And the young man?'

'Peter Finlay. Just graduated from Oxford last summer.'

'Oh? I don't remember ever seeing him there. Which college?'

'James's College, Balliol.'

'Another brilliant youngster granted a place on this most prestigious of digs?'

'A bright enough boy but he's here basically because his father was an old friend of James's and he's dead, the father, I mean — obviously — and James promised . . . something or other, on his deathbed. Keep an eye on the boy, stuff like that.'

'So he's out of his depth among you doctors and professors and the brilliant Robyn?'

'I wouldn't say out of his depth. He feels a bit of an outsider, perhaps. Keeps himself to himself, tends to wander off on his own when he's got any free time.'

'I shall want to talk to them all, eventually.'

'I'm sure you will, Janey Silverman,' Simon said with a faint smile. He drained his glass and got up, indicating that the interview was at an end. 'But will they want to talk to you?'

As he held the door open for her, she

paused and said, 'What's with the Monami boy?'

'Joachim?' Simon shrugged. 'He's epileptic, I think, although I've never seen him actually fit. He's certainly a bit simple as well. Some botch up at birth, I should think. What about him?'

'Was he friendly to Robyn?'

'She was nice to him, tried to coax a few words out of him from time to time. He's harmless, if that's what you're thinking, for all he looks a bit sinister.'

'He can speak, then?'

'He *can*. My guess is he doesn't have anything much to say.'

3

'The house in which a heretic is discovered shall be razed to the ground and the land on which it stands be confiscated.'
Edict of the Council of Toulouse, 1229.

'I have been doing my homework, Dad, reading up on the history of Montprimeur. It's frightening to think of those people — and there were four or five hundred of them in the town at the time of the massacre — stuck there, knowing there was no way out through the armies, waiting.

The awful thing was that they were completely cut off. The only way to get messages in and out of a besieged town was by carrier pigeon and the archers below wouldn't usually miss an easy target like that. You don't think of the Middle Ages in terms of psychological warfare — you hardly think of people having a psyche then — but that was what it was: a not knowing; a silence.

Oh, how I loathe waiting!'

115

Robyn was so exhausted that she slept soundly that night on her hard pallet, but wakened the next morning in the middle of a dream. She'd been eating breakfast with Simon at the Oustal Monami. Simon had been talking as usual but she hadn't really been listening. She had a secret, something that would make Simon sit up and take notice of her, and the professor, and the whole world of Cathar studies. Something that would be the cornerstone, eventually, of her PhD thésis.

But what was it? And did it have any connection with the bang on her head and her present predicament?

If only she could remember.

She missed Simon already, although she thought with a smile that he would cope less well than she with the privations of medieval life. He was a fastidious man, a *bon viveur*. She knew his faults and loved him anyway, as she hadn't loved anyone before.

She knew he wasn't reliable, that he was a spoilt little boy trapped in a thirty-nine-year-old body, but thought she'd been a good influence these last few months. Perhaps he was ready now to grow up, to make the sort of commitment he'd shunned. There was many a devoted family man with fieldsful of wild oats growing behind him.

As an historian and archaeologist, though, he must envy her this experience. It was what they longed for: a time machine. To see what it was *really* like. But would he believe her story? Would anybody?

Would this story — *could* this story — ever be told?

★ ★ ★

'Robert?'

She opened her eyes to find Hugues bending over her, confirming what her nostrils had already told her — that this was no illusion of her dreams.

'Did you sleep well?'

She sat up. That night she'd taken off her tunic and suede jeans and slept in her shirt and she pulled the coarse blanket casually up to her neck to hide any sign of her small but definite breasts. She wondered how they could possibly think she was a male, but presumably it hadn't occurred to them that she could be anything else, unable to get their imaginations past her clothes. She yawned. 'I slept very well.'

'Even through the din?'

'What din?'

'Dias gave birth to twins in the small hours — '

'Twins!'

' — and Jehane is insisting it's proof that she's been fornicating with not one man, but two.' He laughed. 'I've known the purest, most virtuous, most *well-guarded* of wives give birth to twins but the old superstitions die hard.'

Louise d'Ambriers's chronicles had spoken of only one child, Robyn remembered in dismay. Had she been wrong? Were the diaries unreliable?

'Are the babies all right?' she asked.

'Oh, one was born dead.' Hugues spoke matter-of-factly. He sounded indifferent, but the death of a newborn was an everyday occurrence and to have one healthy baby and a surviving mother was as much as any reasonable man could hope for. 'The other seems to be thriving,' he went on. 'A boy. She wants to call him Pietre for some reason.' His austere face softened for an instant, as human faces do at a baby, or the memory of one. 'Such a fine lusty boy child,' he murmured, his human instincts betraying the Cathar doctrine that preferred the suppression of matter and so, logically, the extinction of the species. He recollected himself. 'Anyway, as I was saying, Jehane and Dias were screaming abuse at each other half the night. You must be the only person in town who slept through it.'

Robyn shivered. Jehane frightened her with her rigidity, her moral certainty of her own rightness, her inability to compromise. As bigoted in her way as de Montfort was in his, between them they could only destroy. 'Will you baptise the baby today?' she asked.

He shook his head. 'We baptise men and women, not babes in arms. Let them make their own promises when they reach the age of reason.'

'What if he dies before he grows up?' she objected. 'Is he to be condemned to limbo?'

Hugues was dismissive. 'Limbo, purgatory, hell! Inventions of mankind not of God. The devil has no need of hell; the earth is his domain! And how could a loving God condemn a soul because it didn't live long enough to be baptised? It is madness.' He went out of the front door and she thought that she'd annoyed him with her ignorance, but took the opportunity to pull her clothes on. Her white shirt had lost its starch and felt limp and damp. Her mouth tasted bad. She rubbed a finger squeakily across her teeth and longed for toothpaste.

Hugues had gone only to fetch her breakfast and returned soon with dry bread and an apple from last year's crop, small and wrinkled with age. There was milk too, warm and pungent from the goat. She'd drunk goat's milk once as a child on holiday in Eire and had never felt the need to repeat the experience. She dipped the bread in the milk and swallowed the sops whole, making both more palatable.

The first rule of survival: adapt or perish. Then she glanced up and screamed. Her hand jerked forward and the last of the milk spilled over the floor, trickling away between the rushes.

Filling the doorway was a monster, a grotesque. As Hugues stood up on seeing it, it towered a foot above him. Its head was misshapen, a craggy egg with yellow bristles sparsely sown and two black eyes without lashes, almost no neck. Its legs were too long for its stumpy body, one thin foot twisted at a strange angle. It let out a loud ululating sound, apparently in reaction to her own scream.

'It's all right,' Hugues said, but to the monster not to Robyn. 'It's all right, Joachim. You startled young Master Robert, appearing so silently like that. Come in and say hello. He's far more frightened than you are, Robert.'

Gingerly the creature ducked its head in at the door and stood as far from Robyn as possible, its eyes churning warily. Its arms, crudely long like its legs, were wrapped round a pile of firewood as if they might encircle it twice. 'This is Young Joachim,' Hugues explained. 'Not to be confused with his grandfather, Old Joachim. And best if you don't call him Joachim the Idiot, as some do, either. Joachim,' he spoke slowly and loudly, 'this is Master Robert of Durham, my guest.'

The monster made the ululating noise again and dropped the wood against the hearth before backing away once more. 'Thank you,' Hugues said. 'Joachim's very strong, Robert, and does the heavy work in the town that no one else can do.'

'Hello, Joachim,' Robyn uttered meekly. 'I'm sorry if I frightened you but you startled me.'

'He moves very quietly for one so large,' Hugues said with a note of fondness in his voice. His hand reached up to stroke the monster's shoulder, soothing. He could have been a farmer reassuring his horse. 'Thank you for the wood, Joachim. I'd run out. I'm a poor, sad apology for a housekeeper who'd let the fire go out completely if left to my own devices.'

Joachim made the now familiar noise which seemed to serve for all occasions — as

121

greeting and farewell — and left. 'You startle easily,' Hugues observed, beginning to pile the logs more tidily. 'Every village has its Joachim, surely, even the village of Durham in far-off England.'

'Of course.' Robyn got up to help him, seeing the wasted muscles tighten ineffectually on his skinny arms as his sleeves fell back, the sharp delineation of bone.

'There are those who say his mother mated with a beast,' Hugues remarked, 'but this is foolish talk to my mind. She died bearing him.'

It was rare in the Middle Ages, Robyn knew, to reach adulthood with both parents still living. 'What about his father?' she asked.

'Dead of a wasting fever three years ago.'

'So where does he live?'

'With his grandfather, Old Joachim. They're the last of their line.' A bell rang nearby. 'We begin our service in a few minutes,' the priest said. 'Will you come?'

'Gladly.'

* * *

Bisette was bored. They'd been camped in the same spot for weeks now; she wasn't sure how many weeks, since the days ran easily into each other, but she knew it had been weeks if only because the baron said so. Her senses and the burgeoning countryside told her that it was spring, perhaps as late as May.

She knew she could consider herself lucky that the Baron Henri de Bresse had taken a fancy to her and preferred her company to that of the other camp followers. It meant that she slept in his tent at night and wasn't obliged to seek food and a fresh night's lodgings among the drunken soldiery as each dusk fell. They were fellow countrymen, of course, from the fertile lands around Orleans, and at least he could understand what she said, shared her customs and assumptions.

Henri was essentially a good man, a pious man, now forty-five but still full of manly vigour. He liked to fight because he'd been brought up to believe that was what a gentleman did. He obeyed his overlord, paid his taxes to the king, husbanded his farms and dispensed rough but reasonable justice to his underlings. He'd never had any cause to question the way things were ordered.

He'd fought in the Fourth Crusade and been present at the fall of Constantinople. He wore the crusader's cross on the breast of his cloak by right, and his standard — a hawk displayed sable, a motto *Dieu et Roy* — was flanked by the same cross. He had many stories of hot and distant lands, of strange and savage infidels, to which Bisette listened again and again without rancour.

He'd returned home, after three years absence in the east, to find that his wife, Marie de Rosselet, had decided to enter a Carthusian convent and that his marriage was therefore at an end. A man could hardly kick up a fuss, with the children grown, if his wife dedicated herself to God. They'd been married since they were fifteen, but he felt that he'd never known her. She kept a silent and contemplative devotion and he didn't see her.

He had three daughters, well married and off his hands, and little to occupy him, so that when the call came from Pope Innocent and King Philippe Auguste for good Catholics to ride south to crush the infamous Cathar heresy, Henri had willingly pledged himself, his son, his squire and a handful of knights, at least for a few weeks.

It had been strange at first to fight not against the heathen — that black-skinned, devil-worshipping rascal — but against white and Christian men like any at home in Bresse. He had no real notion what the heresy consisted of, only vague murmurings of a

124

denial of Christ's incarnation and horrifying sexual habits. If his priests said it was heresy, then that was good enough for him.

It was only after he watched his only son, Louis, named for the Dauphin, die from his wounds at Minerve that his involvement became personal, so that when he might, with honour, have gone home to tend his lands, he'd dispatched his knights but elected himself to stay and see the thing through to the end. The boy had just turned nineteen — cut down by a stray arrow in the chest from the watchtower above the main gate at nightfall, missing his heart but piercing the lungs. He'd lost strength hour by hour in a mist of uncomprehending fear, finding it ever harder to catch his breath, coughing up greater and greater gobs of blood, as the doctors flapped uselessly, bleeding and poulticing.

Dying in his father's arms a few minutes before dawn, he whispered, trustingly, 'I will be all right, won't I, sir . . . Father?'

They'd buried him that morning, in alien ground, a hundred leagues from the family tomb.

As Henri dictated a brief letter to his eldest daughter to pass on the terrible news, he swore that he wouldn't go home to Bresse now until he'd seen the last of the heretic scum burnt and filled that bottomless pit of despair inside him with their charcoaled bones.

Sometimes he talked to Bisette about his son, about how he'd loved him, this blond and slender boy, so different from his dark bear of a father. Not merely that he was proud of him, his heir, the one who was to continue his bloodline — his name — into the future, but that he *loved* him, in a way Bisette hadn't known men could love.

Sometimes he would weep and blame himself for bringing the boy with him into this foreign land, but a young nobleman must earn his spurs and never flinch from danger.

Mostly he didn't trouble her much at night; when he did he went straight to be shriven the next morning, lest he die in a state of mortal sin.

★ ★ ★

'*Professor Clements thinks there may be cellars hidden under some of the ruins, cut deep into the limestone as secret storage places and hidey-holes. We have to go slowly, though, so as not to damage anything along the way. The professor says if we do hollow through to one*

I shall have to wriggle into it as I'm the smallest: I do hope he isn't serious. With my claustrophobia, it would give me nightmares.

Dr Guzman says he doesn't think they'd have had the tools to make extensive cellars but the professor says he underestimates the human will, which is capable of anything. He says that if they could raise Notre Dame de Paris then they could dig a bloody hole. I like that idea: that we are capable of anything if we want it enough!

All love, old man
Robyn.'

★ ★ ★

Malcolm was in the dining-room when Janey came down the next morning. Otherwise the room was empty. 'Call this breakfast?' he complained when he saw her. 'Stale bread and jam. *Apricot* jam.' As if this compounded the felony. 'Call that breakfast?'

'I don't call it anything, Malcolm.' She poured herself coffee from the urn, added milk generously and took her place at the table. 'Have you seen Simon? He wasn't in his room just now.' Malcolm shook his head. 'Perhaps he's in the bathroom.'

'Did you want him for anything in particular?'

'I've got lots of questions I need to ask him. I've hardly started.'

'What about the rest of the archaeologists?'

'I haven't forgotten them. Don't worry. We'll go out to the dig again this morning, as soon as we've dealt with the police.'

Madame Monami appeared at that moment with some more bread, and Janey asked for Simon Guzman and was told he was in the garden.

'He takes his breakfast there,' the proprietress explained, 'along with the young lady — ' she lowered her voice, as if a hushed tone made an unpalatable truth less real ' — who is missing. Usually.' She peered at Malcolm with curiosity — like a gawper at a traffic accident, Janey thought. Fortunately, Malcolm was too preoccupied to notice.

'Back in a minute.' Janey picked up her bowl of coffee in both hands and went out of the room leaving Malcolm, who hadn't understood the conversation, staring after her.

She was walking along the dark corridor towards the shaft of light that was the garden door when something moved rapidly out at her from a side room. She let out a squeal of dismay and almost dropped her bowl. Then she saw that it was Joachim. 'Oh, you startled me,' she said crossly, 'lurking about there in the dark. What's the matter with you?'

She made to brush past him but he put a hand on her arm to detain her. It was a big brown hand and she saw that his forearms, like his torso, were covered in dense black hair. His touch was surprisingly light but the fingers looked strong. He said something to her, one word she couldn't make out.

'What?' she snapped. 'Say it again . . . Again, Joachim. Repeat.'

'Robyn?' he said, in a low, thick voice she had to strain to hear.

'Yes,' she said, suddenly very still. 'What about Robyn?'

'Where is Miss Robyn gone?'

She shook his hand off, annoyed. 'I was hoping *you* could tell *me!*'

He called after her, 'Why no goodbye to Joachim?'

She found Simon sitting on a stone bench under an ornamental vine in the pocket-handkerchief courtyard garden. He was leaning against a disused well, overgrown with pot plants, and sipping black coffee but not eating. He was probably worried about middle-aged spread, she thought. He was vain enough. He didn't notice her at first, absorbed in his thoughts, wondering when and how and why everything had gone so wrong.

She sat down beside him. He straightened up, half alarmed. 'Oh, it's you.' His voice was filled with disappointment. 'Just for a second there, I thought . . . Not that you look anything like . . . Not really. Young. Dark hair.'

'Tell me about her,' she said gently. 'I can't rely on Malcolm's account of her — he's biased.'

'And I'm not?'

'Well, not so much. There must have been a time when you looked upon her with fresh eyes not blinkered by . . . affection.'

'If you're the friend of the family you claim to be, how come you don't know Robyn?'

'I'm a very recent friend of the family.'

'How recent?'

Janey glanced at her watch. 'About fourteen hours.'

He blinked but made no comment. Janey Silverman's ability to thrust her way in anywhere was already beyond surprise. 'What do you want to know?'

'We've already had one discrepancy. Malcolm says she's very open. You say she's secretive.'

'I didn't mean secretive in a bad way. She's independent — that's a better word — in that she doesn't like to ask questions or look for guidance. If she has a theory — say, something about Montprimeur — she won't tell us and talk it over, she likes to present us with a *fait accompli*.'

'That may simply be fear of making a fool of herself,' Janey pointed out. 'Not putting forward a theory until she can prove it in case she's ridiculed.'

'Yes. That may be.'

'Not wanting to look foolish in front of you, especially.'

'We're too good friends for that. She trusts me. We trust each other.'

'How long have you known her?'

'Eleven months. Since she joined the dig.'

'And how long have you been a couple?'

'Five, six months.' He smiled. 'It took me longer than usual to make my move. I didn't think she could possibly be interested, you see.'

'Very modest. How would you describe the relationship.'

Simon stirred restlessly. 'I know what you think, that I'm a much older man stringing along a young girl who hero-worships me, but it's not like that. Robyn's not the hero-worshipping type.'

'And you're no hero.'

He ignored the remark. 'She's very mature.

You know her mother died when she was eight?'

'Oh no, I didn't know.'

'Killed in some Belfast horror, some drive-by sectarian shooting where she happened to get in the way.' How closed-up Malcolm was, Janey thought, how hidden. He hadn't mentioned that he'd lost his wife so early and so horribly and that Robyn was all he had. There was more to him than met the eye; he was a survivor. Simon went on. 'Okay, so she's been the apple of Malcolm's eye and he'd probably have spoilt her if she'd been the sort who can be spoilt, but her response to her mother's death was that she was the woman of the household now and she grew up straight away. I was never aware of any age difference between us, not really. We were equals.'

'Perhaps you're immature,' Janey said.

He smiled briefly. 'You don't pull any punches, do you? I bet you weren't bullied at school. Have you many friends, Miss Silverman? Janey? Or have you frightened them away?'

'I don't know why people are so afraid of plain speaking.'

'Then that's something you have yet to learn. Perhaps I *am* immature. And perhaps you have weaknesses too, and perhaps I shall

132

find them out and torment you with them.'

'I have lots of weaknesses but you won't find them out. How old are you?'

'Thirty-nine. Why?'

'Married? Divorced?'

'Neither. Footloose and fancy free, that's me.' He gave a hollow laugh.

'Frightened of commitment?'

'If you like.'

'I hope you're not going to say 'Why keep a cow when you can buy milk'.'

'I wasn't, but thanks for the suggestion.'

'Would I be right in thinking that the blonde woman at the dig is an old girlfriend of yours? What did you call her? Meriel?'

He reddened. 'Shrewd aren't you? Merry and I are old friends, yes, if you must know. We were at university together, at Oxford, back in what you would no doubt call the Dark Ages of the mid-seventies, when you were trying to run the world from your playpen, Janey Silverman.'

'Old friends? Old lovers?'

'We've been lovers from time to time over the years, when neither of us has been heavily involved with anybody else. It's an arrangement that suits us both. We understand each other.'

'And was this 'arrangement' in force when Robyn arrived at the dig?'

'. . . Yes.'

'So it could be said that Robyn took you away from Meriel?'

'I've told you, it's not like that. You young people today are so puritanical! In the seventies people slept together out of mutual lust and companionship without feeling the need to rush out and put a deposit on a three-piece suite immediately after.'

'So you're seriously telling me that this Meriel didn't mind when you dumped her for Robyn?'

'I keep telling you it wasn't like that! Dr Meriel Richards is a world-respected archaeologist, not a love-sick schoolgirl. She frankly doesn't give tuppence for me any more than anyone else ever has, until maybe Robyn.'

'Such self-pity, Simon. So you and Meriel were sharing that room?' She raised her eyes to the first floor, although the room in question was on the other side of the building.

'No. We had separate rooms. I was in the room you're in, as it happens. Come to think of it, Robyn's the first woman who's ever been . . . official.'

'Huh?'

'Actually living together.'

'In a dingy hotel room?'

134

'Hey, that's my home you're talking about. *Our* home.'

'Where's your real home?'

'There's a two up, two down in Jericho but it's let, to a physicist.' That was how they defined you at Oxford, by your subject, not as a man or a woman, a Canadian or a Pakistani, but as a physicist or a philologist.

'There are enough doctors on this dig to staff an NHS hospital,' Janey said,' — well, a run-down one.'

'Is there another sort? It's a very prestigious excavation. Now I have work to do. I'm already a good hour behind the others and there's probably a limit to the allowances they're prepared to make.' He got up, tipped the rest of his coffee over the long-suffering vine and stalked back into the hotel.

'We'll come out to the dig later,' she called after him, 'when we've finished with the police.' Janey sat sipping her own coffee which was almost cold now. She wasn't 100 per cent convinced by 'arrangements' such as those enjoyed by Simon Guzman with Meriel Richards. If they'd been at university together that meant that Meriel, too, was thirty-nine, an age when unmarried women, however successful in their field, often got edgy.

What would her feminist friends say to that? They would bawl her out for incorrect thinking, but it couldn't be helped. It was the simple truth.

The world is as it is and not as we would like it to be.

★ ★ ★

'What's happening?' Malcolm had finished his frugal breakfast by the time Janey returned and was looking restless.

'Simon's gone to join the others at the dig. There's only us here now.'

'I can't understand why Robyn would want to take up with a man like him,' Malcolm said.

'I expect she was looking for a father figure,' Janey said. 'She'd have been better off with the professor. Inside, Simon's about seventeen.'

Malcolm stared at her coldly. 'She's got a father. *I* am her father.'

'Yes, but she became a sort of surrogate wife to you from an early age, didn't she?'

He exploded. 'What the hell do you mean by that?'

'Don't look at me like that, Malcolm. I didn't mean anything you'd have to go on the Oprah Winfrey show about. I meant that she became an adult the day her mother died, that's all.'

'Oh. I don't remember telling you about Ann. My wife.'

'You didn't. I had to hear it from Simon. Why was that?'

'It has nothing to do with the matter. I don't make a point of telling complete strangers about it. Besides . . . I didn't want it to sound as if I was the sort of man that terrible things happen to.' Janey considered this but decided not to probe. 'I treated her as an equal after Ann died,' he said.

'That's the point, Malcolm. Children don't want to be treated as equals by their parents; they want someone strong and powerful to set boundaries and keep them safe. Robyn missed out on her childhood so, paradoxically, finds it hard to grow up.'

'What idiot psychobabble is this?'

'Until she finds a father,' Janey persisted, 'she can't become a woman. Believe me. I know about these things. I could show you three child psychologists I drove to nervous breakdowns.'

'You'd better be careful, Janey Silverman,' Malcolm said. 'From what little you've told me about your family background, you're a bit in need of a father figure yourself.'

'Well!'

'Oh, you can dish it out better than you can take it, I see. Now, if you've finished telling me what an inadequate parent I've been — '

'It's not a question of that.'

'Let's go to the police station.'

★ ★ ★

'Has the young Frenchman remembered where he was heading for yet?' Bruno asked later that morning.

'If you mean me,' Robyn said, 'then no.'

'Nor even where he was coming from? That can't be too difficult.'

'No. My memory hasn't returned. I wish it had.'

'What are you trying to say, Bruno?' Hugues asked.

'Merely that I've been asking around the neighbourhood, as far as Castres in the east, as far as Graulhet and Montréal in the north and Puylaurens to the south, and nobody recalls seeing him. No one remembers a young nobleman on a horse riding into the district two days ago.'

'So what are you suggesting?' Hugues asked. 'That Robert has been spirited to us by the devil?'

'Or that he came from the west,' Bruno

said, 'from Lavaur.'

'That's absurd,' Hugues protested. 'The crusaders are besieging Lavaur and have been these eight weeks. No one can get out of the town.'

'No one,' Bruno agreed, 'unless the devil de Montfort sent him.'

★ ★ ★

'Louise d'Ambriers was born in the summer of 1188 at the château of her father — Odo, Comte d'Ambriers — near the village of Lautrec in the Albigeois, probably in June although exact records are not available.

The child was neglected for the first few days of her life as her mother, Anne de Chambertin, was so ill following the birth that her life was feared for. The baby was probably saved by the old housekeeper who found a suitable wet nurse, one Esclarmonde of Montprimeur. Anne recovered but was advised not to attempt to have further children, so Louise remained the only child of the Comte d'Ambriers.

Although Anne died in 1203, the Comte never remarried and the title died with him.

As was the custom among noblewomen of her era, Louise received no mean education even by modern standards. A chatelaine needed to be able to read and write and keep the household accounts. In the absence of a son, the Comte also saw to it that she studied the rudiments of Latin, mathematics and astronomy, that she might be a companion to him in his old age.

In her youth, Louise travelled extensively with her father, visiting Paris, Rome, Venice, Florence, Barcelona and Madrid but by 1208 the Comte, although still a young man to our eyes, perhaps forty-five, settled into the infirmity of old age and they remained quietly at the ancestral home from then on.

As ill fortune had it, by 1208 war had broken out in the Albigeois; following the murder of the papal legate, Pierre de Castelnau, Pope Innocent III declared all-out war on the Cathar heresy, by then widespread in those parts. Although the Comte d'Ambriers remained a good Catholic until his dying day, Anne de Chambertin had flirted with the new religion and her daughter was raised by its adherents, including the influential Esclarmonde.

In the spring of 1212 Louise married her cousin, Aimeric de Chambertin, and left the Albigeois to pass a more peaceful life on his estates in the Auvergne and in his town house in Paris.

Widowed in 1222, she returned to the d'Ambriers family home, the wars of religion now more or less concluded with total victory for the Catholic faith. With her were her two sons, Aimeric and Louis. She remained there for the rest of her long life and devoted her declining years to literature and scholarship.

It was here, during her widowhood, that Louise wrote the Chansons de Lacaune *for which she is remembered, a long cycle of poems in the* Langue d'Oc, *and collected and preserved the diaries that make up the present volume. She is one of the great medieval voices of this almost forgotten tongue, the matriarch of a dynasty, a scholar, a great lady, a woman I am proud to call my ancestor.'*

Introduction
Diaries of Louise d'Ambriers, Scholar and Matriarch.

ibid.

* * *

A woman's voice hailed them as they crossed the market square.

'Hugues? Is this your wounded nobleman from France that everyone keeps telling me about?'

Hugues's austere face brightened as if lit from within but it wasn't the light of a lover, Robyn realised, but of a proud father or tutor. 'The Demoiselle d'Ambriers. You're welcome, as always.' He laid a hand on her arm in greeting and Robyn realised that this was the first time she'd seen him knowingly make physical contact with a woman.

Robyn looked with interest at Louise d'Ambriers, who returned her stare frankly. She was a young woman, not more than twenty-two or three, a little taller than Robyn, which made her very tall for a woman of her era, taller than Hugues, sturdily built, with the glow of good health, the strong white teeth, that spoke of a childhood in a warm castle with all the good food she could eat. Her clothes were of a finer material than those of the townswomen: a soft linen chemise, visible at the neck of her blue surcoat, gave a frame to her handsome face; her wide sleeves were edged with what looked like squirrel pelt, a russet brown. She wore no ornament or jewel except for a row of gilt buttons down the front of her bodice, carved with a creature half bird, half beast.

She was fairer than the working people, her hair a pale — almost ash — blonde, not hidden by a hat or wimple but displayed proudly in a snood of gold thread, an ivory comb high on each side. Her skin wasn't browned by open-air work, but strawberries and cream. Her voice was high and light. She bore no real resemblance to Silvie de Chambertin, even as she must have looked at the same age, but that was hardly surprising with — what must it be? — some twenty-five generations to dilute her blood.

'This is Robert of Durham,' Hugues said. 'Our guest, as you surmised, but from England not from France. Robert, this is Louise, the daughter of the Comte d'Ambriers whose castle lies some five miles to the north of here. She is of our communion.' Robyn wondered how she was expected to acknowledge the introduction, holding herself back in time from shaking hands. She tried a small bow and was rewarded by a curtsey.

'Hugues,' Louise said, 'I came on the wagon this morning with a load of grain. My father's gift to the town.'

'Thank him from me on our behalves. His present is most timely. The Comte d'Ambriers is not a Cathar,' he explained to

143

Robyn, 'but his wife was and the demoiselle certainly is. Tell me, Louise, is your cousin, the Comte de Chambertin, still visiting you?'

'Aimeric?' Louise made a face. 'No, he's fled back to Paris in dismay, poor soul. He finds us southerners barbarous. I swear he spends half his time walking round with a nosegay pressed to his face like the worst Parisian dandy.'

'I'm sorry for your sake,' Hugues said. 'For he was company for you.'

'Well I'm here now, among my old friends for company. And you've even provided a new friend for me. Are you coming to our meeting?' she asked Robyn, addressing her in French.

'I . . . yes.'

'Then you shall sit with me and I shall explain it to you . . . if that would please you.' Her tone was flirtatious, her blue eyes peeping up from under long pale lashes. Robyn thought how strange it was to change sex, to have women cajoling you, deferring to you, making you feel important. No wonder men had clung to their power for so many centuries.

'That's very kind of you,' she said gravely.

'But first I must take a moment to go and see Dias and her baby.'

'Then I'll come too.' Both Hugues and

Louise looked surprised and Robyn realised that a young man wouldn't normally volunteer himself for a visit to a new mother, but she could hardly draw back now so she mumbled something about her sister having recently been delivered of a son too. They seemed satisfied with this and she and Louise went in search of the lying-in room.

'Don't worry,' Louise called back to Hugues, slipping her arm through Robyn's. 'I shall take good care of him for you.' Hugues gave a rueful shake of the head and went off to prepare for his meeting. It was all very well, Robyn thought, telling people not to marry and procreate, but Mother Nature usually had other plans for handsome, healthy young women like Louise d'Ambriers — and for buxom, lusty girls like Dias.

* * *

Immediately after breakfast Janey and Malcolm made their way on foot to the local *Commissariat de Police*. They walked in silence through the pretty town with its handsome houses. It was a bright spring morning and the sun glittered on the quiet waters of the Agout as they followed it to the town centre, past the sombre Baroque church of St Benoît, and into the functional modernity of the police station on the Carcassonne road.

Malcolm had expected brusqueness, a lot of French hand waving and shrugging, but the local police, like their Belfast counterparts, were kind and sympathetic, if not particularly helpful. He soon gave up any hope of following the conversation between Janey and the policeman at the front desk and passed his time reading the notices on the board, or rather looking at the pictures — identikits and artists' impressions, sharp-faced men who looked capable of anything.

Janey began by explaining who they were and what they wanted but the policeman was nodding assent by the end of the second sentence. Asking her to wait, he picked up the phone, dialled an extension and spoke to someone. 'The inspector will be down in a minute,' he said. Taking Janey for a fellow-countrywoman, the man was more open than he might have been with an intrusive foreigner. He was aware of the problem, he said, had talked to the professor himself when the disappearance had first been reported.

Could the young lady have been taken ill? Janey wondered. Or been knocked down by a car? Or be wandering around suffering from amnesia?

The policeman explained that the local hospitals had been checked and were being monitored, and that Robyn's description had been disseminated to the patrol cars and *Postes de Police* in the villages and small towns of the Albigeois. They were looking out for anyone who might be her, but so far there hadn't been so much as a false sighting.

Janey was disappointed; she'd been hoping that the police had done nothing at all, so that they could now be bullied into action and perhaps find Robyn in a local hospital with nothing worse than a broken ankle.

He'd been on the point of contacting the professor, the policeman added, his voice endowing professorhood with great respect, to see if she'd turned up. If not he intended, this very morning, to pass the description on to other areas, even in the north of the country, in case she'd hopped on a train and was hundreds of miles away by now.

The door that led into the bowels of the police station opened at that moment and another man joined them. He introduced himself as Inspector Guy Laroche, shook hands with Janey and Malcolm and invited them to follow him back to his office. He was about thirty, Janey thought, of medium height and slender build, smartly but casually dressed in plain clothes. A neat little automatic pistol in a shoulder holster was visible inside his sports jacket. Janey never got used to seeing armed police casually wandering the streets — some of them women no older than herself — but Malcolm was accustomed to it.

Sharp features emphasised the thinness of Laroche's face and his thick dark hair fell forward over his eyes every time he moved his head. He was good-looking in a disciplined — military — kind of way, if you liked that sort of thing, which Janey didn't. She noticed for no particular reason that he wore a thick gold wedding band on the middle finger of his right hand. He cleared two seats for them in the cluttered little office and they sat down. He wasn't so easily taken in by Janey as his sergeant had been. 'You speak our language very well,' he remarked. 'I can hardly tell you're not French.'

'I was at the *Lycee Français* in London,' she explained, 'from the age of five. Thank you for seeing us so promptly. Mr Dawson — ' She nodded at Malcolm ' — is very worried about his daughter.'

'Understandably. Poor old man.'

Janey glanced across at Malcolm, testing this description. It occurred to her for the first time what tremendous courage it must have taken to bring him here. There was a steel core inside that unpromising exterior.

'The problem is,' Laroche was saying, 'that there's no evidence that any crime has been committed and, unless or until there is, a full investigation can't be justified. Searching the site of Montprimeur would pose many problems for us: the professor is strongly against it because we might disturb valuable archaeological material and the owners, the Ministry of Defence, are against it because . . . because they like to throw their weight about when dealing with the civil defence forces.'

Janey nodded understanding. Frustrated as she felt, she understood the inspector's position.

'All we have at the moment,' he went on, 'is a woman of twenty-four — by no stretch of the imagination a minor — who's gone away for a few days without informing her colleagues.'

'An action strictly out of character.'

'And yet people *do* act out of character, all the time. Mademoiselle Dawson isn't ill, by all accounts, either physically or mentally. On the contrary, she's described by everyone who knows her as healthy, intelligent and well adjusted. There's been no disagreement between her and her *ami*, Dr Guzman, or if there is he won't admit to it and no one else has seen any evidence of it.'

'All the more reason surely for smelling a rat!' Janey explained about the contraceptive pills. The inspector took the point at once.

'That's interesting, I agree, although if there *has* been a disagreement and she *has* walked out on him, she may have felt she no longer needed those pills.'

'No sensible woman would stop in the middle of a cycle like that.'

Laroche shrugged apologetically. 'A woman, alas, is not sensible at such moments. I'm sorry, but I can't justify any more manpower at the moment. If once we had a body . . . ' He broke off and looked a little shamefacedly at Malcolm who was watching them both eagerly, hoping that the length of their conversation meant there was some news, even if it wasn't good news. The inspector had twin baby daughters of his own and knew that, even in an age that paid lip-service to sexual equality, a missing son could never provoke quite this anguish.

'It's all right,' Janey said to him. 'He doesn't understand anything we're saying.' The policeman looked unconvinced. Like all monolingual speakers, he knew that he spoke God's own language, whose meaning was self-evident, encrypted in its syllables. *Une rose est une rose est une rose* and foreigners merely pretended not to understand that for devious reasons of their own. So language students the world over ask their teacher, What does this outlandish word *mean*? The old man with the sad eyes was merely feigning incomprehension.

'What does he say?' Malcolm asked. Janey explained. 'So they are doing something?'

'I'm sure it's only a matter of time before some rural bobby spots her.'

'But they're not going to come out to the dig, to the hotel, question her colleagues?'

'Not at present.'

'What they want is a body,' he said. 'Then they'll do something — when it's too damn late.'

Janey wondered for a second if he'd understood after all.

Then wondered for another second if it was too damn late already.

★ ★ ★

'My mother had a saying, a sort of proverb from her village in the Gers,' Laroche said, as he saw them out. 'A disappearance is often easier than an explanation.' He handed Janey a small white business card. 'My direct line. Ring me if you find anything concrete.'

151

As they left the station, Laroche was suddenly at their side again. 'Wait!' He took his card back, produced a pen from his jacket pocket and scribbled another number under the official one. 'My home number. Any time.'

★ ★ ★

Malcolm stood on the pavement, thoughtful. 'It's been a hectic couple of days. I didn't know I had it in me to chase halfway across Europe like that.'

'We none of us know what we're capable of until disaster strikes.'

'If Grandfather McCreedy could see me now, perhaps he wouldn't despise me so much.'

'Who?'

'My mother's father. He was a hard man, worked in the shipyards for forty-five years, hands like mallets, high up in the Orange Order. I wasn't the grandson he wanted.' That was another reason Grandfather McCreedy had treated 'the office boy' with contempt — that he wouldn't join the order, wouldn't take part in the rallies and marches, or sing the songs of hate. 'I told you about him,' he said. 'He was the one who built the *Titanic*.'

'Well he wasn't such a great man after all then,' Janey said. 'The bloody thing sank!'

A few seconds passed while Malcolm considered this, then began to laugh. 'I'd never thought of it in those terms. He was so proud of it, more than anything. Damn me, you're right.'

★ ★ ★

'The Languedoc was one of the few places in Europe where Jews could lay their heads in safety,' Janey told Malcolm as they drove to the dig. 'The counts of Toulouse and Foix recognised their skills as bankers and accountants and often made them their chancellors.'

'Isn't the notion that Jews are good with money inherently racist?' he objected. 'Like saying black people have natural rhythm. There must be some Jews who can't balance their own chequebooks or stick to a budget, just as there are blacks with two left feet, and teetotal, humourless Irishmen.'

'Who rattled your cage?'

'It's just that minority groups like to complain about unflattering stereotypes while conniving at flattering ones. You can't have it both ways.'

'Point taken. Whatever the reason, Jews

153

were accepted in the south-west and lived alongside Christians and socialised with them.'

'Bet they didn't intermarry.'

'Well, maybe not. But what everybody forgets is that they lost out in the crusades, too, since they fled into Spain — where they lived in comparative peace until Ferdinand and Isabella came along and set them off on their travels again. They weren't going to hang around on the off chance that de Montfort would be too busy slitting the throats of Cathar babies to bother about them.'

'He might well have left them in peace,' Malcolm said. 'Heresy is more of a danger than another religion. It's more tempting to the faithful, you see, not such a quantum leap.' Janey looked at him in surprise. 'I reached that conclusion last night,' he explained, 'lying awake in bed. Thinking it through stopped me thinking about . . . other things.' He yawned and rubbed his eyes. They were silent for a moment while Malcolm worked himself up to something. 'Do you think Dr Guzman is Jewish?' he asked finally.

'He could well be. Why?'

'Can't you tell?'

'Not unless he suddenly yelps 'Oy, veh!'

at me, no. You could ask him, I suppose, if you thought it was important.'

'It's not that I'm anti-Semitic — '

'It's just that you don't like Jews.'

'No, of course not! I mean it's not that I like Jews — not that I *don't* like Jews ... You're getting me confused now.'

'Spit it out, Malcolm.'

'All I think is that a ... relationship stands the best chance of success if people come from a similar background — same class, religion, race, generation — that's all.'

'The boy next door?'

'Well, why not?' Malcolm's voice turned defensive. 'Ann and I grew up four streets apart, went to the same school. We knew each other since we were children, knew each other's families, understood each other's ways. It's hard to think of one's child marrying a *stranger*.'

'But most people,' Janey pointed out, 'do marry a stranger — in the sense you define it.' She decided that discretion was the better part of valour and didn't tell Malcolm that Simon had been threatening to marry his daughter. Clearly, being her official fiance wouldn't have made Malcolm like him any the better, rather the reverse. 'You want a good mix of genes,' she said, as she parked at the dig, 'to ensure the health of future generations.'

They got out of the car and Janey locked up. Malcolm looked about him and sighed. 'You know, she's been away so much these last six years, and for so long, come home so seldom, that there have been times I've begun to wonder if she still existed.'

★ ★ ★

'I keep thinking about the girl called Dias, Dad, the laundrymaid with the fatherless baby son. She was younger than me, about nineteen according to Louise d'Ambriers. The Cathars weren't keen on sex, even within marriage, yet Dias was cared for and not censured or cast out into the snow.

They were a compassionate people. They didn't believe in capital punishment and thought criminals should be counselled instead of punished. No wonder the Catholic church wanted to crush them: Guardian readers to a man, I shouldn't wonder!'

★ ★ ★

Louise led Robyn through the thronged market-place with its mêlée of stalls, its smell of hot pies, its shouting, squabbling vendors, past the old church and two rows of prosperous housing, before plunging into an alleyway, perhaps six feet wide, which sloped sharply down towards the eastern walls. A channel ran along the middle in which the local inhabitants clearly dumped their household slops. This, Robyn deduced, was the less salubrious part of town.

Louise let go of Robyn's arm to hold her skirts clear of the trickle of waste matter and wrinkled her nose, inviting her companion to share her amused distaste. Dias's hovel was indistinguishable from half a dozen others, a flat-roofed terrace of wooden huts which seemed to prop each other up. The door stood open and Louise walked straight in. Robyn blinked as she entered, for the hut had no windows, and she squinted until her eyes became accustomed to the semi-darkness.

The first thing that struck her was how empty the room was. There was only the smallest fire, unlike the great hearth in Hugues's house which was big enough for a man to walk into. Dias must do her cooking at a communal oven. The bed was a straw mattress on a raised trestle, like the one Robyn herself had been sleeping on. A crude chest lay at the foot of the bed to hold clothes and household effects and a wooden trough, which presumably served some purpose in the laundrywoman's art, lay in the corner filled with what looked like a mess of wet wood ash.

Jehane had swaddled the baby into a limbless parcel, with nothing but a fierce red face jutting out and a hungry mouth. It was wrapped in white linen from head to foot; like a winding sheet, Robyn thought, making of the tiny creature the corpse he would soon become.

He could expect no cradle, this poor maid's bastard, only a share of his mother's palliasse and a hope she wouldn't roll on him in her sleep.

Dias, looking very pleased with herself, was suckling the child and made no attempt to cover herself when her visitors entered, although Jehane looked askance at them both. Robyn had visualised her as an apple-cheeked country maiden, a picture of robust wholesomeness, an earth mother. Now she saw a fat, stupid-looking girl, her flesh billowing in pale folds below the feeding baby, her hips and thighs wide and mottled, her cheeks plump and as red as raspberries. Her teeth, as she smiled a greeting, were discoloured where they were not missing. Above all, Robyn could hardly avert her eyes from the girl's huge flaccid breasts, so different from her own as to render

Dias, surely, a member of another — a mysterious third — gender. She wondered what it could be like to carry that weight around with you all the time, slung about your neck like gourds.

Louise went to stand close to the mother and peered into the baby's wizened face. 'Does he resemble his father?' she asked.

Dias laughed. The baby's paternity was obviously a longstanding joke between them. 'That's for me to know.'

'If he does it was a very old man,' Louise commented. 'See how wrinkled and toothless he is. I bet it was Old Joachim.'

'Aw no, miss!' Dias said. ' 'Ee were a young and lusty man, I can promise you.' They both thought this was very funny and Jehane gave a snort of disgust and left the room.

'Well, thank goodness she's gone,' Louise uttered. She sat down on the bed, her booted feet scuffling the packed dry earth. Robyn felt it best to stay where she was by the doorway. Dias's uneducated dialect, her lack of grammar and her fatigue-slurred diction made her all but unintelligible anyway. Louise pulled the blanket up to make Dias a little more decent for mixed company. 'How are you, dear?'

'Aw, it hurt something terrible, miss. I can't tell you.'

'But Jehane stayed with you all night?'

'Yes,' the girl admitted, answering Louise's questions while all the time ogling Robyn with huge but vacant eyes. 'She done what she could to help. Then washed the baby over all nice in salt and put some honey on his gums.' She concluded eagerly, 'And she took the other one away what was all black and nasty and shrivelled, and buried it.'

Another young woman appeared in Dias's doorway, starting away in alarm when she saw Robyn. Louise rose swiftly and called her back. 'Mengarde! Don't go on our account.'

She came reluctantly back into the hovel and dropped a graceful curtsey to Louise. She was in her mid-twenties, Robyn thought, neither a low-class slattern like Dias nor a lady like Louise but the nearest thing the era had to a respectable middle-class housewife. She was dressed like Jehane, simply, in a clean brown dress with a snowy wimple covering her neat dark hair.

'I expect you've come to look at the new baby,' Louise encouraged her.

Mengarde said in a very low voice, 'I've come to *see*, my lady.'

'Nothing like, Na Piquier,' Dias called

cheerily from the bed. 'But you're welcome to look.'

'We'll leave you to it.' Louise opened the little velvet pocket which hung from her belt and took something dull and metallic out — a copper obol. She pressed the coin into Dias's eager hand and received a rapturous smile of gratitude. Then she motioned Robyn to go and they both slipped out into the street as Mengarde Piquier very slowly and cautiously approached the bed.

'What did she mean?' Robyn asked. 'See?'

'The souls of those who die in childhood return. Did you not know?'

'Metempsychosis?' Robyn said.

Louise rolled her eyes coquettishly. 'Too difficult for me, Master Robert. Mengarde lost her first baby six months ago. Her husband wasn't pleased. She's come to see if she recognises its soul in Pietre.'

'Is that a comfort to her?'

'No doubt it is, although Dias might not be your first choice of custodian for your poor baby's soul, don't you think?' She began to laugh as she turned and led Robyn through the town, slipping her arm through her companion's once more. 'But there's no harm in her,' she said after a moment. 'Dias, I mean. Nor in Na Piquier neither, come to that!'

'You behave to Dias like a friend.'

'You think that wrong? That her ladyship demeans herself? And who are my friends to be exactly? There are few of my rank for a hundred miles around and a girl can't always be lonely.'

'You mistake me. I don't think it wrong.'

'No? Jehane does? She thinks I should make a friend of *her* if I'm that desperate. Now, that would be loneliness!'

'Who's the baby's father? Do you know?'

'She won't tell anyone, not even Hugues. Perhaps she's not sure herself. Some passing tradesman would be my guess. There were plenty of them around last summer before the fighting got dangerously near. One of the itinerant shepherds? I dare say his name was Pietre — or so he told her.'

Some mercenary soldier, Robyn wondered, on his way to join the crusaders? Or some deserter, met one starlit night and tumbled under a haystack? An abiding fantasy for Dias's ill-informed imagination.

Louise turned kittenish again. 'You men care so little where you sow your seed!' Louise might be a Cathar, Robyn reflected, but she was obviously a long way from committing herself to being a Perfect and leading the ascetic life Hugues had adopted. She'd eventually married her cousin de

Chambertin, of course, the Parisian dandy she spoke so slightingly of, and had borne him two sons, so hadn't dedicated her life to her faith.

'Who will see to the laundry while Dias is laid up?' she asked.

'Why, she'll be back about her work tomorrow,' Louise said in surprise. 'How else are she and her baby to eat if she doesn't work?'

'Of course. I wasn't thinking.'

'Tell me,' the young noblewoman asked, abruptly changing the subject, 'what does your father do in England, Master Robert?'

The question took her by surprise. ' . . . He's retired from active work.'

'Indeed? He must be a wealthy man. What *did* he do, then, or did he manage his own estates, act as magistrate for the district and so forth, like my own father?'

'He sort of gave advice to the monarchy,' Robyn said helplessly. This description of her father's minor position in the Northern Ireland civil service pleased her and she smiled.

Louise looked duly impressed. 'He's King John's man? One of his right hand men? Advising him on matters of state?'

'Something like that.'

'And he goes often to court?'

'He's certainly been there.' Robyn excused this lie to herself with memories of a childhood visit to Windsor Castle.

'And are you his eldest son?'

I am all the daughters of my father's house, and all the brothers too.

'I'm his only . . . child.'

She remembered too late that she'd spoken of a sister — lying had never been her strong point — but her new friend didn't seem to notice the discrepancy and was apparently pleased with this reply. Was it possible, Robyn wondered, that she was being sized up as a suitable husband?

'And you've studied at the university?' Louise went on.

'I've studied in Paris,' Robyn replied, glad of a grain of truth in her tale, 'and in England before that.'

'Is there a university in England?' Louise opened her eyes wide. 'I thought only the kingdom of France was so favoured.'

★ ★ ★

'I like her. We all do. I hope she's okay. Obviously I do.'

Dr Meriel Richards examined her archaeological instruments with the cold eye of a surgeon before selecting a four-inch pointed

164

trowel, a small shovel and a wire sieve. She might have chosen a set of what looked remarkably like dentist's picks, or a common kitchen spoon, or even a soft green toothbrush.

They weren't on the summit of Montprimeur but on a small strip of land, perhaps twenty feet wide, between the hill and the wire fence.

'This is where the bodies are buried,' Meriel added.

'What?' Janey took an involuntary step back. The ground beneath her feet looked no different from the rest.

'What was left at the end of hours of non-stop bloodshed, much of it burnt beyond recognition. They dug a shallow trench, here, at the foot of the hill, piled the bodies in and sealed them with quicklime to prevent infection. There were no rite-of-passage ceremonies, but then there was no one left to mourn.' She concluded, 'Just about where you're standing now,' and smiled as Janey jerked away again. 'There is no risk of infection after all this time,' she said clinically, 'and no ghosts walk. If it were a plague pit, now . . . '

'Are you going to dig them up?'

'I expect so. What's left of them. Eventually. There's no hurry. Anything of value would have been stripped from the bodies before or after death, possibly even their clothes.' Her voice was light and unconcerned, as if she was discussing the weather.

Janey, who no sooner thought or felt a thing than found it on her tongue, didn't know what to make of this woman, so alien was her temperament. 'Still waters run deep' was a phrase that came into her mind and she wondered briefly if it was one of those 'truisms' that are true or one of those that aren't. Sleeping waters are the worst, the French said, carrying with it an implicit threat absent from the English proverb.

Meriel — Janey found it hard to think of her as Merry since she seemed, if anything, rather grave — looked younger than her years. If she'd told you she was thirty-two you wouldn't have said 'Pull the other one'. Her style was one of cool sophistication which Janey would have liked to admire but didn't, preferring her own so very unchic English ramshackle.

The archaeologist's body was thin and muscular and Janey was prepared to bet she never ate puddings. Her straight blonde hair was cut blunt to the shoulder and moved smoothly and heavily every time she turned her head. Her lightly-tanned skin was unblemished and largely unlined.

She wore sunglasses, which prevented Janey from seeing her eyes. Her lips were a little on the thin side and she pursed them in concentration, increasing the effect.

She wore linen trousers the colour of bitter chocolate and a beige blouse in a lighter material, possibly silk. Clothes much too good for a dig, surely, but they might be the scruffiest she owned. Her leather shoes were old but good and she wore no socks or tights. She looked elegant and cool despite the fact that she was currently on her knees on a mat in the dust, trowelling soil. She would scrape off a layer with the edge of the trowel into the hand shovel, then sift it into a bucket, working in strips about a foot wide.

A very different type, surely, from Robyn Dawson. Did Simon Guzman have catholic taste in women? 'So what's your theory?' Janey asked, after Meriel had worked for some minutes in silence.

Meriel looked up in surprise as if she'd assumed Janey to be gone. She took off her sunglasses to reveal blue eyes much the colour of the spring sky above them — very pretty, but offering no convenient window to the soul. She put one end of the sunglasses in her mouth and nibbled at the plastic earpiece while she thought. 'I haven't

167

got one,' she said eventually. She put her glasses back on and carried on with what she was doing through the ensuing conversation, having no difficulty in giving her mind to two things at once.

'But people don't simply disappear,' Janey said.

'Actually, you know, they do, all the time, thousands of them every year. I have a friend who's with the police. He's an assistant chief constable in West Lothian — ' she added hastily, in case Janey might think she was friends with mere beat-pounders, ' — and he says mostly it's voluntary — a conscious decision to run out on an impossible situation: an unhappy marriage, huge debts . . . whatever.'

'That hardly applies in this case, though, does it?'

'I'm basically a scientist,' the older woman said. 'I observe data and draw logical conclusions therefrom. But if you want my opinion, I suspect that she and Simon had a row and she packed her case and took off for a few days to teach him a lesson. Simple as that. She's young enough to think that might work and — who knows? — perhaps it will. When she comes back and finds this hysteria — the police called in, her father summoned from home in panic — she's going to be one very embarrassed little girl.'

Janey explained about the contraceptive pills, wondering if she should be keeping this vital piece of evidence up her sleeve. If whoever was responsible for Robyn's disappearance realised that no one was taken in by the impromptu holiday theory, they might take fright. Then anything could happen.

Meriel thought about it for a minute. 'It's the oldest trick in the book when it comes to trapping a man,' she pointed out, her voice a little sour. 'Getting yourself knocked-up,' she elucidated, in case Janey hadn't got the point. She picked up a small brush and began to examine the contents of her sieve more minutely. 'We had something in common,' she said, 'Robyn and I, come to think of it. We both lost our mothers young and were raised by our fathers.' She glanced up, sitting back on her heels, and smiled for the first time. It was a broad and generous smile and she was suddenly Merry after all. 'My father was a professor of philology at Edinburgh,' she explained. 'He hadn't a clue about children but he wouldn't have a nanny fussing about the house, so we muddled by as best we could.'

'It sounds idyllic.' Janey had worked her way through a number of fussy nannies until the agency refused to send any more.

'In many ways,' Merry agreed. 'He used to read me his learned articles instead of bedtime stories, even when I was six and couldn't understand a word. How funny. I'd all but forgotten.'

'When did you see her last?' Janey asked, moving in on the new sense of goodwill.

'It was after lunch, the day before yesterday. I was in the middle of something I wanted to get on with so I grabbed a sandwich on the run.' She got up, rising gracefully with a straight back, and pointed. 'I was round there, where the hill makes a sharp turn and the rest of the group were over there, under those trees.' She frowned. 'At least I think they were all there.'

Janey followed the direction of her finger. 'You can't see one place from the other,' she said.

'No,' Merry agreed. 'Then Robyn appeared round the corner. I must have started slightly, because she waved a sort of apology and called out that she was going to stretch her legs. Then she went on round the next outcrop and was out of my sight.'

'And were you there all afternoon?'

She thought. 'Yes. Nipped into the bushes for a minute at one point.'

'What for?' Merry gave her a sardonic

look. 'Oh, I see. And did anyone else come past you?'

'No one. Simon and the professor were digging around the path where we found some treasures a few weeks ago — a ring, a belt buckle, stuff like that. Pete was with them, I think. Silvie was up in the town itself, pottering about in the place that was supposed to be the Perfect's house. She seems to think that's her special domain.'

Janey did a mental check-off. There was one short. 'What about the American?'

'Of course. I'd forgotten. Dexter took the minibus into St Paul to see if he could find a doctor. He'd gashed his finger badly on a rusty billhook he'd turned up — '

'A what?'

'A billhook — a hedge trimmer, bit like a scythe.'

'Did people have hedges in a hill town?'

'I expect one of the refugees brought it in as a weapon. Anyway, Dexter wanted a couple of stitches and a tetanus shot to be on the safe side.'

As they stood looking at the stark hill, Malcolm came into view about a hundred yards away, wandering disconsolately along the path that circled the site, the one Robyn had walked that mysterious day, his hands in his pockets. He was wearing shiny 'stayprest' trousers, a checked shirt and his tweed jacket and looked very out of place, hot and uncomfortable. He was too wrapped up in his thoughts to see the two women. After a moment his path took him behind some bushes and he vanished from their view.

'Poor little man,' Meriel said soberly. 'When Robyn does turn up, I shall have something pretty sharp to say to her.'

'*If* she turns up.'

Dr Richards gave a little shiver, the way people do when they say someone has walked over their grave, but she made no comment on it. She kneeled down again and continued with what she was doing. 'To lose a child,' she said, 'is the worst thing in the world. It's not right, to have your children die before you. It's not the way Nature intended things to be.'

Janey looked at her sharply. Had there been a child, Simon's child, back in those carefree days of the seventies? The oldest trick in the book, failed? Aborted or adopted, long forgotten by Simon but not by Meriel?

'Dr Guzman will take it pretty hard, too, if she doesn't turn up,' she suggested, to see the effect.

'Simon cares for nobody but himself.' She said the words without judgement, as if she was saying 'Simon has dark hair and brown eyes' — a statement of fact.

Simon had told Janey that Robyn was the best thing that had ever happened to him. Was that just talk, pious cant, or did he feel that way about all his women in the beginning, or had Robyn really been special?

'You can get another lover, even another husband or wife,' the archaeologist went on, 'but not another mother and father and not another child, not a replacement for the one you've lost anyway, and certainly not at Mr Dawson's age.'

'You must know Dr Guzman well.'

She looked up and smiled very faintly and Janey sensed that she knew the reasoning behind the question and that it didn't offend her but, if anything, amused her. 'We're old friends.'

She didn't elaborate. It occurred to Janey that if Meriel was responsible for the loss of Robyn, then she would have disposed very carefully of the body and that she wasn't going to break down and confess. 'So it seems you were the last person to see Robyn.'

'She said she was going right round the hill,' Meriel pointed out, 'which means that she might have met someone coming in the other direction. Or she might have finished her walk and got back to work.'

'How long had you known her?'

'Since she got here — what was it? — eight, nine months ago, something like that.' She frowned again, a scientist, a stickler for accuracy. 'Come to think of it, it must be nearly a year.'

'Was she an asset to the group?'

'She was bright, methodical. I told you, I liked her. Could you . . . You're in my light there, Miss Silverman.' The dismissal was clear. Merry had gone again and only Meriel was there. Janey apologised and moved away.

France was a much bigger country than England, its rural areas more remote, more deserted. You could ramble for hours without meeting the hikers and dog-walkers that were such a feature of the English landscape. Solitude and privacy were useful accomplices to crime. There had been a few cases of tourists — often English, campers and cyclists — being abducted and murdered in wilderness France, the culprit usually an inarticulate, heavy-eyed victim of rural inbreeding, left too much to his own devices by his slightly ashamed family.

Janey stood looking into the distance, her arms folded across her chest. *Robyn* — she willed the thought out into the still countryside — *where are you, Robyn? Are you alive?*

Unsurprisingly, there was no reply.

★ ★ ★

The Cathar meeting-room was full, what with the refugees who were pouring into the town, but Robyn found herself the centre of attention as she came in behind Louise, with everyone present craning their necks to look her over as a whisper licked round the congregation like fire in hay.

As Hugues had indicated, the room was austere, even bare, with whitewashed walls and windows of oiled parchment, torn in places. Almost everyone she'd met was there, except Dias and the other woman; what was her name? Mengarde Piquier. Bruno and Jehane claimed pride of place near the front. Young Joachim was only too visible, towering above the others against one wall. At his side a man with a face like Old Father Time stooped against a rough stick.

'Is that Old Joachim?' she whispered to her escort.

'Mmm? Yes. I think he's older than anyone I've ever known.'

The handful of wooden benches were full and latecomers had to stand, but two middle-aged men hastily offered their seats to Robyn and Louise and the latter accepted for them both with a gracious smile which said, nevertheless, that it was no more than her due.

As they waited for the ceremony to begin, Louise pointed out prominent citizens. Sometimes they heard their names and turned to look, not self-conscious at being singled out by the young noblewoman and the mysterious stranger, flattered. 'That is Bruna the baker and Philippa the alewife, who runs the tavern in the square.' Two fat women who might have been sisters in their matching green kirtles sat up very straight in their seats, their heads bowed in private prayer. 'Gaston the carpenter, Pons the tanner, Vital the tinker who mends our cooking pots.'

Robyn grinned, recalling some scandalous gossip about Vital and the oh-so-respectable-looking Bruna in Louise's diaries. Presumably taking her journals to be forever private, this demure young woman didn't bother to mince her words. 'What's amusing you?' Louise asked.

'Nothing. You talk like a native of the town,' she said.

'I've known this place all my life.'

'Your wet nurse came from here,' she remembered.

Louise turned to her in startled amazement. 'How can you know that? Are you a mystic?'

'Hugues must have mentioned it.'

'Yes. My dear Esclarmonde died but two years ago this autumn.'

At the end of the room stood a table laid with a spotless white cloth. On it was a copy of the gospels, a basin and ewer and some white candles of the best wax. Napkins, as white as the cloth, lay barely visible on it.

'Today we make the public act of contrition,' Louise whispered.

Robyn looked at her in alarm. She'd heard of evangelical groups where people stood up and announced their sins to the assembly. Before she could ask for clarification, Hugues entered the room through another door, Bruno stepped forward to serve him as acolyte, and the meeting began. Those who were seated rose and bowed three times towards the white table chanting, 'Pray God to make a good Christian of me.'

Hugues looked majestic as he intoned in response, *'Adoremus patrem et filium et spiritum sanctum.'*

To Robyn's relief the act of contrition was a general one and no one was called upon to admit publicly to any sins of commission or omission. The only prayer the Cathars

177

favoured was the Lord's Prayer and this was repeated several times along with some other readings from the gospels, especially the Revelation of St John the Divine, whose apocalyptic fervour seemed appropriate at this dangerous time.

The kings of the earth, and the great men, and the rich men, and the chief captains, and the mighty men, and every bondman, and every free man, hid themselves in the dens and in the rocks of the mountains. And said to the mountains and rocks, Fall on us, and hide us from the face of him that sitteth upon the throne, and from the wrath of the Lamb: For the great day of his wrath had come; and who shall be able to stand?

'My friends,' Hugues said, washing his hands for the last time and patting them dry on a white napkin, 'we are living at the end of civilisation, I'm convinced of it. For three years our land, our people, have suffered War, Famine, Pestilence and Death — the Four Horsemen of the Apocalypse. The end of the material world — the world of the devil — is in sight.'

Young Joachim howled ardently.

Death seemed superfluous, Robyn reflected, already encompassed as it was by the other three. And every generation believed itself to be living at the end of civilisation. In 1945 the atom bomb had seemed to seal all their dooms, yet man survived to swarm over the earth, a victim of his own genetic success.

'Let us offer each other the kiss of peace,' Hugues said.

Louise turned her face to Robyn's and Robyn hastily planted a small kiss on her cheek. She smiled and said roguishly, 'We're not Perfects yet, Master Robert,' and kissed her in return on the corner of her mouth.

'It is my intention to hold a mass Consolamentum next Sunday,' Hugues went on. 'I know that not everyone believes themselves yet to be ready for such a step, but under the shadow of death I will make it available to anyone who asks. The Consolamentum *des mourants*. Let those who wish to seek it keep the fast this week and pray God to give us the strength to die for our faith if that is His will.'

★ ★ ★

Dexter Mooney was about forty-five and, to Janey's eye, a singularly unattractive man. He had the Irish look about him that is so difficult to breed out — the coarse red hair, fading now, the ruddy face, the regular but undistinguished features, the thin lips, the thick neck — but he was taller than most

Irish, a good six feet, suggesting at least a generation in high-protein America, if not two. He was a little overweight but didn't hold himself straight which made him appear more so.

He hadn't been keen to be questioned by Janey, giving it as his opinion that they should leave the police to look for Robyn, since that was what they were paid for, and get on with their vital work of excavating Montprimeur. There had been a whispered consultation between him, Simon and the professor which had resulted in his reluctant acquiescence.

'What time did you leave the dig the day before yesterday?' she asked.

'Soon after the lunch break. Say, about two?'

Dexter interested her especially since he'd been the one person absent from the dig on the afternoon of Robyn's disappearance and, crucially, in possession of the group's minibus. Suppose he'd seen Robyn walking along the road, had stopped to offer her a lift, had quarrelled with her, perhaps when she rebuffed an unwanted sexual advance, accidentally killed her with those strong-looking hands of his, digging those oblong fingers with their blunt nails into her neck, hidden the body somewhere or even coolly left it in the minibus, gone back to the hotel, sneaked in while Madame Monami was having her siesta and stolen the case . . .

She took a covert look at Mooney's right hand which was neatly bandaged — not the sort of thing you could easily do yourself with your left. 'You got your hand seen to then?' She tried to sound sympathetic. 'Dr Richards said you'd given it a nasty gash.'

'Huh? Oh, yeah. Just a scratch really, but you can't be too careful. Blood poisoning can kill.'

'Did you manage to find a doctor locally?'

'I decided to go back to Castres so I could ask the old beldame at the hotel to recommend a doctor. You don't know what you're going to get otherwise — some quack horse doctor, like as not.' He grinned at her suddenly; his teeth were even and white in a way that must have put some Massachusetts dentist's children through school.

How convenient, she thought. Ask Madame Monami for a doctor and, while she's phoning, nip quietly upstairs to steal Robyn's bag, with a few spare clothes and her toothbrush to make it look right, shove them out of sight in the boot of the minibus, get your pathetic tetanus jab and dump the bag — and maybe even Robyn's body along with it — somewhere where it wouldn't be found for a good long time.

Where would you choose, Dexter Mooney?

'Did you pass anyone along the road?' she asked.

'No one on foot, although there were a few cars going in both directions. They're not big walkers round here — even the little kids have those mini scooter things to barge about on. Guess it was siesta time too. They close the shops down from twelve till four in these villages, you know, or even later. Crazy. You can't get a can of Coke, not even petrol sometimes.'

'What time did you get back to the dig?'

'Four — four-thirty. More like quarter to five, maybe, because it wasn't that much later, not much more than an hour, that lovesick Simon came bleating that the kid had disappeared and we spent the next three hours getting real hot and sweaty looking for her and yelling for her. I called her some names under my breath, I can tell you.'

Almost three hours to drive to Castres, talk to Madame Monami, get his hand bandaged and his arm punctured and get back to the dig? A pretty slow business. It seemed that Dr Dexter Mooney had had plenty of time to dispose of a body and a bag.

★ ★ ★

As Robyn and Louise left the meeting they passed a man who'd been standing at the back of the room. He followed them into the street and stood expectantly, clearly wanting to talk to Louise but prepared to be infinitely patient. She turned to him with a smile.

'This is Thibaut of Béziers,' she said to Robyn, 'the blood-letter.' She laughed at her companion's startled look. 'Thibaut is the town barber,' she explained. 'He lets blood too, when necessary, for we have no healer in the town.'

Doctors, Robyn knew, were a rare luxury; there might be one in Albi at a pinch, but certainly not in a small country hill town. Surgeons, unlike their modern namesakes, were lesser mortals who amputated limbs in a manner little short of butchery and usually resulting in death.

Thibaut touched his cap respectfully. He was a sturdy man of about thirty-five, plain and ruddy of face, well-muscled, looking more like a soldier than a peaceable workman. He was the only man Robyn had seen who didn't have either a beard or a three-day growth of stubble — a perk of his trade, no doubt. His hair, which was thick and gingery, certainly looked as if he trimmed it himself. 'I'll be glad to give you a shave any day soon, young master,' he said. 'My shop is over the way.' He pointed down a narrow alley where the upper storeys of the opposing houses leaned towards each other like whisperers.

'Thank you,' she said, having no way to explain that she couldn't possibly be in need of his services.

'Why Master Robert is a beardless youth as yet,' Louise exclaimed.

'Well, I'll gladly pull your teeth then,' Thibaut said, as if conferring a great favour.

'I'll think about it,' Robyn said.

'You'll need to make up your mind soon, young sir, since I'll be on my way before the week's out. That's why I wanted to speak to you, my lady, to ask if my lord your father would give me shelter for one night and perhaps sell me a decent horse from his stables. I can pay the proper price for it. I have some money saved.'

'Thibaut fled here from Béziers after the massacre there three years ago,' Louise told Robyn.

'I can't bear it again.' The man looked shamefaced but determined. 'I've lived through two sieges already, remember? I was at Carcassonne too. You damn heretics may not want to live; you may want to shrug off your mortal coat as soon as you may and find a life of everlasting bliss in the spirit, but spare a thought for the rest of us.'

'You're not a member of the sect?' Robyn asked.

'I'm a good Catholic,' he said gruffly, 'but one who wants to live and let live. I can't stand to see good men die whatever the name of their God.'

'But you were in the meeting just now.'

'As were you, young sir. There's no church nearby so I attend Hugues's services as better than nothing for my immortal soul, although there's many would disagree.'

'Violently!' Robyn was impressed by this spirit of ecumenism. 'Where will you go?' she asked.

'I shall keep heading north and west, eventually into Aquitaine. The Jews have already left for Spain. The Languedoc is finished, dead.'

'Not while I'm alive!' Louise said.

Robyn sympathised with this. She looked at the barber with tacit scorn and thought him a coward, since in her young life she'd never known real danger or real fear. She wouldn't run away. She would fight, yes, and die if need be. She was still young enough to believe, somewhere darkly below her rational exterior, that she was immortal and that, even if this proved not to be the case, to die was better than to live in shame.

The barber wasn't offended, only a little saddened. 'You haven't been through it, my lady, my lord, haven't seen what I've seen. You might sing a different tune if you had.'

'Will you tell me about it?' Robyn asked. 'About Béziers?' Her pulse quickened: a first-hand account, an eye-witness; what James Clements would give for this.

'They called upon us Catholics to surrender the heretics,' Thibaut said. 'Neighbour to betray neighbour, do you understand? Even brother to betray brother in some cases. The Catholics would save their lives that way and watch their friends burn in agony at the stake.' He spat into the gutter. 'What sort of people did they think we were?'

'So you refused?'

'So we refused and prepared for a long siege — the first of many. But something strange happened, I don't understand it to this day, the townspeople panicked and suddenly the crusaders were inside our walls. They sacked the city and slaughtered everyone. Women and children were dragged from the church of St Mary Magdalene where they'd sought sanctuary. Some were thrown into the wells and had stones dropped on them, or were left there to starve. Some were buried or boiled alive.' He concluded, 'They saw the ease with which the city fell as proof that God was on their side, of course.'

'They say no vultures follow de Montfort's army,' Louise put in. 'Because he loses no men for them to feed on.'

'He provides them with plenty of other fodder,' Thibaut pointed out angrily. 'It's a foolish myth, begging your pardon, my lady, as you'll maybe see for yourself.'

'But you got out of Béziers?' Robyn asked.

Thibaut's face closed up. 'I escaped,' he said, without elaboration, 'and fled north to Narbonne, but word had gone even faster than me of the atrocities at Béziers. The Narbonnais were terrified and surrendered without a fight. They handed over the Cathars to be burnt and gave food and provisions to de Montfort.' The barber was silent for a moment, awed by his own memories. 'It was the same story all the way inland,' he continued finally. 'People were fleeing before the invading army, burning their crops rather than leaving them to feed the enemy. Every town, every village, every hamlet was empty of souls, the fields ashes and the houses smoking ruins. It was like a journey through hell. I reached Carcassonne towards the end of July with the army only two days behind me, so fast do they move. The town was full to bursting, of course, with the refugees coming from miles around and townspeople from the suburbs forced to retreat within the walls.'

'Like here?' Robyn said.

'Like here, only more so, the town that much bigger.'

'We're small fry compared to Carcassonne,' Louise murmured.

Thibaut continued. 'In better times we might have stood out for months, but it had been a blazing hot summer and the wells were all but dried up — more proof of the righteousness of the crusaders' cause. And no man can survive without water. In no time the pestilence was among us. Fortunately, de Montfort wanted the town as intact as possible so he could use it as his own headquarters, and he agreed to negotiate a surrender. We Catholics were allowed to leave the town in the clothes we stood up in.'

'And the Cathars?' Robyn asked timidly.

'Public burning. I can still taste the stench of it in my nostrils as I sleep. It has made cooked meat as foul to me as it is to Hugues and I get my strength on milk and eggs. You look pale, my young sir. I can tell you much more about what de Montfort is capable of if you will hear it.'

'I think the Sire of Durham has heard

enough,' Louise said quickly, since Robyn did indeed look as if she might faint.

But the barber went on relentlessly. 'At Bram the following year, he blinded every man of the defeated garrison, except one. That one was left to lead his comrades to Cabaret to serve as an awful warning.'

How, Robyn wondered in horror, was the one lucky man chosen? And how could he live with his guilt?

'What happened to the laws of war?' Thibaut asked, his voice rising in a cry of disbelief that seemed to echo across the ages. 'The laws that say a surrendering garrison must be treated decently, honourably? What happened to chivalry? To simple humanity? To de Montfort the Cathars are no more than soulless animals.'

'Enough!' Louise said. 'Our friend is still recovering his strength. I will speak to my father, Thibaut, I promise you. Are you all right, Master Robert?'

Robyn nodded dumbly. It was strange, she thought, that man had always felt the need to draw up rules for warfare, that most unregulated of his major occupations, from chivalry to the Geneva Convention; rules that no tyrant ever hesitated to break when it suited him, justifying it by denying his enemy's humanity.

'So now you know why I'm leaving, master,' Thibaut of Béziers concluded, 'and why you will too if you've an ounce of sense.'

Robyn no longer felt scorn for him. Louise took her arm firmly and marched her back to Hugues's house.

★ ★ ★

'Shall we be here much longer?' Bisette complained one evening to her friend, a redhead from the Roussillon they called La Vierge, because she wore a ragged cloak of Marian blue.

There was a constant flow of camp followers: a girl could appear one day and nobody ask where she came from; another girl would disappear and no one notice or care. Once, a young woman had been found strangled in the river at dawn, her face shorn of all character, all emotion, even surprise, and had been quietly buried.

Insofar as Bisette had a friend, La Vierge was it. The redhead had taken her under her wing, taught her how to take care of herself, rather as an older sister might, by using a plug of wool soaked in vinegar and honey.

'Not long.' La Vierge answered her in her liquid southern vowels. She listened to

190

what the soldiers said around the campfire at night. She found the war interesting as her friend didn't.

'It goes on forever,' Bisette complained.

'The town will fall any day now.' Her voice turned sour. When the town wall was finally breached the soldiers would avail themselves freely of its womenfolk and she, La Vierge, would sleep under a hedge, hungry, that night. She flinched suddenly, rummaged in her bodice and removed a fat flea. She examined it for a second, then squeezed it dead between her fingers with a satisfying popping sound.

The two women sat on the banks of the Agout, their bare feet dragging in the water. It had been a hot day. Bisette was no more than eighteen but La Vierge was twenty-five and had few years left to her trade. Part of her envied the younger girl not only her ripe youth but her tenuous security with the Sire de Bresse, but Nature had made her an optimist and given her a generous spirit and she couldn't begrudge her friend her good fortune for long.

She was a big-boned girl who would have been fleshy if she didn't so often go to bed hungry. She was tanned darker than a redhead had a right to be and her face and arms were sprinkled with freckles. There were men who said a redhead smelt different from other women, men who liked that difference and men who didn't.

'What is this place called again?' Bisette asked.

La Vierge sighed and rolled her eyes. 'Lavaur,' she said, with exaggerated patience. She was fond of the younger girl but found her profoundly dim.

'They all look the same, these hill towns.'

Their eyes ranged across the scattered camp. They saw upwards of five thousand men, of any age from sixteen to sixty, of all complexions and accents, bearded and beardless, tall, short, fat, thin. They were calling a halt to the day's bombardment as the sun lowered in the sky, withdrawing to a safe distance, setting fires in the open, putting carcasses to spit for their dinner.

The girls watched as they trundled back the great catapult they called Malevoisine, the one the Earl of Leicester supervised himself.

La Vierge shaded her eyes against the fierce red of the southern sun. 'Tomorrow,' she said. 'Mark my words. Tomorrow it will be over.'

★ ★ ★

Janey asked Mooney to introduce her to Silvie de Chambertin and he led her over to the south face of the summit where the elderly French woman was to be found. To her surprise she heard him address the older woman in fluent and barely accented French. For some reason she'd assumed him to be a linguistic no-hoper — shouting at the natives in English enhanced by meaningless hand gestures, until they got the point.

Mooney had depths.

She asked politely in French if the old lady could spare a few minutes to talk about Robyn, but Madame de Chambertin replied in excellent English and the conversation continued in that language.

'You speak English so well,' Janey commented.

'I was there in the war, as a teenager. My father was in London with de Gaulle. Adolescents want to blend into the background so I soon learnt.'

She must be seventy, Janey now saw, although she held her slender figure so erect that from a distance she looked like a much younger woman. She kept her hair short and had let it go uncompromisingly grey. She wore no make-up and her skin was a mosaic of fine, dry lines. Although she had a wedding ring on her right hand,

Janey assumed her to be a widow, filling her old age with a passion for history and archaeology where others might garden or make jam. She wore old clothes, a tweed skirt bagging in the seat, a cotton sweater with a hole in one cuff and a silver brooch off the left shoulder. Her legs were thin in tan tights ending in lace-up shoes in brown leather. She looked nothing like the chic Frenchwoman of myth; Meriel Richards was far smarter than she.

'You must have seen so many changes,' Janey said.

'In a way, and yet in another way man's greeds and passions remain the same.' She gestured at the ruined house beside her, the site indicating a one-roomed building, although there was no knowing what the height of it might have been. They could hardly have built high on these limestone foundations, Janey thought, not if they wanted to sleep at night.

The Frenchwoman's hands were small and, like her face, sun-worn and wrinkled, a blue-roped vein prominent on the right one, like a pointer to the ring. 'The Perfect's house,' she explained. 'Where the Cathar leader lived. Normally there would have been more than one of them — the idea being, I suppose, that they helped keep each other on the straight and narrow — but Montprimeur seems to have had only one Perfect at the time of the massacre, the former — technically, the extant — parish priest, Father Hugues de Lizier.'

'Was that usual?' Janey asked. 'For a Catholic to turn heretic like that?'

'Not out of the ordinary. There were even bishops appointed by the Pope who kept the Cathar rituals instead. After all, it was basically the local religion and some of the less educated parishioners adopted the Cathar rites without realising that it wasn't the strict teaching of old Mother Church.'

'So the Perfect was the Cathar priest?'

'There's not an exact correspondence,' the Frenchwoman said. 'Any member of the faith might become a Perfect after a lengthy noviciate — the Abstinentia — and a ceremony called the Consolamentum, but the life of a Perfect was so ascetic that most people postponed making that final commitment until their deathbeds. It meant adopting a vegan diet, you see, fasting several days a week on bread and water and giving up women, naturally. I expect you know that the Cathars didn't approve of sex even inside marriage, let alone out.'

'That sounds convenient,' Janey said wryly. 'Putting it off, I mean, until it becomes academic. We can all swear to be good on our deathbeds.'

The other woman smiled agreement, her blue eyes benign. ' 'Lord make me chaste and continent, but not yet', as St Augustin says. But there is always,' she added more soberly, 'the possibility that death will come unheralded, like the thief in the night, leaving us no time for repentance.'

Which reminded both of them of Robyn.

'She was very special,' Silvie de Chambertin said. 'A good girl — honest, hard-working, clever, with no malice in her. She had a gift for happiness that is rare today when people are spoilt in their expectations, rare especially when childhood has been blighted by tragedy, as hers was.'

'You mean the murder of her mother?'

The older woman inclined her head. 'Just so.'

'When did you see her last, madame?'

'When she went off after lunch saying she wanted some exercise. She was young, little more than a child, and the young need to run around and let off steam.'

Janey, who never did much running, asked, 'And where were you?'

'I came back up here shortly after. This is my special study, this little house. I was here all afternoon.'

'Alone?' She nodded. 'What do you think has happened to Robyn?'

The old woman turned away for a moment and looked out over the purple hills and fields of the Agout Valley. 'My family have lived here for countless generations,' she said. The remark seemed irrelevant but Janey waited patiently. Silvie didn't strike her as a self-centred woman and she was sure there was some point to this. 'I'm descended from the d'Ambriers who were the noble family hereabouts at the time of the massacre. I am a mere epigone, you see.'

'A what? I'm sorry.'

'An epigone — the undistinguished descendant of some great man, or woman. The great poetess Louise d'Ambriers married Aimeric de Chambertin, who was her cousin, and that was my maiden as well as my married name since I, too, married my cousin, Etienne.' She smiled, self-deprecatingly. 'The de Chambertins have often intermarried, you see, believing that no one else was good enough for them.

'I've grown up with these hills and valleys and rivers, with their history and mystery. The most terrible evil was done here, Miss Silverman, one of the worst evils in the history of Christendom, as neighbours betrayed and slaughtered each other in the name of tiny

197

differences of doctrine. Do you believe in evil as a force, a . . . a reality?'

'I don't know,' Janey said. 'I've never thought, but yes, I think I do.'

'My Cathar ancestors did and so do I. You see, I believe that evil gained so strong a hold in this country seven or eight hundred years ago that it lingers here to this day, as the very hills and valleys weep for the lost civilisation of the Languedoc and its dead language whose mellifluous syllables put the harsh northern *Langue d'Oïl* to shame . . . Most girls your age would be embarrassed by such talk.'

'I don't embarrass easily.' In fact, there was a prickling of discomfort at the back of Janey's neck as if someone had put a hairy hand there in the dark when she'd thought herself alone.

'The hills and valleys are crying out for revenge,' the Frenchwoman said, 'and innocent bystanders sometimes get hurt in the mêlée.'

'You don't . . . you can't think that some evil spirit has abducted Robyn?'

'Stranger things have happened. Any local will tell you there's a curse on this place, that the ghosts of the townspeople can't rest quietly in such graves as they have.'

'But you're not afraid to be here?'

'I'm not afraid of anything much at my advanced age — except a long, slow, lonely, painful and confused death in the hospital, perhaps. Besides, if there are ghosts then many of them are the ghosts of my ancestors and I like to think that they will watch over me and spare me.' She sighed. 'Nothing in the world matters more than family.'

It sounded crazy and Janey didn't believe in spirits, good or bad, or in anything she couldn't see with her excellent eyesight, but the old lady was obviously perfectly sane and, suddenly, on that rocky summit, in the strong spring sun, looking down over a vertiginous drop, she felt that anything was possible. Then Silvie de Chambertin's hand was warm on her bare arm. 'My dear! I wish you would come away from the edge. The rocks aren't especially stable and no one could survive a fall like that.'

'No.' Janey turned shakily away from the sheer drop and smiled into the old woman's kindly eyes. 'Thank you.'

'You should invest in a shady hat,' she said. 'Northerners find the sun surprisingly powerful this far south even in spring, especially up on a hill like this, without any cover.'

'I, er, yes. I will.'

'Thibaut didn't explain how he got out of Béziers,' Robyn pointed out when she was feeling better. 'In fact, he was at pains not to explain it.'

She was sharing a dish of jugged hare with Louise — another gift from Jehane's prolific kitchen — while Hugues ate bread and an overripe pear from last year's stock, brown against his fingers. Robyn could see the bones stark on the backs of his hands and realised that Hugues was only a matter of weeks away from death by starvation. She'd heard of the Endura — the fatal fast which was the ultimate sacrifice of the Perfect — but had never expected to see it occurring before her eyes.

Hugues and Louise exchanged glances. 'Thibaut has suffered a great deal,' Hugues said. 'Of your mercy, don't press him for details he would rather not give.'

He changed the subject, but Robyn was suspicious. Thibaut was a Catholic by his own admission; he seemed to have had more than his fair share of luck in surviving sieges so far. The crusaders would be arriving at their walls in a few days — angry, dangerous men. But how much more dangerous was the enemy within?

At that moment a prosperous-looking man appeared in the open doorway, clearly confident of a welcome anywhere. Like most of the men Robyn saw in the streets he wore hose, a shirt and a tunic, but the sleeves of the shirt, visible beneath his surcoat, were of best white linen and he wore shoes of soft leather instead of rough boots. Robyn remembered seeing him at the meeting, seated near the front with a pious look on his face. Now that same handsome face was pinched with annoyance. He carried a torch in his hand, a neatly turned piece of wood, its hollow top stuffed with straw.

'Friend Jaufré Piquier,' Hugues said, by way of greeting.

'Your pardon, Hugues, but can you spare some fire for our Ostal? Mengarde has let it go out. Again.'

'Help yourself.' Hugues gestured. 'I was sorry not to see Mengarde at the meeting. Is she well?'

'Well enough!' The man called Jaufré bent over the fire. 'She's wasted half the morning with that slut Dias. If she took more care of the Ostal this would never have happened. It is not as if she has anything else to do all day!' He stood back from the fire, satisfied with his torch, nodded to Robyn, made a

201

small bow to Louise and left as abruptly as he'd come.

'It was an ill day that joined those two,' Hugues said, with a sigh. 'But he wanted into the Ostal Piquier — '

'Please,' Robyn asked, 'what is an Ostal?'

'Why . . . ' Hugues looked momentarily perplexed. 'It's the house, the hearth, the home, the family, the very centre of our life and culture.'

'Not to mention our ancestors,' Louise added drily. 'Mengarde Piquier's Ostal was a wealthy one, by the standards of Montprimeur, and Jaufré was glad enough to marry into it, but that was five years ago and Mengarde hasn't given him the son he craves and when she finally did, six months ago — '

'The baby died,' Robyn supplied.

'As babies will,' Hugues said. 'The Piquiers have been of our communion for many years and Jaufré claimed to join it when he married her, and yet he longs for a son, a material stake in the future. There's no gainsaying him.'

'Is he a local man?' Robyn asked.

'No,' Hugues said. 'He comes from Castres.'

'And what do the Piquiers do?'

'They make cloth,' Hugues replied. 'They

keep sheep down in the valley and card and spin and weave their own stuffs. They make simple clothes in wool and linen for the local people, but also finer stuff for trade throughout the region. Mengarde embroiders exquisitely.' As he spoke, he took two apples from the barrel in the corner and forced a thin stick through them both, then put them in the fire to bake for his guests.

'It wouldn't surprise me,' Louise mused, as the caramel smell filled the room, 'if Mengarde met with a nasty accident one night. That way Jaufré can keep the wealth of her Ostal and take a fertile woman to wife.'

★ ★ ★

'So is the Consolamentum like Extreme Unction?' Robyn asked, when they'd satisfied their hunger.

'Not exactly,' Hugues said. 'Many — perhaps most — do leave it until their deathbeds, because they don't feel able to promise to leave their wives and homes and give up eating animal flesh, even though the prophet Christ told us that freely surrendering everything we had was the only way to salvation.'

'Not everyone has your willpower, Hugues,' Louise said gently. 'But the number of

Perfects is growing with every year.'
Persecution, as ever, served only to reinforce
what it was intended to crush.

'Do any of them recant?' Robyn asked.

'Precious few,' Hugues replied. 'And those
who do seldom save their lives by it. When
the crusaders enter a town they lay about
them with sword and fire. At Béziers they
cut down even those who were holding up
crucifixes and reliquaries as a sign of their
apostasy.'

'My friend,' Louise laid her hand on
Hugues's arm, 'you're too despondent. You
will see off de Montfort and his men. You
know as well as I do that he holds our
country mainly through bluff. His men aren't
committed to their cause, as we are. The
core of his army is a band of mercenaries
— adventurers and fortune hunters. And
the ones who come to earn Pope Innocent's
favour go home after a few weeks when they
feel they have done enough.'

'I don't know,' Hugues replied. 'I have a
bad feeling about it. You must be sure to
stay safe in the Château d'Ambriers from
now on, Louise. That they have no excuse
to touch and they will not dare. You would
do well to go with her, Robert, if she'll
take you.'

'Of course I'll take him!'

But Robyn shook her head. 'We're agreed, Hugues. My place is here, to the end.'

★ ★ ★

Janey went to look for Malcolm and found him deep in conversation with Peter Finlay. They didn't hear her coming and she was able to observe them both at her leisure.

Peter was an unremarkable boy, looking like most of the young men Janey knew at Oxford. Public school, she decided — something in the tall, healthy blondness of him, the excellence of the teeth in the smile he fixed on Malcolm, the casual way he stood and moved, a cotton sweater slung round his shoulders over a short-sleeved shirt, in contrast to Malcolm's diffident shuffle and comfortless, too neat clothes, his shoulders low with worry.

He was enthusing boyishly about his chosen career, his eyes bright with zeal. 'Think of finding buried treasure,' he was saying as Janey approached them, 'treasure beyond price. Imagine how Howard Carter felt when he made his way into King Tut's tomb and saw riches beyond the dreams of avarice. 'I can see wonderful things!' There can be nothing like it.'

'But that's a once-in-a-generation find,

surely,' Janey interrupted. 'Once-in-a-century, more like. Mostly it's bits of broken pottery and half a plough.'

'I can dream,' he said with a small laugh.

'They wouldn't have had much here,' Malcolm said. 'Poor people, peasants, scratching a living.'

'And then everything looted by the soldiers after the massacre,' Janey added.

'Maybe.' Peter shaded his eyes and looked up the hill. 'There've always been rumours of hidden cellars, caches, folds in the rock, in the town. Most places had them in a time when no one had serious locks on their doors. Who knows that the townspeople didn't squirrel away their valuables — jewellery, some old coins, manuscripts — before the blow fell?'

'They would have been found,' Janey said scornfully, 'during the last eight hundred years. Especially if there are legends about it.'

'But there was supposed to be a curse on the place,' he reminded her.

'All the more reason for small boys to explore it,' Malcolm put in, 'if I remember anything about being a small boy.' Janey smiled gently, picturing a very earnest little Malcolm in short trousers and an Aertex shirt, out and about on his bicycle but never late for his tea. 'It would be a matter of honour to them to come, you see,' he added, wistful for a long-gone, unworried boyhood during and after the war. 'A dare!'

The young man shrugged. 'I can dream,' he repeated. 'And there are those who say that the last known resting place of the Holy Grail was with the Cathars of the Midi, that it was kept in secret at one of their strongholds, that it vanished without trace during the crusades.'

'Children's stories,' Malcolm scoffed.

'There was supposed to be a curse on King Tut's tomb, too,' Janey pointed out, 'not that that stopped Lord Carnarvon and Howard Carter.'

'But it stopped everyone else, for thousands of years in that case.'

'Even if there was treasure,' Malcolm said, 'it wouldn't belong to you. It would be treasure trove, or something.'

'True,' the young man said with a sigh. 'Very true.'

Malcolm remembered Robyn's letter about the chess piece and wondered if young Finlay would be as scrupulous as she.

Janey asked him the usual questions. He'd liked Robyn — although he would hardly have said otherwise in front of Malcolm — describing her as a nice kid. He must be a year or two younger than Robyn, Janey thought, so why the nice kid? Was it just that she was shorter, smaller than he, or because she was female, or because of her residue of working-class Ulster accent, her comprehensive school background?

He'd been pleased to have someone his own age on the dig even though she'd spent most of her free time with Dr Guzman — he grimaced apologetically at this point and Malcolm nodded reassurance. The others were so much older, so experienced, weighed down by their doctorates and professorships or, in the case of Madame de Chambertin, her distantly prewar manners. Janey understood now: Robyn's relationship with Simon placed her among the grown-ups, leaving young Peter on his own, perhaps a little lonely.

He wasn't prepared to offer any theory in explanation of her disappearance, professing himself baffled. He'd heard her say to Simon that she was going for a stroll before resuming work, had watched her — in the sense that he happened to be looking in her direction — until she rounded the corner. That had been the last time he'd seen her.

He'd spent the afternoon sketching a map, a floor plan of the town, since his talents included that of drawing. Almost every day brought some change in the way they viewed the town, some new insight into its layout and the uses to which the disparate buildings had been put. He was kept busy updating their plans.

'Don't you use photographs?' Janey asked.

'We do take photos but a sketch is more useful since it can concentrate on the important things where the camera can't discriminate. I do stratigraphs too — cross-sections of the layers of a site — although Montprimeur existed as a human dwelling place for such a short period of time, perhaps two hundred years, that there aren't really layers here.'

He also did artist's impressions of various parts of the town, he added, mostly for his own amusement. He offered to show them his drawings some time, which offer Janey accepted.

As they left the young man to get on with his work, Malcolm said under his breath, 'Holy Grail, indeed!'

* * *

'You're very fond of the lady Louise,' Robyn said at nightfall. The young woman had left them to spend the night at the home of a respectable widow of her acquaintance.

'You must understand that until you came along, Robert, Louise was the only person I could talk to. The people of Montprimeur are dear, good people, loyal and hard-working, but they're uneducated and simple and one can't converse with them as equals. Louise can read a little Latin as well as French and Occitan. She's travelled with her father, in former times, before the wars, has been to Paris and even further afield. She's read a little philosophy and logic. She knows the rudiments of arithmetic and astronomy. She understands music and literature. I thank God daily for her good friendship.' Hugues smiled. 'Except that she wouldn't learn chess. She says she prefers a game with an element of luck to it!'

'She must find it dull round here,' Robyn suggested. 'In general.'

The priest shrugged. 'It's the way of the world. Her father's old now and has no more use for travel and gaiety. Louise, as his only child, must be both companion and nursemaid to him, unless or until she marries.'

'Do you think she will marry?'

Hugues lifted his shoulders again. 'She meets no young men of her own rank so it is hard to see whom she may marry. I hope she'll be spared that temptation. No, like so many young women before her, she must find her pleasure in doing her duty and in country pursuits.'

'Her mother died, I think, a few years ago.' Hugues's pale face went red, his struggle between truth and discretion almost tangible. Lying was anathema to him. Sensing his distress Robyn said gently, 'Hugues?'

'Why do I find it so hard to dissemble with you, Robert? The lady Anne is not dead.'

'But I thought — '

'She's kept . . . locked away, at the Château d'Ambriers.'

'But why? I don't understand.'

'She's sick, sick in her mind — oh, she's danger to nobody but herself. She's safe, loved, attended. Her every comfort is secured.'

'She's mad?' Hugues nodded. 'Oh, poor Louise!'

'It has been so since Louise was born. She . . . she tried to kill her own baby within hours of the birth.'

Post-natal psychosis, Robyn thought, and they'd locked her up for life.

'That's why the Count has never remarried. He's not free. That's why he travelled so widely in his youth: he couldn't bear it at home, seeing the woman he loved . . . '

The story seemed familiar to Robyn, as if

211

she had heard something like it, and not at all long ago, except that she couldn't remember. Hugues rose and poked the fire, putting a log on to see them through the night. 'Time for sleep; I think. Let's get our rest while we can.'

★ ★ ★

That same evening Bisette stood watching in a group of a dozen or so soldiers as La Vierge danced to the music of a lute and tabor. Late at night, when she was drunk, she would do wild gipsy dances, swirling among the crowds, from bonfire to bonfire, like a giant firefly; but now her movements were slow and sinuous, designed to arouse custom. Bisette clapped along with the rhythm, tossing her head from side to side, thinking that there was no better place to be on a fine spring dusk.

The music came to a sudden cacophonic stop as two riders entered the camp near them, passing the guardpost without pausing, clearly expected by the soldiers there. One pulled his grey horse to a halt beside their little party, surveying them down his broad nose. He was a small, dark man of about forty, tonsured and wearing a white robe. La Vierge stopped her dance and dropped a little curtsey but Bisette could see, behind her back, that her fingers made the sign against the evil eye.

His companion was younger, about twenty-five, tall and blond, handsome, richly dressed, mounted on a mettlesome black pony. Neither a soldier nor a monk, Bisette thought, more of an easy-living nobleman. He regarded the two girls with a more benign eye than his friend, flickering from one to the other before settling on Bisette. He winked at her. She tried to give him a frosty look but couldn't keep it up. She began to giggle, putting her hand across her mouth.

The first man stared at them for a moment in haughty contempt, then gathered up his reins and, kicking his horse in the side, said, 'Come, my lord, let us not tarry,' and rode briskly away towards the centre of the camp. His companion doffed his cap with exaggerated respect to Bisette, who giggled even harder, before following the white-robed cleric.

'Who was that?' Bisette asked.

La Vierge shrugged. She had no business with monks and priests. It wasn't that they were indifferent to her wares, just that they never wanted to pay, deeming a blessing and some mumbled prayers sufficient recompense. A light voice with a gutteral accent answered her in adequate French. 'His name is Dominic, a monk and a priest, a Spaniard.' The speaker was Heinz, a redheaded Rhinelander, thin as a whippet, a mercenary but a good-natured man who wasn't mean with his drink. 'He is the Pope's envoy,' he went on, 'sent to preach against the heretic. He and de Montfort are old friends.'

'I meant the other one.'

'Him I have not seen before. Dominic will have heard that we are about to breach the wall and come to watch them burn.'

'You see,' La Vierge whispered to her friend. 'I told you it would be soon.' The soldiers were calling to her to dance some more but her movements had served their purpose. Heinz took her by the hand and led her unceremoniously away to groans and catcalls from the others.

A young man, a sweet-faced lad of perhaps twenty-one who had fought against the Moors as a fourteen-year-old, began to sing a crusader's song. The lutenist picked up the tune and the tabor soon joined in, resounding in marching time.

Chevalier, mult estes guariz,
Quant Deu a vus fait sa clamur.

Bisette slipped away into the night, humming the tune to herself, trying to recall the words. Knights, you are fortunate that God has called to you.

★ ★ ★

'This would have been the market square. This was the centre of town and had the valuable attribute of being flat.' James Clements stood in the middle of the hilltop and spread his arms to embrace the space. He looked cool in cream cotton trousers and a pistachio-coloured shirt, his customary straw hat shielding his dark eyes. He seemed happy with an audience, even of only two, a man accustomed to public attention, accepting it as his due.

'Montprimeur was a thriving little town until the crusades began,' he explained, 'and there would have been stalls here most days. People would come to shop and exchange gossip. This was truly the heart of the town with its location next to the church.'

Malcolm followed his pointing finger. The crusaders hadn't destroyed the church — time and climate alone had done that, plant and animal life, wind and rain, frost and intense sunlight — and its crumbling walls still rose eight feet in the air to the east of the square, its inside ruined and empty. Compared to the rest of the town it was a conspicuous survivor.

'What did these people believe, anyway?' he asked, gesturing at the dilapidation around him, 'that they must be *annihilated*?'

'They were dualists,' the professor said.

Malcolm turned and looked at him steadily, and the professor apologised and explained. 'Orthodox Christianity believes that God is the supreme power — a power for good that will eventually triumph over the devil at the last reckoning. Dualists, on the other hand, believe that good and evil are *equal* powers, engaged in a struggle in which first one and then the other gains the whip hand, for eternity.'

Malcolm thought about this for a moment. 'That makes perfectly good sense to me,' he said finally.

'But thinking so, or at least saying so, would have got you burnt as a heretic eight hundred years ago. In fact, Christian dualism is as old as Christianity itself; the Gnostics began it in the first century after Christ.'

'I suppose,' Malcolm said, 'that the moment they looked about them and perceived the problem of evil, they had to find an explanation. And theirs is as good as any I've come across.'

'It seems to me,' Janey put in, 'that if good and evil are equal forces, then evil will triumph in the end because, when it comes to the crunch, it'll fight dirty.'

'Also,' James said, 'the Cathars believed that worldly matter was the work of the evil power and only the spirit world belonged to God.' He quoted: ' 'The soul is a point of light, trapped in the darkness of the body.' '

Malcolm slowly shook his head. 'Now that I don't agree with. Life is laughter and weeping, birth and death, pain and rapture; and the remembrance of those things.'

'Hear, hear!' James said.

'You can say that,' Janey burst out, 'after what happened to your wife?'

'Every time I stand by her grave,' Malcolm answered simply, 'I remember the great joy she gave me: the day I put my ring on her finger, the moment she placed Robyn in my arms, a Sunday hike together across the hills of Antrim, stopping for a picnic when we were too tired to go on.' He smiled thinly, a little embarrassed, and ran his fingers through his hair.

James, respecting his confusion, talked on. 'Farmers' wives brought their eggs, milk, butter and honey here to sell. The cobbler would sell you a pair of shoes if he could or, more likely, mend an old pair for you. The potter would bring his wares. Itinerant knife grinders would mend tools or sharpen blades. There would be hot pie stalls on feast days. That might be the only hot food the very poor got. If you hadn't got your own fireplace, you used the communal oven or lived on black bread and herbs.'

'I suppose there were a lot of very poor people?' Malcolm ventured.

'Not especially. Perhaps ten per cent, like the underclass of today — the level of poverty being strictly relative, of course. Everyone else managed; they didn't go hungry or cold, or not often; they kept themselves decent, tended their sick and buried their dead. It was the same sort of people who went under, too: the old, the disabled and chronically ill, widows, single mothers, the unemployed and unskilled.'

'How would they live?' Malcolm asked.

'There was a little private charity, but essentially old people had to live with their children or grandchildren if they were to survive. People who remained childless could look forward to a rough old age. That's one reason that, unless you went into the church, marriage was more or less obligatory.'

Malcolm nodded, comprehending. 'When people ask why the starving of the Third

World don't stop breeding, they misunderstand the nature of peasant farming communities. You see it a lot in rural Ireland. A man needs sons to do the hard work on the land for little pay, and daughters to milk the cows and bake and sew. The childless are the poor.'

'But the Cathars rejected marriage and childbearing,' James explained. 'Theirs was essentially a self-limiting system, in that, if it has succeeded, they must eventually have died out anyway. It is a religion without hope and doesn't, therefore, appeal to me personally.'

'But you would defend to the death their right to their beliefs,' Malcolm said with a small smile.

'Perhaps not to the death,' James replied.

'And the Church,' Malcolm murmured. 'Always dominating everything.' It seemed at once familiar and alien.

As if reading his thoughts, the professor continued, 'Things didn't change all that much in the next six hundred years. It was only with the coming of the railways that human life took a great leap forward. After that there was no stopping us: gas, electricity, sewerage, the internal combustion engine, powered flight, heart transplants, space travel. All — in terms of historical perspective — in the blinking of an eye.'

'Why do you drive this car, anyway?' Malcolm asked, as they rattled over a pothole, shaking the suspension. 'Inverted snobbery?'

'It annoys my mother to see it parked in the driveway of her elegant Surrey mansion. She offered to buy me a new car for my twenty-first birthday in February, anything within reason, but I said no.'

'I do call that cutting off your nose to spite your face.'

'My Reliant gets me from A to B. Who could ask for more?' Janey grinned. 'She doesn't like the way I talk either.'

'Poor little rich girl,' Malcolm said wryly.

★ ★ ★

Sleep didn't come easily to Robyn that night and her thoughts were full of home, in the 1990s, of her real life, of Simon — things that were starting to seem part of a dream world. It was like the Chinese philosopher who dreamt he was a butterfly and could never after be sure that he wasn't a butterfly dreaming it was a Chinese philosopher.

Sex had been something new with Simon, different from the hasty fumblings of her

Durham classmates. Like many women, she'd reached the age of twenty-three disappointed by her experiences with men — messy and unsatisfying couplings, so far removed from the adolescent's fevered imaginings, fuelled by television and cheap novels.

She hadn't been brought up to think of sex as dirty: her parents had been reserved rather than prudish and they were physically demonstrative, both with each other and with their only daughter. Their own mutual passion was still evident in early middle age, even to the child Robyn.

On her twelfth birthday her father had given her a book on the subject — a dry book with complicated diagrams — and mumbled his sorrow that her mother wasn't there to guide her on this point. He'd offered, bravely, to answer any questions that might arise from her reading, but she'd spared him that embarrassment and turned to a sympathetic form teacher who had been informative and at ease with the subject.

So when she reached Durham in the autumn of 1990 it was in the eager expectation of careful experiment. There had been no shortage of willing partners but somehow the experience wasn't what she'd hoped for and soon she began to concentrate on her studies and on her large circle of friends — both male and female — dismissing fictional orgasms as advertising hype, written by men.

During her post-graduate year at Nanterre she'd had a French lover for a few months, an earnest twenty-five-year-old schoolteacher from Neuilly, the sort who thought you could change the world by going on marches; but if she'd hoped for better things in leaving behind the notoriously inhibited English for the famously passionate French, Thierry had failed to live up to his race's reputation, and she'd said goodbye to him without regret when June came and her master's thesis was finished.

She'd been in awe of Simon at first, struck by his handsome person and impressed by his academic qualifications and his man-of-the-world manner. She'd no more thought of him as a potential lover than she had the professor, assuming him to be, among other things, out of her league. It wasn't that she thought herself unattractive — she was athletic and healthy and had always felt what the French called *bien dans sa peau*, which seemed, perhaps significantly, to have no English translation — but in her limited experience men who looked like Simon kept company with beautiful, sophisticated, well-groomed women — women such as Meriel

Richards — not with gamine girls.

Until one evening, four or five months after her arrival, they'd been hunched together over some maps, their faces necessarily close. He'd turned his head towards her to emphasise some point and their lips had been mere inches apart. And then not even inches, as they'd moved instinctively forward to kiss. It was a gentle exchange, inquisitive, which raised more questions than it answered. They'd straightened up, their map forgotten, and looked at each other in silent query. Then Simon said, 'I've wanted to do that for a long time', and they both began to laugh because it sounded so cornily like a line from an old film.

'What about Merry?' she asked him scrupulously.

'I told her weeks ago that I was falling for you. She wished me luck, said you would be good for me.'

'You make me sound like a medicine.'

He said, 'You taste nicer than any medicine I've ever swallowed.' And tasted her some more.

So, first in her little attic room and then in the big shared chamber on the first floor, she'd experienced the deep, slow ripples of pleasure she'd given up dreaming of. She'd never felt so relaxed; it was like those rare hot nights of her Belfast childhood when she'd slept, naked and warm, her arms and legs limply disposed under the white cotton sheet like those of a rag doll, a sleep of perfect peace.

It was time to sleep now, time to cry herself to sleep. As so often when she found herself wakeful, she thought about the terraced house in Jericho that Simon had described to her, imagining them living there together. It gave a sort of comfort but her cheeks were soon wet with the inescapable thought that that happy future might never be.

She did remember one thing her father had said to her, not long after giving her the book of diagrams: do not confuse passion with love.

★ ★ ★

Madame Monami was pacing the hall when Janey and Malcolm entered the hotel half an hour later, wearing her usual black dress and a clean apron. She seemed almost literally to be wringing her hands. As soon as she saw them she darted forward. 'Have you seen my Joachim?'

'No,' Janey said startled, 'but we've

come straight from the dig, straight from Montprimeur.'

'Montprimeur.' The woman spat the word out. 'That place is accursed. I said no good would come of interfering with it after all this time. First the girl and now this.'

'Whatever's the matter with her?' Malcolm asked.

'I don't know. Something about Joachim. What is it, madame?'

'He went out after lunch as usual. He should have been back here a good hour ago to lay the table and help with the supper, but he isn't here.'

'It's only an hour,' Janey pointed out.

'You don't understand. He's never late.'

'Where does he go in the afternoons?'

The woman shrugged. 'Nowhere much. Occasionally he goes to the cinema if there's a children's film on. Mostly he hangs about, looks in shop windows, walks by the river, sits in the square and reads his comic books.'

'Have you tried his friends?'

Madame Monami looked at her as if she were mad. 'He has no friends.'

'What is it?' Malcolm asked insistently. Janey explained. He went pale. 'You don't think there's a connection?'

'How can there be?' The telephone on

225

the reception desk began to ring at that moment. 'There,' Janey said to the frantic mother, 'that'll be him now.'

The woman gave her a look of contempt. 'He doesn't use the phone.'

They stood there in the hall as the telephone went on in long, unbroken rings unlike the English two-tone. 'Well, someone had better answer it,' Malcolm pointed out.

Janey snatched up the receiver. '*Allo, oui? Non, l'hotel est complet en ce moment. Je suis desolée. Oui. Au revoir.*' She hung up. 'Just someone wanting to book a room.'

The back door opened again and Madame Monami looked up hopefully but it was only Simon and Dr Mooney, both come back in Simon's car.

'I hope dinner's ready,' the American said. 'I'm starving . . . What's up?'

'I don't think there's going to be any dinner,' Janey said. She explained.

Mooney whistled. 'Okay,' he said. 'Let's keep calm here but let's not waste time like we did before. The kid's probably lost track of how late it is, but we're not taking any chances. It's getting dark out there. Janey, Simon, you come with me on foot. Mr Dawson, you wait here for the others, tell them what's happened and get them to go out again in the minibus.'

They followed him meekly out of the front door. 'Okay,' he said again, 'Janey, you take the main route to the town centre. Simon, cut through the park by the river. I'll go round by the one-way system. Ask everyone you meet if they've seen him — he must be a familiar sight to the locals. Meet up outside the *Bon Marché* in twenty minutes.'

'What was that?' Janey said.

They looked in the direction she'd turned. Both men could hear it now too, a grunting like an animal in great pain coming from a blind alleyway a few yards up the street. They ran towards it. Simon, the fittest of the three, got there first but the others were only seconds behind him.

'Shit!' Mooney said. 'Janey, run back to the hotel and get an ambulance.' She obeyed at once. 'Joachim? Can you hear me, pal? One grunt for yes.'

The boy grunted.

'He's taken a hell of a beating,' Simon said. 'Look at his face.'

'I'm kinda trying not to look, thanks.'

Janey was back in five minutes, severely short of puff. She stood doubled over, panting. 'Nod your head if the ambulance is on its way,' Mooney said. She nodded.

'Good girl.' Simon put his arm protectively round her as she straightened up. Joachim began to crawl away from them, heading for the hotel on all fours. 'Whoa!' Mooney said. 'You're not going anywhere, boy.'

'He's crawled a long way already by the look of it,' Simon pointed out, indicating a trail of blood along the pavement from the corner. 'Making for home.' Joachim with a surge of strength, pushed Mooney out of the way, got to his feet and lurched along the road.

'What's that in his hand?' Simon asked as they caught up with him.

'It's a scrap of torn material,' Janey said. She prised it out of his tenacious fingers. 'Give, Joachim.' She held up a ragged piece of cotton perhaps four inches by six, hemmed along one edge. 'Bit of a tee shirt, I think,' she said.

It was blue, with the tail end of a gold fleur-de-lys.

Madame Monami appeared in the doorway at that moment, with James hard on her heels. At the sight of her only son — his torn lip, his broken nose, his blackened eye, his blood-soaked clothes — she screamed long and hard. 'Jojo!'

'It's not as bad as it looks, *Maman*,' the boy said, coherently. He put his arms round her, bloodying the crisp white collar of her blouse, as they heard the sirens a few streets away.

★ ★ ★

'The *Enfants de France*, naturally,' the professor said, when he got back from the hospital with Madame Monami four hours later. They were gathered in the dining-room and the woman had silently opened a bottle of brandy and poured a large one for each of them. It was her way of thanking them.

'Poor kid,' James went on. 'Seems one of them was someone he was at school with, considered more or less a mate. He's totally bewildered as to why his old pal Eric wanted to beat the shit out of him.'

'Well, why did they?' Janey asked. 'He's not black or Jewish or Arab.'

'No, but he's subnormal. Mentally unfit, as our fascist friends would have it. Got to be stamped out to preserve the purity of the master race, the white race.'

'That's sick!'

They were speaking in English and Madame Monami turned to stare at each speaker in turn as if concentration might bring enlightenment.

'He *is* going to be all right?' Malcolm asked.

'He hasn't any broken bones, more by luck than any mercy of our thuggish friends. As he said himself, it's not as bad as it looks, just an awful lot of blood. He won't win any beauty competitions, but then he wouldn't have yesterday.'

'Will I be able to play the piano, doctor?' Mooney said. 'Sure you will. That's great, because I couldn't before.'

'The charming Eric, that fount of friendship, is being questioned at the police station at the moment,' James went on, 'but his loving mum has alibied him. It seems he was at home with her all afternoon and evening watching TV, except that he can't remember what it was he was watching — some film, apparently! I expect she'll crack eventually.'

'I think I could identify the one who spat at me last night,' Janey said.

'What good will that do?' James asked. 'It could have been any one of two hundred youths who did this. The town is crawling with them. The Languedoc is the most economically depressed area of France. It has the worst unemployment in the country. The perfect breeding ground for this sort of thing.'

230

'How long are they keeping him in?' Mooney asked.

'He'll be home in the morning,' James said. 'A few days rest is prescribed. He'll be fine . . . this time.'

4

'I have preached and prayed. I have wept.
Where I can't bring blessing
I shall bring the sword.'

St Dominic

*'We have at last learned the fate of our
kinsmen at Lavaur. It seems that Aimery
de Montréal, who had taken eighty men
to reinforce the town, escaped lightly: he
was hanged. His men had their throats cut,
also quick if not exactly merciful.*

*Aimery's sister Guiraude, Lady of Lavaur,
fared less well. De Montfort gave her to
his soldiers to do with as they pleased.
When they had done with her they threw
her down the well and stoned her to death
over a period of several hours.*

*In her place, I think I would have turned
my knife upon myself as the crusaders
entered the town.*

*My father is very low in spirits. He
feels it terribly. We both do. He thinks
the nobility have a duty to stand together,
not to kill each other.*

We wait in fear now, to hear the news

from Montprimeur.'

Diaries of Louise d'Ambriers, Scholar and Matriarch.

ibid

* * *

Robyn was awake early the following morning. As she rose from her bed she heard something scuttle away into the corner and hoped it was only a mouse. She took a bucket and slipped out to the nearest well to fill it. The bell was tolling as she made her way through the crowded streets and queued for her turn. Back at Hugues's house she poured boiling water from the perennial kettle into a basin and cooled it with water from her bucket. She refilled the kettle with cold water and set it back in the fire to boil.

It felt like a routine. She washed herself from head to toe in the basin. Even without soap, it was bliss. She was safely dressed again and finishing off her hands and face when Hugues appeared in the doorway, his expression grim. 'Don't take water from the well,' was his only comment on observing her activity. 'We shall need it soon, every drop of it. Young Joachim brings water up from the river every morning, noon and evening. It's a good job for him: it allows him to use the

233

great strength, which he has, and demands no thought, which he lacks.'

'Why's the bell tolling?' she asked.

'Lavaur has fallen.'

Robyn took the basin to the door and emptied the dirty water into the gutter while she digested these three devastating words. Lavaur was only ten miles to the north-west. History recorded that de Montfort had taken it by force on 3 May 1211. He would pause for the minimum time to secure the town before marching on.

Which meant that he would be in Montprimeur within three days.

'I shall hold the Consolamentum this evening,' Hugues went on. 'Next Sunday may now be too late.'

* * *

Malcolm was sitting on a bench in the *Jardin de l'Evéché* in the centre of Castres, on the banks of the river. He'd been there for most of the morning. The serene beauty of the narrow daub-and-wattle houses he'd passed on the way, their balconies overhanging the river in vertiginous slope, made him think he might have been hasty in disliking this place.

Every time a young woman with dark hair

came into view he would sit up eagerly, but it was never Robyn. Janey had asked if she might read Robyn's letters and he'd agreed after some thought, since there seemed no good reason why she shouldn't. He'd left her in the hotel dining-room after breakfast, the miscellany of papers spread out on the table in front of her. Clearly she viewed this as an act of scholarship.

Not knowing what else to do, he'd found this park and claimed the seat with the best view. There was a pair of swans on the river with two gawky brown cygnets. Plenty of people had come by, many of them dog walkers like at home, even one or two sweating joggers. The dogs were what he thought of as silly, useless dogs — poodles, chihuahuas, pekes — fashion accessories. An old lady had thrown stale bread to the eager birds and made some comment to Malcolm to which he nodded and smiled, assuming it to be about the fine spring weather or the pretty chicks. She seemed satisfied. It was odd, he thought, how easily this park might be in Belfast — the same people with the same faces, the same preoccupations.

He'd left his post only once, to go in search of a cup of coffee mid-morning; he'd been unable to find anything he recognised as a café and had ended up at a bar where the barman had understood the one English word, coffee, and hadn't overcharged him too grossly for being a foreigner and unable to understand the currency.

The place hadn't been busy and he'd shown the barman the photograph of Robyn in her graduate robes but he'd been unable to frame the necessary question. Have you seen this girl? Or rather, Have you seen her *lately*. The barman had simply nodded and smiled and said, *'Jolie fille'* with a relish which Malcolm didn't much like, wondering if the young man thought he was offering her for sale.

On the way back he'd passed a newsagent with a rack of English papers outside and had bought the *Daily Mail* at five times its normal price. It was only as he settled back on the bench that he realised the paper was two days old and that he'd read it on the plane to Gatwick. He crumpled it in disgust and put it in the waste bin beside him.

The sun was high in the sky now and soon he would have to venture out again in search of something to eat.

'Sorry I've been such a time. It took longer than I thought.'

He hadn't heard Janey come up alongside him until she sat down and spoke. 'Oh, hello,' he said.

'Here.' Janey handed him a white paper bag. He looked inside it and found a baguette oozing with ripe Camembert garnished with lettuce, tomatoes and mayonnaise. The bread was fresh and crisp. 'Lunch,' Janey said. She pulled an identical sandwich from an identical bag and bit into it. Malcolm emulated her. It tasted good.

'How did you get on?' he asked, munching.

'She sounds like . . . fun,' Janey said, after a pause for thought.

'Yes,' Malcolm said in surprise. 'She was. Is. She's fun.'

'Only the way everyone spoke about her, being so mature and clever and everything, I somehow had this idea that she might be a bit of a stuffed shirt, the school swot.'

Malcolm didn't take offence. He said, 'No, never that.'

Janey had drawn a few conclusions from the letters. As Malcolm had said there was no intimate mention of Simon; indeed, she referred to him as Dr Guzman, but it was there if you cared to read between the lines, in that she lost no opportunity to mention his name, as lovers do. Talk of a trip to Barcelona at Easter for 'a few of us' certainly meant a group of two.

The other thing that struck her was how seldom Robyn went home to Belfast, particularly since her arrival in Castres, making a number of reasonable excuses over the months. Was it just a long and troublesome journey, a wish not to be parted from her beloved, or a desire not to see her father? She didn't think she could ask.

She went home rarely herself. She didn't dislike her present stepfather: she thought him generally a kind man and good for her mother, and he made her welcome in his house. Last summer they'd gone fishing together, much to her mother's annoyance. Part of her didn't want to get too attached to him as experience suggested he wouldn't last long. She loved her mother but had nothing in common with her and they ended up arguing, however good their intentions. Mostly she felt like the parent, with her mother — now morosely squaring up to forty-five and facelifts — the feckless child.

'How did you and Robyn get on when she was home?' she asked.

His face glowed. 'That was wonderful. We would go for long walks and talk about all manner of things and she would take me out to dinner and make me go to films and plays I wouldn't normally bother with.'

'You looked forward to her visits.'

'Oh, yes. I counted the weeks between them.' Brought up to be strictly truthful, he amended this. 'The months.'

'You would have liked her to come more often?'

'She had her life to lead. Old men are dull for young women, and I'm duller than most.'

'I wouldn't say that.'

'Wouldn't you?' He turned a sweet, knowing smile on her. 'That's the first bit of tact I've heard from you, Janey.'

'I mean it. I don't think you're dull.'

'That's because I'm in an extraordinary situation,' he said. 'An object of interest for the moment, of pity.'

'No, not pity. I think you're very strong, Malcolm. I think you're a survivor.'

'Is that good?'

'Of course it is.'

'I don't know. Sometimes I wonder if it isn't easier to let go, to stop swimming and let the waters close over your head.' He swallowed the last of his baguette, stood up and squared his shoulders. He became a taller and more forceful man. He crumpled his empty paper bag into a ball and dropped it into the bin on top of the unwanted newspaper. 'Come along,' he said to Janey.

He turned without another word and began to walk away, back towards the hotel. Janey jumped up and scuttled after him, leaving her own bag to the will of the wind. 'Where are we going?'

'We've wasted enough time. Let's go and look for Robyn's suitcase. That must be the key to this.'

'Whoever took the bag did it in a hurry,' Janey mused as they walked briskly through the quiet streets. 'Probably in a panic, cramming in a few things to make it look as if she'd taken off. If it was Dr Mooney, then he had the minibus; anyone else would have been on foot.'

'Except Dr Guzman.'

'Except Simon. Even Dr Mooney wouldn't have taken it very far, I don't think. He wouldn't have needed to. If we can find it, it will be proof that there's been some sort of foul play and then the police will have no excuse not to treat our complaint seriously. You'd recognise it?'

'I suppose so. Yes, she's had it for years. It's like a gym bag only in soft black leather, not very big, literally for weekends.'

'The hotel is the obvious place to start, assuming the perpetrator was on foot.'

'It has to be one of them, doesn't it?' he said. 'But they seem so . . . nice,' he finished lamely.

'I don't see how it can be anyone else. If she'd just disappeared, okay, it could be any

240

passing nutter, but it always comes back to the bag.'

'Six of them,' he mused. 'Is it more likely to be a man? One feels somehow that it is.'

'She's small, isn't she?' Janey replied doubtfully. 'It wouldn't take much strength to . . . er . . . knock her out, even shift her.'

But Malcolm went on, as if not hearing. 'Four men: the professor, Dr Guzman, Dr Mooney and Peter Finlay. Quite a disparate bunch, wouldn't you say?'

She nodded, agreeing. 'Differences in age, certainly, nationality, temperament. None of them strikes me as a cold — ' She stopped abruptly.

'Cold-blooded killer.' He finished the sentence for her. 'Stop pussyfooting around me, Janey Silverman. I know she might be dead.' He stopped and banged one fist with the other, hard. 'I'm not an idiot and I won't be treated like one.'

'Be angry, Malcolm: anger drives out fear.'

He subsided. 'I've been used to suppressing anger. That was what I was taught as a child. I can't keep it up for long. It seems wrong.'

'Be angry with me. I can take it.'

'After all you've done for me?' He shook

his head. 'You are my good angel, Janey Silverman.' He stood for a moment looking moodily at his surroundings, now so alien where earlier they'd seemed almost familiar. Then he walked on. 'I want to think that I'd know if she was dead,' he said, his eyes fixed firmly on the pavement ahead, 'that she's part of me, that it would be like my heart had been torn out of my body, except that it isn't like that; it comes at you out of a clear sky, like when they came to tell me that Ann had been killed . . . '

He stopped speaking for a moment and Janey prompted him, curious. 'I'm listening, if you want to talk about it.'

'We both used to come home from work for lunch since our offices weren't far away and I got home that day and she wasn't there and I remembered she was going into town to get Robyn's Christmas present. I pottered about, cutting myself some bread and cheese, making a pot of tea, thinking she must be back in a minute, planning a wonderful family Christmas for us all.'

He paused to collect himself. 'Then the doorbell rang and there were two police there, a man and a woman — they send a woman in case you break down, to make you a nice cup of tea — and still I didn't get it, still I didn't damn well get it, just stood there beaming at them, wondering what they wanted, if Ann had got another parking ticket she hadn't paid.'

He smiled in recollection. 'She was a very laid-back parker — I was always telling her that she'd come back to her car one day and find that the bomb squad had blown it up.' He added soberly, 'She'd been dead an hour by then.' Janey said nothing: there wasn't anything adequate to say. 'At least this time,' he concluded, 'I'll be ready for it. This time it won't creep up on me unawares and knock me sideways.'

★ ★ ★

'You were suspicious about Thibaut,' Louise said. 'About how he escaped from Béziers.'

'I was . . . curious.'

'Hugues doesn't like to speak of it since it distresses him, but we both know the full story.'

'The story the barber told you, you mean.'

Louise frowned. 'How literal you are, young Master Robert. Very well then, I shan't tell you.'

'No, please do.'

'I think not.' It was obvious that she wanted to tell but Robyn had to tease her for some time before she would give in.

243

'It's not something he cares to speak about,' she began, her pretty face turning grave, 'especially to strangers, but what happened was this. He managed to overpower one of the crusaders — a humble foot soldier — and stole his weapons and surcoat with his master's livery on it. He tried to leave the town in this disguise but he was co-opted into a lynching party on the way out. There was no excuse he could make; he had to assist at a burning for hours before he could steal away under cover of darkness.'

'How horrible!'

'Some of the victims were people he knew, his friends. He says that one of them burnt there at the stake, his eyes fixed unflinchingly on Thibaut until the smoke finally obscured him from view.'

'How can . . . how can any human being treat another so?'

'Cathars aren't human to them. They accuse us of every imaginable vice: they say that our men lie with other men and not with women, that our women lie with beasts, that we sacrifice children.'

The sacrifice of children: the last, worst crime of which outsiders were always accused. 'What rational being could believe such nonsense?' Robyn said quietly.

'They believe what it suits them to

believe — especially when they're offered land and plunder as well as relief from the torment of their purgatory in the form of papal indulgences. So you see,' Louise went on, 'why Thibaut doesn't readily speak of it. It haunts him still. He sees that man's eyes in his dreams. Well, does that satisfy your curiosity?'

'It wasn't idle curiosity, my lady, I assure you.'

'You know that Lavaur has fallen.'

'Hugues told me.'

'Their town wasn't as high as ours, nor their hill as steep, nor their walls as sturdy.'

'I'm glad to hear it.'

Louise wore the same clothes as yesterday and had probably slept in her shift. Robyn hadn't noticed anyone change their clothes in the three days she'd been there, but then nor had she. She was afraid she was starting to smell, but who would notice? Louise wore some flowery cologne — jasmine? — rather strong, presumably to mask the odour of sweat.

'Tell me,' Robyn said, 'how long have you known Hugues?'

'Oh, since I was a child, eight years old perhaps. He's been a favourite uncle to me.'

'Do you know anything about his background?'

'You could ask him yourself if you're so curious but, as he makes no secret of it, there's no reason not to tell. He's the youngest son of a wealthy man, the Sire de Lizier of Narbonne. They're distantly related to the Trencavals who are the greatest landowners in these parts, after Count Raymond himself. He went to Paris as a young man to study at the university.'

'Hence his fluency in French?'

'As you say. He was studying the Trivium — grammar, rhetoric and logic — and, like all young men of good family, he did his share of drinking, gambling and womanising.'

'I take it he had some sort of Damascene conversion.'

'I don't think it was anything so dramatic,' Louise said, after a short pause for consideration. 'Just a sickening with the futility and emptiness of it all. So he abandoned his studies and decided to become a priest instead. That led to a breach with his family.'

'But it's common, surely, for younger sons to make a career in the Church.'

'To make a *career*, just so. His father would happily have used his influence to ensure that Hugues became chaplain to some great man and, eventually, a bishop, but that

246

wasn't what Hugues had in mind. His plan was to be a humble parish priest, perhaps even a mere itinerant preacher, walking the byways of France and the Languedoc, often hungry, always footsore. *That* the Sire de Lizier couldn't stomach. It dishonoured his noble family. He forbade any of his kin or acquaintance to help his rebellious son.'

'And so Hugues came here?'

'An old tutor of his at the university took pity on his plight and knew of this place and here he came. But soon he became as disillusioned with the Catholic Church as he'd been with the scholastic life. He found there was as much drinking, gaming and whoring among priests as among the most dissipated of students. And so he came quickly into our Christian communion where he has found his peace at last.'

'And his family has never forgiven him?'

She said sombrely, 'When word came that his mother lay dying, four years ago, he made the journey to Narbonne. He went the whole way on foot as he'd no money to pay for a mule and he didn't pause long enough to ask for help or my father would surely have lent him one. He was many days on the road with little food or rest.'

'And what happened when he got there?'

'They shut the door in his face.'

'His mother?'

'Died, never knowing that he'd come to say farewell.'

★ ★ ★

'You know what,' Malcolm said, as they stood in Simon and Robyn's room a few minutes later. 'If I were Dr Guzman and I'd hidden the bag, do you know where I'd hide it? Here, that's where. In this room. Double bluff.'

They stood looking at the bright room again. It was sparsely furnished: the high double bed with night tables on either side; a massive wooden wardrobe; a polished but well-scratched desk by the window with an upright chair beside it; a slipper chair with a loose cover in faded forget-me-nots. A chest of drawers filled the space between the table and the washbasin and a blue and white rug covered half the polished floorboards.

'Lucky he doesn't lock his door,' Janey commented. 'Or is it? If it was him he'd have to claim he'd left the door unlocked so the thief could get at the bag.' She made an exasperated noise. 'But I can't believe it was Simon. You can see the misery in him, growing like a tumour.'

'There's many a man who's strangled

his ... his mistress in a fit of jealousy or passion, then been stricken to the heart by what he's done,' Malcolm said grimly, as if such happenings were an everyday experience for him. 'It proves nothing.'

Janey bent and looked under the bed. She felt foolish, like an elderly spinster checking hopefully before lights out. Nothing, not even dust. The Oustal Monami might be shabby but it was clean.

'I don't feel we ought to be in here without permission,' Malcolm said.

'All's fair in love and war,' Janey replied, 'and this is war. Besides, it's Robyn's room too, and you've got a right to check her things, surely.'

'Good point.' He opened the wardrobe. Simon's clothes hung there — jackets, trousers folded over hangers; shirts and sweaters were arranged neatly on shelves. He was a tidy man. He recognised a dress of Robyn's; she didn't often wear dresses but this one — soft cool cotton, hanging almost to her feet, in reddish hues that flattered her dark colouring — was one she liked for best in summer. He went to take it out, to see if it smelled of her, to hold it away from himself and inspect it, remembering the last time he'd seen her in it, last October, an Indian summer, when she'd been home for a few days and had insisted on taking him out for dinner, but the hangers were the sort you couldn't steal and it took him some time to work them out and then the moment had passed.

There was the black jacket she wore either with the dress or with jeans. It had been 'good' when she bought it in a sale and had lasted well. Her blouses and sweaters were less neat than Simon's, rolled into balls and stacked like bales of hay. He pulled the hard chair over and stepped on it, examining the top of the wardrobe. There was a suitcase, a grey nylon zip-up one, easy to cram with things and light to carry. He hadn't seen it before and supposed it to be Simon's. It was empty.

There was also the trunk that Robyn had proudly carted off to Durham with her six years earlier, not realising that people didn't have trunks any more like in her Enid Blyton boarding school stories, but stuffed their books and teddy bears and joint-rollers into cardboard boxes and tea chests and the boots of battered cars.

'Here.' He handed the suitcase down to Janey, then the trunk.

'Bloody hell,' Janey said, 'That's a weight.' She opened it, clicking the unlocked catches and throwing the lid back. Nothing. 'What-ever must it weigh when it's full?' she asked rhetorically.

'Nothing behind them.' He heaved the two cases back up and descended from his chair. He pulled open the drawers of the chest one by one, although it was obvious that none of them was large enough to conceal her overnight bag. Knickers, handkerchiefs, some paperback books, a swimsuit of Robyn's, a travel iron with a multi-voltage adapter, socks in all colours and patterns and materials. 'She could never resist buying socks,' he remarked, 'of all the odd things.'

There wasn't anywhere else in the room to look. Janey peered out of the window which gave onto the flat top of the front porch, but there was nothing there either except a spider's web and some bird droppings.

They looked at each other. 'I suppose we can't search anyone else's room,' Janey said, in a way that suggested she was hoping, for once, to be contradicted.

'Not even if they left them open,' Malcolm said, 'which is unlikely.'

'There was no one at reception when we came in.'

'So?'

'All the keys were hanging up there.'

After a moment's thought, Malcolm vetoed

this idea. 'We don't want to be chucked out of the hotel,' he pointed out, 'or find *ourselves* being arrested by the police. We have too much to do.'

'No one saw us come in,' Janey said thoughtfully. 'As Dr Mooney says, everywhere closes down from noon until four. Madame Monami says she didn't see any member of the dig — except Mooney — that afternoon, but anyone could have wandered in unseen, as we did.'

'Including Robyn,' Malcolm said.

'May I ask what you think you're doing in my room?' Simon's edgy voice cut in from the doorway, making them both jump. Meriel Richards stood behind him and to one side. She looked embarrassed by the little scene.

'We weren't expecting you,' Janey said.

'So I see.' Simon stood with his hands on his hips. 'That doesn't answer my question.'

'It's Robyn's room too,' Janey pointed out again, 'and Malcolm, not you, is her next of kin.' Those three words, usually used in the context of a death, fell like stones in the warm room.

'Thank you so much for reminding me,' Simon said.

Meriel said, 'Thanks for the lift, Simon. I'll leave you to it, if you don't mind.'

He turned solicitously after her, then back

to the two intruders, uncertain who to deal with first. 'We'll talk about this later,' he said, addressing himself principally to Janey, his finger pointed at her in admonition. 'I've brought Meriel back as she isn't feeling well.'

'Oh, I'm sorry to hear that, Dr Richards,' Malcolm said.

'Bad period pains. She gets them every month.'

'Thank you, Simon. Mr Dawson doesn't want to hear details.'

'I'll give you a hand.' Janey came out onto the landing and took Meriel's arm. The older woman looked pale and her normally erect figure was hunched forward, seeking solace for cramps.

'Thanks,' Meriel said weakly.

'I'd better get back then, Merry,' Simon said. 'Since you're so obviously — ' he looked coolly at Janey, undeceived by her ministering angel act ' — in good hands.' Meriel unlocked the door of the room opposite and the two women went in. Simon moved forward into his own room and shut the door behind him. 'I take it you're not planning to move Robyn's personal effects out yet, Mr Dawson.'

'No, of course not.' Malcolm ran his hand agitatedly through his hair. 'We were just — '

'I know what you were *just* doing. And I know what you thought I was *just* doing here with Merry in the middle of the afternoon. And you're bloody well wrong on both counts.'

'I didn't think anything,' Malcolm protested. 'About you and Dr Richards, I mean. The thought never crossed my mind.'

'Oh, really?'

'Really, although apparently it crossed yours. If you ask me you've got a guilty conscience.'

'Now if you'll excuse me,' Simon snapped, 'I've got work to do back at the dig!' He wrenched open the door and left. Malcolm heard his angry footsteps clattering down the stairs, then the slamming of the back door.

* * *

Hugues's door was open except when he slept, to admit as much light as possible, and callers were inclined to walk in without ceremony. As the light was briefly blotted out, Robyn looked up from her frugal lunch to see a small but strong-looking man standing in the doorway. He was of indeterminate age, his clothes dusty from travel but of good quality. His boots were thick-soled but well worn. He had a deep-lipped tray slung in front of him with a number of what looked like animal skins, bulging sleekly, upon it. More skins hung from it on either side and from a yoke on his shoulders which were hunched by the weight.

He had to turn sideways to come through the doorway, like a lady in a farthingale. 'Friend Guilabert,' Hugues said, 'what can I do for you?'

The man flashed the slick smile of a used-car salesman, his thick blond hair falling forward over his weathered face. 'I heard that you had a guest, Hugues, a young gentleman from Paris, so I thought you would be in need of some extra wine, some *good* wine. I have some wine from the vines of Maitre Tavernier, all the way from Gaillac, which would grace Count Raymond's own table in Toulouse.'

Hugues laughed and shook his head. 'You'd better take it to Count Raymond, then. The local wine is good enough for me. Besides, I've no money to pay for your wares and nothing left to exchange for them.'

The man's face fell. Business had clearly not been good that day. The people of Montprimeur had more important things to think about than stocking their cellars, although the moment might come when they sought oblivion and freedom from fear in a wineskin. But Guilabert of Mazamet didn't give up so easily. He took on a wounded tone, as one forced to witness a social solecism. 'I thought you an educated man, Hugues, one who understood the responsibilities of hospitality.'

Hugues bit his lip and gave a sideways glance at Robyn. She was surprised by how much easier she found it to follow what people were saying, even after only three days' practise. It obviously did matter to Hugues that the supposed young nobleman he'd taken in shouldn't think him lacking as a host. There wasn't much she could do about that, but she wouldn't lack as a guest. She got up. 'Let me buy some wine,' she said. 'To thank you for your hospitality, Hugues.'

He made a gesture which she chose to take as acquiescence.

The wine seller cheered up and began to unload skins, loosing a patter of names and vineyards that meant nothing to Robyn. She held up a hand to stop him and selected two fat skins at random. After the smallest hesitation, she pulled the silver ring from her finger and offered it to the man. He took it eagerly and returned to the doorway, where he examined it in the light. It was small and light, easy to carry and acceptable anywhere, the sort of currency you needed in wartime.

'That's far too valuable for a couple of skins of wine,' Hugues intervened. 'It's pure silver.'

'I'm not so sure,' Guilabert said, 'I think it may be mixed with baser metal.' Hugues looked momentarily offended on behalf of his guest but Robyn assured him that she considered the deal a fair one. Hugues fell silent, perhaps remembering the worthless metal medallions he'd found in his guest's purse on his arrival. 'So it's a deal?' Guilabert pocketed the ring deftly, spat on his hand and offered it to Robyn, who gingerly shook. 'I bid you good day, then, gentlemen. I must be in Albi in two days. I'm expected.'

'He must be out of the line of fire, he means,' Hugues grumbled, when the man had gone and Robyn was wiping her hand discreetly on her shirt. 'Pity, we could use his strength in the battle to come, but he's right, it's not his quarrel.'

'All those wine skins must weigh a ton,' Robyn said. 'Here, Hugues,' she handed him her new acquisition, 'put these in your larder.'

'We'd best drink them up,' Hugues said gloomily, 'for they'll not keep, not if I know Guilabert and his wares.'

Meriel had tried to make something of her room, even to the importation of a cream sofa with red cushions, a little cramped in one corner. Red silk curtains hung at the windows. Instead of the usual dreary boarding-house pictures — bad landscapes and sad-eyed clowns — she'd put up some framed prints, mostly modern French, Olivier Raab and Renée Halpern. It seemed she had a nesting instinct.

'Here.' Janey helped her onto the bed where she sank back and closed her eyes. She'd wondered cynically if either Simon or Meriel, alarmed at their absence from Montprimeur that morning, had made an excuse to come and look for them, but Meriel was clearly well below par. 'There must be something I can get you,' she said.

'There's some soluble aspirin in my sponge bag on the sink. If you could mix two up in a glass of water, I'd be grateful.'

Janey busied herself about this task. 'Shall I go down and see if they've got a hot-water bottle?'

'There aren't any,' Merry said. 'I've tried. The French think hot-water bottles are what the British have instead of sex.'

Janey laughed, conceding the truth of this.

'Is it like this every month?'

'For the last six months or so. It took me by surprise this afternoon; I wasn't expecting it until the weekend or I'd have taken the day off.'

'Shouldn't you see a doctor?'

'I will when I get back home, see about having a hysterectomy.'

'Isn't that a bit drastic?'

'Why? I've never wanted children and it'd solve the problem at one fell swoop. Save having to worry about contraception for the next ten years.'

'Can't you get it done here?'

'Certainly, but it's a major operation and requires several weeks convalescence. Besides, I know it sounds vaguely xenophobic but somehow one feels safer at home where the doctors speak English. It'll have to wait till my sabbatical is over in the autumn.'

Janey swished the milky granules with her finger. 'Here. Drink this.' Meriel sat up and accepted the glass. She held her nose and swilled the medicine down in one gulp.

'Ugh!' she said. 'The pills are tasteless but they take longer to work.'

Janey sat down on the sofa and curled her feet up under her, manoeuvring a cushion into the small of her back. The barriers had broken down between them in this union of feminine troubles and now they were two women in sympathy. 'You've made it nice,' she said.

Meriel closed her eyes again. 'Most of the others don't seem to notice if they're comfortable or not, but I do. We're out here for months on end and the further you are from home, the more important it is to have a few of your things about you.'

'Where do you live,' Janey asked. 'When you're in England?'

'I live in Edinburgh,' Meriel said mildly, 'which wasn't in England last time I looked.'

'Sorry.' Meriel didn't have a Scottish accent, but that wasn't unusual among people from Edinburgh.

'Oh, I know. England is synonymous with Britain — if you happen to live south of the Cheviots or east of the Severn Bridge. I live in my father's house, in fact, in Regent Gardens, ludicrously big for one woman, but it's been in the family for four generations. I sleep in the room where I was born.'

'It's unusual these days to live in the house where you were born. Must be nice.'

Meriel nodded. She fingered a gold filigree chain round her neck. 'I suppose it gives me a base, somewhere perfectly secure from which to venture out into the world.'

'Do you let it while you're away?'

The older woman shook her head. 'I should. It's a crime to leave that great house empty, but I don't like the thought of strangers in it.'

'Must be expensive to keep up.'

'Money isn't a problem.'

'Oh.' They sat in silence for a moment, then Janey said, 'You've known Simon longer than anyone here.'

'Twenty years or more.'

'Tell me about him.'

Merry sucked at the gold chain thoughtfully. 'One thing you have to say about Simon is that what you see is what you get. He's not devious, he's not deceitful. He's a hopeless liar, transparent as a window pane.'

'I suppose those are rare qualities,' Janey admitted.

'Sure, he's a Peter Pan. Sure, he's never wanted to grow up. Sure, he's had affairs with dozens of women, but he's never made them any promises, never pretended to be ideal husband material.'

'But sometimes women hear promises that have never been made.'

'Wishful thinking? I suppose. He genuinely *likes* women, enjoys their company. It took him six years to finish his PhD, you know, since he liked being a student so much he didn't want to give it up and venture out into the real world — if that's what this is. I understand Simon because we're alike. Neither of us wants to be tied down.'

'You've never been tempted?' Janey felt confident that she would marry some day, even given her experience of serially monogamist parents, even given the fact that she'd yet to meet anyone she thought was halfway good enough for her.

'My father became very dependent on me towards the end of his life,' Dr Richards said. 'I found that stifling. I couldn't go through that again.'

'So what happened when Simon became interested in Robyn?'

'He told me, frankly and openly, that he was falling for her. I was pleased for him. She was good for him.'

'Where's he from, originally?'

'Surrey. Comfortable middle-class household. His father was a barrister and is now enjoying a prosperous old age in Bournemouth. There's a sister, Rachel, comfortably married to another barrister.' She smiled with almost a mother's fondness. 'I suspect Simon has never had anything to worry or vex him in the whole of his thirty-nine years.'

'Until now,' Janey said.

Meriel's mouth twisted down again. 'Until now.' She let out a long sigh and rubbed her abdomen with the flat of her hand.

'Any improvement?' Janey asked.

'It'll take a while. I don't want to be inhospitable, Janey, but I think I'll get some sleep if I can. Then a warm bath and I should be vaguely human by supper time.'

'Okay, I can take a hint.' Janey sprang up. 'See you later.'

★ ★ ★

'I wish I could be more of a friend to Mengarde Piquier, who's a deserving young woman, and an unhappy one. But I don't like to go too often to her house, since I fear that her husband seeks my company solely out of a desire for social advancement. Or perhaps he's afraid of what she'll say to me when we're intimate.

Whatever the reason, he comes to interrupt our conversation, even if he must leave his work to do it. And how he bows and smirks and compliments me and would kiss my hand if I'd let him. I think the maidservant, a sly girl, informs him of my arrival.

I remember Mengarde when we were both girls of perhaps twelve or thirteen, she a year or two older than I. How much life she had in her then, such a spirit of mischief. What tricks we two played on her father, Bertrand Piquier.

She was busy then, running the family business, taking more and more responsibility as old Bertrand grew frail, dealing with the silk merchants, bullying the apprentices, weaving and sewing and embroidering herself far into the night by the light of a single candle.

But that was before Jaufré Arsen came first to the house.

How strange to see that spirit crushed from her, as if she is become a different person. Is this what marriage does to women?

The loss of a friend is, in its own way, as poignant as the loss of a lover.'

Diaries of Louise d'Ambriers — Scholar and Matriarch.

ibid.

★ ★ ★

The Piquiers' house was a neat building in the best part of town, a little to the west of the market square, convenient for the town's amenities but with fresh air from the prevailing winds. It was wider than

Hugues's little hut and most of the houses in Montprimeur would have fitted into it twice. Both storeys were of stone and had windows fitted with oiled parchment like the ones in the meeting-room, except that this parchment was new and untorn.

Next to the house was a barn or stable in which Robyn could see a mule, a cow and a nanny goat with two boisterous kids. Above them was a loft with a wooden ladder leading to it and Robyn could make out supplies of hay and barrels of apples. Here was a prosperous and flourishing family.

The ground floor at the front was the workroom and shop. Hugues had explained that with the entry of Jaufré into the Ostal, they'd become merchants as well as manufacturers and grown yet richer, with the result that Mengarde — though trained in every aspect of the trade — no longer worked in the business at all. 'Which is a pity, since it means she has too much time to brood,' Hugues had said.

'About the baby she lost?'

'Among other things,' he'd said, obscurely.

The shutters were pushed back leaving the shop front open to the street, giving the workers inside as much natural light as possible. Even so, Robyn had to adjust her eyes to the comparative gloom of the interior. She could see a spinning-wheel and a massive loom, currently half full with a fine blue material. A girl was teasing hanks of raw wool, while an underfed apprentice weighed coins in a balance to ensure they'd not been clipped. The boy came forward at once to ask the visitor's business in a polite tone.

'Is your master at home?' Robyn asked him. He nodded towards a curtain that screened off the back of the house. She pulled it to one side and called out a greeting. After half a minute, she was confronted by a maidservant, a pert-looking girl of eighteen, neatly dressed in a grey tunic and a white apron with clogs on her feet. Quite pretty, with a neat figure and shiny black hair visible at the edges of her wimple.

'Are your master and mistress at home?' Robyn asked. 'I have a message for them from Hugues.'

Jaufré Piquier's voice called from somewhere in the house, 'Who is it, Raymonde?'

The girl turned back into the room and said in a shrill whisper, 'I don't know, but he talks very funny.' Then, realising that Robyn must have heard her, she held her apron up to her mouth and giggled.

Piquier flung back the curtain and looked at Robyn without recognition. Since everyone else she'd met in the town had stared at her as if memorising her face for a photofit, this argued a fierce introspection on the part of this wealthy man. 'We met yesterday,' Robyn reminded him. 'I'm Robert of Durham, staying with Hugues.'

The name seemed already to belong to her.

'What do you want?' Piquier asked.

'May I come in?' Since he didn't seem to want her in his Ostal, Robyn was the more determined to barge her way in. After a moment's consideration, Piquier shrugged and backed away, leaving her to follow. 'I hope I'm not interrupting your midday meal,' she said politely.

But there was no sign that dinner was imminent. The room had more furniture than the other homes she'd visited; concrete symbols of wealth. A rug covered much of the hardpacked floor and there were a number of wooden chests, a large dining table and six chairs. A yellowing tapestry hung on the far wall, a hunting scene with a wounded stag in the foreground being set upon by the hounds.

'You needn't wait,' he said to his maid. 'I'm sure there's lots for you to be getting on with in the kitchen.'

'As you wish . . . sir.'

As she bobbed an insolent curtsey and

left the room, passing through a doorless doorway into a second chamber from which cooking smells drifted, he added to Robyn by way of belated introduction, 'Raymonde is my cousin.'

'Oh, I'm sorry. I thought she was a servant.'

He looked surprised. 'She is. She came to us two years ago, a penniless orphan. She naturally expects to earn her keep.'

'Is Na Piquier in?'

'She's resting upstairs. Why?'

'Hugues sent me to tell you he's holding the Consolamentum tonight.'

He frowned. 'Why us in particular?'

'Oh no. I'm seeing lots of people. Half the town.'

'Tonight? That's sudden.'

Robyn said apologetically, 'With Lavaur fallen . . . '

'Yes, of course.'

'He would like to know if you and . . . Mengarde wish to take the Consolamentum tonight.'

Piquier ran his hand across his face, tugging at his small black beard, losing his cool façade as he might throw off a cloak. 'It was an ill day that I came to this accursed place!' he said savagely. 'This barren hole where no crops grow and children wither in the womb. The old priest expects us to die, doesn't he?'

'It's merely a precaution.'

'Save those platitudes for the stupid and the credulous. I should have got out while I had the chance, gone home to Castres — '

'But you didn't.' Mengarde had entered the room, unheard by either of them, and stood in the shadows, one hand resting, balled into a fist, on the table. 'And why? Because there's nothing for you there, because you were as penniless as that slut Raymonde until my father took you in and I was fool enough to think I loved you.'

'Oh yes,' he said, his mouth clenched like lockjaw. 'You took me in and how often you've thrown that in my face. And what have you given me in the end? The ultimate prize: an early and brutal death.'

'You, Jaufré, have made death no enemy to me. You've turned him into a friend.' She walked forward into the light of the open window. She looked very pale but Robyn could see, loud as a shout in a cave, fresh bruises on her face and neck.

She said, 'Tell Hugues that I, for one, will take the sacrament tonight.'

★ ★ ★

269

If the Piquiers kept a servant, Robyn thought as she left the house, why had Jaufré come himself to fetch fire from Hugues? Surely it would be more natural to send the help, especially for a man with such a good opinion of himself. And there must have been someone nearer he could have asked. Had he hoped to eavesdrop on the conversation between herself, Louise and Hugues? Had he lingered outside a while before making his presence known? She tried to remember what they'd been talking of, but couldn't think that it had been significant.

'Excuse me!'

Robyn had been almost knocked off her feet, saved from falling by a gnarled pair of hands that seized her by the shoulders. Thibaut of Béziers.

'No, it was my fault,' she said. 'I wasn't looking where I was going.'

The barber released her. 'No harm done. Now, if you'll excuse me, my lord . . . ' He walked through the workshop, continuing through the curtain into the private quarters without bothering to announce his presence.

That was what they'd been talking about, of course. She, Robyn, had been expressing scepticism about Thibaut's repeated good fortune in escaping from de Montfort with his life and Piquier had made his entrance only after Hugues had changed the subject.

What were those two men plotting together? Or had Thibaut just been invited for his dinner?

Speaking of dinner: Robyn saw that the iron cooking pot which stood on its triple legs in the centre of the fire had been filled in her absence and steam was starting to rise from it. Closer inspection revealed a couple of handfuls of dried peas, a shredded onion and some stalks of cabbage, lost in several pints of water. 'I thought I'd better make some soup,' Hugues said, seeing her looking. 'I can't rely on the charity of my neighbours to feed my guests at every meal.'

'How long will it be?' Robyn looked without much hope at the little peas, half of them black, obviously as hard as gravel. Perhaps if she'd hung around *chez* Piquier long enough they'd have felt obliged to feed her.

'Oh, it'll be fit by nightfall,' Hugues assured her. 'I'm not much of a cook, I'm afraid, but we're simple people and used to rough fare. I'm sorry, it's the best I can do.'

'I'm sure it'll be delicious.' Robyn gave

the pot a stir with a wooden ladle that lay, charred, by the fire, and hoped for the best.

★ ★ ★

It was the custom of the archaeologists to eat together at the Oustal Monami most evenings for convenience and at seven-thirty that night everyone was gathered in the dining-room except for Silvie de Chambertin who was nowhere to be found. After a couple of doses of painkiller and a rest, Meriel was now well enough to join them.

As they took their seats at the one long table, the professor at the head, Janey said, 'Does this place never have other guests?'

'It's out of season,' Simon reminded her. 'We had one or two strange faces last summer, as I recall, although none of them stayed more than two nights. It doesn't take long to 'do' Castres. Mostly they do very nicely out of caring for us. Means they only have to change the sheets once a week.'

Madame Monami came in at that moment with two baskets of bread which she put at either end of the table and a dish of mixed salad which she placed in the middle. Joachim followed her, echoing her movements, but much larger, like a shadow at twilight, bearing two jugs of red wine and two bottles of Evian on a tray. He was limping and his bruises looked like a thunderous sunset, but otherwise he was much as normal. Malcolm jumped up and offered to help the boy with his burden but was silently refused. Feeling foolish, he resumed his seat.

The professor shook out his napkin and dropped it in his lap as the Monamis went back and forth. Next an open dish of carrots and peas was dumped in front of him by the boy, and his mother was about to place a covered dish beside it when Silvie de Chambertin arrived in the doorway looking dishevelled. She had something small and pale clutched between the fingers of her right hand. 'Sorry I'm late,' she said. 'But I found these.' She opened out her fingers to display three capped fungi.

'Mushrooms?' Janey asked.

Madame Monami turned to look, screamed, crashed the dish she was holding down on the table and ran out of the room, throwing her apron up over her face. Joachim followed her more slowly. As he passed Silvie in the doorway he hissed, *'Vous êtes folle'* at her.

'Oh dear,' Silvie said. 'Perhaps that wasn't very wise. I didn't think.'

'Not mushrooms then,' Janey said, hoping for enlightenment.

Silvie turned the toadstools so that their white undersides were visible. 'Mushrooms are dark under here. Promise me you'll never eat a mushroom with a white underside, Janey.'

'What are they?' Meriel asked when Janey didn't reply.

'Amanita Verna — the destroying angel. A pretty name in a funny way. I haven't seen any in thirty years. That was the main reason I was so excited.'

'Poisonous?' Simon asked.

'Horribly. I thought I'd take a little walk in the park before supper and I found these growing in the dark, wet soil in the shade of a felled oak tree. It's rare to find them this early in the year. I have to report them so they can be destroyed. If a child were to eat them . . . '

'Are they that dangerous?' Malcolm enquired. They looked inoffensive. Not much different from the outlandish things he'd noticed on sale in the local market that morning. Personally, he wouldn't dream of eating any fungus that wasn't a button mushroom fresh from the supermarket or, better still, out of a tin.

'They're one of the most poisonous things

known to man,' Silvie said. 'If I were to lick my fingers now, I should be dead in minutes.'

'Silvie,' the professor said gently, 'there is a time and a place and I don't think — '

'Yes, I'm a foolish old woman to bring them into the dining-room. It was thoughtless. I'm sorry. I'll get rid of them safely and then I'll go and see about getting the rest of them destroyed. Don't wait supper for me. I'll get something later.'

And with that she left the room, still cradling her treasure.

'And for Chrissake don't forget to wash your hands!' Dexter Mooney called after her. 'Now, I don't know about anyone else but I'm starving.' He reached cavalierly across James and lifted the lid from the covered dish to reveal a number of pieces of chicken chasseur, the mushrooms brown and succulent on top.

'Ah, shit!' Mooney said. Nobody spoke for about a minute then he resumed. 'Well, I guess I'll be the first to take my life in my hands.' He lifted a leg of chicken onto his plate and spooned a generous helping of the sauce over it. He tasted it. 'Not bad. Pass the carrots, James. If I'm dead by eight o'clock you can have my portable TV.'

As the others began to serve themselves

Janey slipped out of the room. She met Silvie coming out of the kitchen wiping her wet hands on a dishcloth. Madame Monami pursued her, speaking quietly and very fast in some sort of local patois which Janey couldn't attempt to follow. Her tone managed to be simultaneously hectoring and respectful.

Silvie merely answered '*Oui, je sais*' or '*Ça va*' at intervals when the hotel owner paused for breath. Then she thrust the cloth into the other woman's hands, said '*Calme-toi, Julie,*' and headed for the door with her brisk, bird-like step.

'Madame!' Janey hurried after her. 'I was wondering if I could take a look in your room this evening.'

'My room? Did you want to borrow something?'

'We're looking for Robyn's missing bag,' Janey said, with a faint blush on her cheek. 'The others have agreed.'

'Oh, I see.'

'It's not that . . . I mean someone might have hidden it in your room — '

'That's all right, Janey. My room isn't locked. Help yourself. A *bientôt.*' And with a slight click of her low heels across the flagstones of the corridor Silvie left the hotel. Through the open kitchen door Janey saw Madame Monami thrust the dishcloth into the fire of the range with a pair of blackened tongs.

Janey stood for a moment in the hallway. She still couldn't shake off the feeling that someone was watching her every move, that a fearsome and cruel intelligence observed her actions, always one step ahead. But all these people were alarmingly intelligent so she was none the wiser. She smiled at her own imaginings, shook her head and went back into the dining-room. Everyone else was eating and she helped herself to a plateful and joined them.

'Charming as eccentricity can be . . . ' Simon was saying.

'It would be a dull world if we were all the same,' Meriel interrupted. This surprised Janey; she hadn't seen Meriel as a woman who talked in clichés.

'In old age,' Simon continued, raising his voice, 'it can turn into mere tiresomeness.'

Meriel put her fork down with a clatter, her pale cheeks reddening. 'I hope you're not talking about my father, Simon!'

'My dear Merry — '

'I'm not *your* dear Merry, nor anybody's dear Merry, for that matter.'

' — You must admit that your father did get a bit odd towards the end.'

'I will admit nothing of the sort. He was

in his perfect senses till the day he died.'

Simon sighed and a hostile silence fell between them. To Janey's surprise it was Dexter Mooney who politely started a new conversational hare. 'So what brings you to this part of the world, Janey?'

'I'm the English language assistant at the grammar school in Muret,' she explained.

'Ah, Muret!' James Clements exclaimed.

'You know it?'

'The last battle,' Simon murmured.

'Not the last,' James corrected him, 'by any means.'

'But the most decisive and, in that sense, the last. The triumph of bigotry over freedom of worship.'

'You've been to the battleground, of course,' James told Janey.

'Er, 'fraid not. No.'

'Oh you must! Picture it.' The professor put his knife and fork down and threw himself into his story. His hands traced pictures in the air. 'No siege here, but two armies head to head in battle on a plain on the banks of the Garonne, a couple of miles from the castle of Muret. A hot August day in 1213.'

'Imagine lurching about head to foot in armour in the middle of summer,' Simon said.

James didn't seem to hear the interruption. His face was rapt. 'The crusaders outnumbered two to one by the Occitan army who were, moreover, on their home ground, commanded — bizarrely — by a Catholic, a Spaniard, a veteran crusader against the Moors, King Pedro II of Aragon, brother-in-law to Raymond of Toulouse.'

'What was he doing there?' Malcolm asked, entranced.

'Defending the glorious civilisation of the south against the northern barbarians, of course.'

'Of course.'

'And family is family,' Janey murmured.

'Shhh!' Malcolm said. 'Listen to the professor.' He was beginning to understand for the first time what had drawn his daughter to this fateful land.

'De Montfort had given orders that Pedro must die, whatever the cost, but the king had changed his clothes and armour with a simple soldier who was soon killed. The moment they realised their mistake, the French accused King Pedro of cowardice at which he instantly revealed himself — '

'As what man of honour wouldn't?' Dexter muttered sarcastically.

'Shhh!' Malcolm said again.

' — and was cut down by a dozen

swords. That was it! The Occitan army panicked. The French drove them back into the river. Twenty thousand were cut down or drowned in a matter of hours, struggling against the tug of the Garonne in full armour.'

'They should have won!' Malcolm exclaimed, the excitement of battle overcoming his natural diffidence. 'With a bigger army and a knowledge of the terrain, how could they not win?'

'St Dominic was in the church at Muret all the while praying for a Catholic victory.' The professor picked up a hunk of bread and began to wipe up his sauce chasseur with it. He seemed deflated.

'So someone was clearly listening,' Dexter Mooney concluded, 'and told Dominic to set up the good old Inquisition while he was on a roll. 'They tell me God is on my side, sitting high on my shoulder all the way, means that anything I do is A-OK.' Remember that song? Remember Woodstock?'

But nobody answered him.

★ ★ ★

'Jaufré Piquier has left his wife and hearth,' Hugues told Robyn later that afternoon. 'He took the family mule, everything of value he

280

could load on it, and left by the main gate above an hour ago.'

'Where's he gone?' Robyn asked. The news came as no surprise.

'Home, I assume, to Castres. He'll be safe there since the town submitted peacefully to the crusaders early in the war. He'll see the priest and make his confession and be taken back into the bosom of Mother Church in good time.'

'Did Raymonde go with him?'

Hugues shook his head. 'The Ostal had only one mule and a pillion passenger would have slowed it down too much for Master Jaufré's liking, but Mengarde has thrown her out after him and she was last seen setting off east on foot. She's young and healthy and will be in Castres by nightfall.'

'He and Raymonde, were they . . . ?' Robyn felt indignant that the man should abandon not only his wife but his mistress in this way.

'I never asked,' Hugues said. 'I preferred not to know.'

'Are we sure he's headed for Castres?'

'Where else?'

'What if he went west instead?'

'Then he'd run headlong into de Montfort's army!'

'Precisely!'

Hugues considered this. 'He was definitely heading east. We have men on the walls round the clock now and he was watched out of sight.'

'Is he . . . was he . . . did Piquier know any of the town's secrets?'

'No,' Hugues said, understanding her. 'He was an outsider and never fully gained our trust and never formed part of our town council. But he has no time for politics, in any case. All he cares about is saving his own skin.'

'So he doesn't know the location of the secret pathway,' Robyn persisted. 'Or the gate?'

Hugues flushed. After a short pause he said without much conviction, 'What secret pathway?'

'Oh, come on, Hugues.'

'No,' the holy man said flatly. 'He doesn't know.'

'Poor Mengarde,' Robyn mused. 'All alone now.' Left to die alone, without even her unsatisfactory servant for company.

'Did I not say?' Hugues said. 'How forgetful I'm becoming. She's taken in Dias and the baby. There's plenty of room in her house for Dias to ply her trade and to care for her son in greater comfort.'

'That's generous of her.'

Hugues said, 'It gives her daily access to the child.'

'Does she really think little Pietre is *her* baby.'

'I think it's enough that he's *a* baby,' Hugues said.

★ ★ ★

The day Lavaur fell Bisette saved half her supper for La Vierge.

'What's the matter?' Henri de Bresse asked, seeing her apparent lack of appetite. 'Is it not to your taste, my fine lady?'

'I'm not so hungry tonight, sir.' This was no more than the truth. She'd been chastened by what she'd seen that day. She'd known many people die in her young life — it was a rare month in her village of Sainte-Marie-la-Source that didn't see a funeral, including that of her own mother, gentle Margot, coughing her life away one bitter January — but she'd seen nothing like this.

Some of the heretics, waiting their turn at the stake, had torn free of their captors and hurled themselves voluntarily onto the pyres. The fires still burnt fiercely and would do so, by all accounts, for several days. A human body wasn't quickly or easily reduced to ashes. The soldiers stood around laying bets on which of the screaming bodies would fall silent first.

'I thought I would keep some aside for La Vierge,' she said, seeing that her master was still awaiting an explanation.

Henri growled, 'Don't call her that. It's blasphemous.'

Bisette shrugged. As far as she knew her friend had no other name, any more than she any longer had a name, other than Bisette — little kiss — although her family wouldn't know her by it. She put the dish hastily aside before he could offer to finish it for her and went to sit on his lap. He smelt of gunpowder that night and there was dried blood on his shirt.

She'd observed that an orgy of killing stimulated man's appetite for women and since mid-afternoon the smell of burning heretic had vied with that of roasting capon on the still air. Sure enough, Henri left his own food to cool and, stripping off as few of his clothes as he needed to achieve his end, pushed her back onto the straw pallet and was swiftly done.

This was better than life at home, Bisette thought, as she rearranged her skirt. She didn't have to rise early every morning to milk the cow but might lie abed half the day if she chose. She did no housework, no rough work at all, and her hands weren't reddened by constant immersion in water. There was no stepmother to nag her, resenting this pretty memorial to her predecessor who took food from her own children's mouths.

What she really wanted, though, was to find her way to a town, where there were market stalls and street entertainers — the sort of diversions La Vierge had described to her.

Sometimes she remembered the less pleasant times, on her first arrival at the camp, when it had been a different man each day, usually more than one, until the Sire de Bresse had picked her out some weeks ago, staring at her corn-fed fairness, his gloomy face brightening at the sound of her accent. 'From Orleans? Where? I know it well.'

But she was young and thought mostly of the future and those days were gone.

★ ★ ★

Silvie de Chambertin's room was almost bare, but then Janey remembered that Simon had said she had a house in the village of Cordes on the far side of Albi, so this room was presumably a pied-à-terre for her.

Even so, considering it was her home from

home for several days a week, perhaps for years to come, it had an air of unoccupancy about it. Perhaps it was just that Silvie was tidy and left no clothes strewn about the furniture as most people did. The bed had been made, tight as a soldier's. There was a small run of books on the dressing table, old editions of French classics, mostly Balzac and Hugo, their titles in alphabetical order.

The bedside table housed an alarm clock and an ancient monochrome photograph of a tall man, his clothes dating, Janey guessed, from the fifties. He was leaning on a shotgun, a shooting hat planted firmly on his clipped dark hair, shading his prominent features, his dark eyes and long nose. A black labrador sat at his feet, the image of eager obedience.

She picked up the silver frame and passed it to Malcolm. The room was so impersonal that she didn't feel like an intruder.

'Her late husband?' Malcolm guessed.

'I assume so. He looks a bit glum.'

Malcolm examined the picture carefully. 'People did in those days. They weren't so used to the camera as we are. I've got some photos of my parents glaring out at me and they were the most mild-mannered of people.'

'I can imagine,' Janey said affectionately.

'He was handsome, wasn't he, Monsieur de Chambertin?'

'In a saturnine sort of way,' Malcolm agreed. 'He has a stern mouth.'

Janey thought you could better call it cruel. 'I suppose he resented coming down in the world,' she mused. 'The aristocracy never like falling on hard times, descending among the hoi polloi, like us.'

'Have they fallen on hard times?'

'Judging by the shabbiness of Silvie's clothes and so on, I assume so, but maybe it's just that she's not bothered, one of Nature's ascetics.'

She crossed to the narrow French windows which gave out onto a balcony, opened them and went out. Silvie's room was at the back, overlooking the courtyard. The wrought iron of the balcony was rusted in more than one place and the railing rattled under Janey's firm hand. 'Nowhere to hide anything here.' She stood on tiptoe, craning up at the roof, but there was nothing but old guttering overflowing with last year's leaves. 'This place is either quaintly picturesque or seedy,' she said, 'depending on your point of view.'

'I think I might like it in other circumstances.' Malcolm joined her on the balcony. They had to stand close together.

Janey wasn't sure it could hold two and went back in. Her plans for the Easter holidays had taken a turn for the unexpected but they still didn't include ending up with a broken leg on a load of flagstones in a cheap hotel in Castres.

'I suppose archaeologists like old things by definition,' she remarked.

She pulled open the oaken door of the wardrobe to reveal three tweedy skirts, a number of high-necked blouses, a navy-blue Guernsey pullover, and two cardigans. A pair of stout brown shoes, lace-ups, stood toe-to-toe on the floor next to, a little unexpectedly, a pair of white leather trainers. Silvie had very small feet, Janey noticed, perhaps an English size three. Odd how having small feet automatically made a woman seem ladylike.

A Burberry raincoat and a dressing-gown, hanging on a hook on the back of the door, seemed to complete the old Frenchwoman's supply of clothes. She examined the sink, purely out of curiosity. It seemed the old lady used no cosmetics, although there was a tube of sun block, half empty.

Malcolm came back in. It was getting dark and he closed and bolted the wooden shutters a little fussily. He got down on his hands and knees to look under the bed. Nothing. He sat back on his heels. 'I feel we're looking for the sake of looking,' he said.

As they left Silvie's room, Janey became aware of a presence in the gloom of the landing, masculine and young. Joachim. She shrank automatically back against Malcolm who put out paternal hands to steady her. Then the young man stepped forward into the light and she let out an involuntary sigh of relief. It was Peter Finlay.

'Did you want to look at my drawings now?' he asked.

Janey found her voice. 'Sure. This is as good a time as any.'

'I'm up here.'

He turned and led the way up a narrow flight of stairs to the second floor. The hotel's main staircase, from the ground to the first floor, dated from more prosperous times, stone with a carved oak banister which Madame Monami polished every morning, but this one was shabby and uncarpeted, fit only for servants. He switched the landing light on as he reached the top and Janey and Malcolm could see three closed doors leading off it. Peter pushed one of them open and they followed him in.

If Silvie's room had been bare, this was a boy's study-bedroom, probably identical to the one he'd recently vacated at Oxford. There were clothes, books, old newspapers, mugs with dried-in coffee. He'd even put posters up on the walls, including one of the great Tutankhamun exhibition at the British Museum in the early seventies, an event which surely, Janey thought, preceded his birth.

The window was small here, admitting little light at the best of times and none at all in the encroaching dusk. Peter switched on a lamp on the bedside table and another on the desk. The floorboards were bare except for a blue-green rag rug by the bed and dust motes spiralled upwards in the lamplight as they watched. 'The chambermaid has given up on me,' he said with a boyish grin. 'Or, rather, I told her I'd manage for myself.'

He hadn't made his bed, presumably for several days, and the sheets lay rumpled with one pillow trailing on the floor. Above the chaotic desk were a number of sketches, mostly architectural. There was one portrait, head and shoulders, of a woman, a girl, blonde-haired and fair of face, noble and ascetic. Peter's girlfriend waiting patiently for him in England? Or his ideal woman?

'Are you the only one on this floor?' Janey asked.

'Unless the hotel has other guests. I much prefer being on my own under the eaves. Robyn was up here too at first, of course — the professor said our legs were the youngest and best able to deal with two sets of stairs — but then she moved down to share with — '

'Where do the Monamis sleep?' Janey interjected.

'On the ground floor, at the back, next to the kitchen. There's two rooms. Joachim sleeps in the sitting-room.'

'Do they run the hotel with just the two of them?'

'There's a sister-in-law, a *Miss* Monami comes in to help out but she doesn't sleep in.'

'Is there a Mr Monami?'

'If there is he's awfully quiet and apparently invisible.'

'What happened to him?' Malcolm asked.

The young man shrugged. 'Dead or decamped. I've no idea.' He picked up an artist's folder, about two feet by three, unfastened the ribbons and laid it open on the end of the bed.

Malcolm gave an exclamation of pleasure and picked up the topmost picture. It was a charcoal sketch of a village street, narrow, cobbled, with a drainage channel running down the middle. Two vivid men gambled on the corner, crouching on the ground to examine the runes of two bone dice. Each had a purse slung from his belt. One purse was very fat, the other very thin. The man with the thin purse had a look of bewildered desperation on his face. 'This is really good,' Malcolm said.

'Not bad,' the boy replied, without false modesty. 'Not bad at all.'

'I don't know anything about it, but I'd have thought you could've done this professionally.'

'It was art or archaeology. My father was keen it should be the latter and I decided I hadn't enough of the artistic temperament to see me through the precariousness of an artist's existence.'

'Drinking and loose women, you mean?' Janey said.

'Drink makes me sleepy and I've never had the good fortune to meet a loose woman. Anyway, I like it best as a hobby.'

Above the dicers, and unbeknown to them, a plump woman was about to empty a chamber pot on their heads from an upstairs window.

'Everyday life in Montprimeur?' Malcolm asked.

'Or any town or village in the region for that matter.'

Malcolm passed the picture to Janey and helped himself to the next one. It was the main gate of a medieval town, set into a thick stone wall, a turret on either side. The wall was perhaps twenty feet high and the turrets thirty. Armed men were visible, peeping out nervously from behind the crenellations. The stout wooden gates, which would fit snugly when shut, were open and a rickety cart loaded with wineskins was negotiating the entrance behind a skinny horse.

'Is that how it was?' Malcolm sighed.

'Montprimeur is too badly damaged for us to know for sure,' Peter said, 'but this is how it is at Montségur, say, or at Puylaurens where most of the wall has survived.'

'A wine merchant,' Janey remarked. 'They had their priorities right.'

'Quite a rich one too,' Peter said. 'Got his own horse and cart.'

Janey pulled a handkerchief from her pocket sending a small tinkle of coins onto the floor. She bent to pick them up. There was a suitcase under the bed but it was a rigid oblong, nothing like the bag described by Malcolm. It had to be Peter's own case. She pocketed the coins, blew her nose unnecessarily and put her handkerchief away.

'Merry's a keen photographer,' Peter was saying. 'We've got vague ideas of mounting an exhibition eventually, her photographs of all that remains with my sketches of how it was before the fall.'

'That could work,' Janey said, only half listening. 'Aren't you a bit cramped here?' She pulled open the wardrobe. 'You must be very dedicated to live in hotels for so long, out of suitcases.'

Peter looked at her with mild amusement. 'If you want to search my room, Janey, you have only to ask.' She shut the door again, embarrassed. The wardrobe contained nothing but men's clothes. She'd exhausted the possible hiding spaces in this attic.

'No one could have hidden Robyn's bag in here,' Peter said. 'I keep my door locked, even if there aren't any other guests. Call me paranoid — '

'No, I wasn't thinking that anyone *else* might have left it here.'

'Oh, I see. And what on earth do you imagine my motive for spiriting Robyn away might be?'

'That's just it,' Malcolm said. 'We can't see that anyone has a motive to harm my daughter.'

They fell silent for a moment, then, 'Who's the girl?' Janey asked, nodding at the portrait above the desk. 'She looks vaguely familiar. Do I know her?'

Peter laughed and shook his head. 'Not

unless you see ghosts. It's my idea of Louise d'Ambriers. Since no portraits of her survive, I've made her look like Silvie must have fifty years ago.'

'Ah, that explains it.' It occurred to her that Silvie de Chambertin, for all her mottled brown hands, her grey halo of hair, her wrinkles, had the sort of beauty that time couldn't wither.

'Which was Robyn's room?' Janey asked as they were leaving.

Peter pointed. Janey tried the door and it opened. The room was the mirror image of the one they'd left. The wardrobe door hung open to reveal only coathangers. The bed wasn't made, the blankets and counterpane folded neatly in squares. No one had slept here since Robyn went to join the grown-ups.

The third door led to an even smaller room with a tiny bed, a child's bed perhaps, under a sloping roof. This had an attic window out onto a flat roof with a selection of chimneys and a view to the mountains of Lacaune.

Neither room was hiding Robyn's bag.

★ ★ ★

'I feel I should be doing something,' Hugues said, 'but I can't think what.' He stood moodily in the doorway of his house, watching as the people of Montprimeur bustled about their business. There was a buzz of fear in the air but also of excitement, every sense heightened with the thrill of imminent battle: of a great victory or certain death.

'I'm sure you've done everything you can,' Robyn said.

He nodded, listing, almost to himself, what was done and what was yet to be done. 'Bruno and some of the other able-bodied men are inspecting the walls for any breach or weak point, ensuring that everyone is armed who needs to be, that they've had archery practice, that the mangonels are oiled and ready.' He struck his palm with his other fist. 'The boulders for the mangonels! I must make sure we have a steady supply to rain down on the invaders. There! I knew there was something I'd forgotten.'

'Bruno said he'd organise that,' she reminded him. 'It's a good job to set Young Joachim to. You're not strong enough to manhandle rocks.'

'I'm no weakling, Robert.'

'I didn't say that.' Although she saw that he used his thick black robe to mask a dangerously cadaverous figure, bulking himself out with wool as an anorexic will hide her condition. 'Physical strength is ... well, it's a gift from God, and Young Joachim has it to compensate him for his missing wits.'

'The grain is stored in a good dry place,' Hugues went on, apparently convinced, 'and several small boys have been detailed to sleep with it and keep the rats away. The town elders will meet later, after the Consolamentum, to decide what each family's allocation of grain and milk and eggs is to be for each week the siege lasts.'

Rationing, Robyn thought. How was it done? Did they start with the minimum to conserve stocks or with the maximum they dared, to keep up strength? She asked. Hugues frowned. 'That's one of the things we shall decide. We may be eating those same rats before summer comes. Or rather, *you* may be.' Which made Robyn wish that she was a vegetarian too. 'At least we shan't send our old and sick out of the town to be slaughtered to save our meagre rations.'

'Does that happen?'

'Frequently! At Montprimeur we shall survive or die together.'

'Come and sit down, Hugues. Everything is under control.'

'You're right.' He turned into the room with a sigh. 'We've done what we can and are now in God's blessed hands and I've never felt so helpless.'

'You said something about chess the other day,' she reminded him. 'Do you want to play, to keep your mind off things?'

'An excellent idea!' He opened the cupboard which was a rudimentary affair of planks nailed to posts, placed in the corner to keep it upright. Two of the planks were split where they'd warped in the heat from the fire and the door opened only with difficulty.

Robyn gave a gasp of pleasure as he shook the pieces out of a soft cotton bag — like the gym-shoe bag she'd had at school — onto the trestle. 'Oh Hugues, these are beautiful!'

He was pleased, a look of pride creeping into his sombre face for the first time. 'I carved them myself.' He went on hastily as if he had to justify this indulgence. 'It seemed an honest task, working with my hands, which I don't do enough of. It's a game that keeps the mind agile, too, and not a mere foolish timewaste like dice. I often stay up late when everyone else is abed. I can carve by feel, you see, without light.'

'You don't need to explain or apologise. They're wonderful.'

Hugues rubbed his fingers down the furrows between his eyebrows, the lines that the short-sighted develop when they

298

have no spectacles. 'Too much close work hurts my eyes,' he admitted.

He laid out a length of linen painted with black and white squares and began to place the pieces for play, but as fast as he did so Robyn picked them up again, holding them to the door to examine the glorious detail: the king's face proud above his neat beard, the castle with each stone separately delineated. The pawns were little workmen, all different, some with scythes, some aprons, a butcher with his axe aloft, a farmer carrying his seedbox. She remembered how she'd found the one surviving pawn all those years in the future and had longed to see its fellows and had thought she never would. 'How long did they take you?' she asked.

'Perhaps three years.' He took the pieces gently back from her and laid them out in their starting positions. 'Do you want black or white?'

'White.' White moved first and she'd probably need the advantage as she hadn't played since leaving her father's home. Her king, taller than the other pieces with a long flowing robe, stood in the correct spot but next to him Hugues had placed another figure, similar but smaller, wearing a skull cap instead of a crown.

'What's this one?'

'The king's minister,' he said, surprised. 'But where's the queen?'

'The queen!' He was puzzled.

'The most powerful piece on the board, the one that can move any distance in any direction in a straight line, provided her way is clear.'

He laughed uneasily, as if he thought she was teasing him and didn't know what to make of it. 'There's no piece that powerful. The king's minister is his advisor and shadows his every move.'

'What's the point,' Robyn asked tartly, 'of that?'

'You play by the new rules,' he said with a sigh. 'I'd heard some talk of it, but didn't believe it since there seemed no point in changing a perfectly good game for the sake of it. Besides,' he added, 'whoever heard of a queen who wandered around doing as she liked without her lord's permission?' A thought struck him and he chuckled at his own wit. 'Except for Eleanor of Aquitaine, obviously.'

'Obviously.'

'What a nuisance.' Hugues looked for a second like a small boy robbed of his best toy.

'Never mind, Hugues. Teach me your rules. I'll soon pick it up.'

'Really? You don't mind?' He seized the suggestion and for the next two hours he and Robyn played increasingly aggressive games of chess in which Hugues, initially, won all the time while Robyn eventually began to snatch the odd game from him.

'Have you nothing better to do than play children's games, either of you?' Bruno's voice interrupted them rudely, his face full of suspicion as usual as he looked at Robyn.

Hugues jumped guiltily to his feet. 'I was trying to take my mind off things, Bruno.' He glanced out of the door, surprised at the position of the sun. 'I didn't realise so much time had passed.'

Bruno picked up a black figure, a baker-pawn that Hugues had lost, and threw it across the room where it disappeared with a thud into the dark corner, into a crack between the floor and the wall. The vandal of every age, Robyn thought: destroying that which he didn't understand, but paradoxically, in this case, preserving one small chessman for a young woman to find in another world.

She couldn't like the man, try as she might.

'We shall need diversions if we're cooped up in here for weeks,' Hugues pointed out, 'with no way out, no fishing, no hunting, no riding or walking the countryside.'

'That's as may be, but at the moment what we need most is willing men with strong arms. Do you know how many de Montfort has burnt alive at Lavaur? Four hundred, that's how many.'

'How do you know?' Robyn asked, stunned.

'Because bad news flies like the wind, young sir, indeed it flies *with* the wind, in the ashes of good men brutally murdered, and that's what's waiting for us too if we don't look sharp.'

He pointed at Hugues. 'You, *Bonhomme*, go and prepare for the Consolamentum, and you, Robert of Durham — if that *is* your name, which I doubt — come and help Young Joachim with the boulders.'

They both went, very meekly, to do as Bruno bade them.

★ ★ ★

'Baron de Bresse? Are you in?'

Bisette shrank back as the tent flap opened and the Earl of Leicester, Simon de Montfort himself, entered. He was a huge man, well over six feet tall and powerfully built even, as now, without his armour. He wore hose and a mail shirt under his crusader's cloak with its great red cross. He was a year or two senior to de Bresse although in Bisette's eyes they were both incalculably old.

Henri gestured to her to make herself scarce and she slipped out past the great warlord, making herself as small and fleet as a zephyr wind.

De Montfort tolerated camp followers so long as he didn't have to look at them. It was all very well for him, the men grumbled. He could visit his wife, Alix de Montmorency, herself more at home in chain mail than fine gowns, safely installed at his headquarters in the castle at Carcassonne.

Bisette slid round the back of the tent and sat, her long legs stretched out on the grass before her, her ear pressed to the canvas.

'Are you with us for Montprimeur?' de Montfort was asking.

She heard no reply from her lord but clearly he'd nodded assent since she heard de Montfort clap him on the shoulder and say, 'There's no better life for a man than to fight for righteousness, to reconquer souls, no better destiny than to give his life for his faith.'

La Vierge had gone. With Lavaur fallen, a number of the mercenaries had decided to call it a day, at least for this year. La Vierge had set off for Toulouse with Heinz. 'I shall be dead by the time I'm thirty,' she'd told her friend. 'So I'll live for the moment and go and make merry in town.' She added laughing, 'Heinz may be small but he has plenty of stamina!'

Not to mention a purse full from the spoils of war.

5

*'Your towers will be destroyed and your
walls razed. You will be enslaved.
Force will prevail
where kindness failed.'*

St Dominic

'*In the beginning was the Word,*' Hugues
intoned, '*and the Word was with God, and
the Word was God . . . All things were made
by him; and without him wasn't anything
made that was made.*'
The white room was crammed as the
people of Montprimeur, far from preparing
to abandon their doomed faith, queued to
be received into its inner circle. Mengarde
Piquier displayed her bruised face with pride,
her whey-faced apprentice respectful behind
her, holding her woollen cloak folded over
his arm. Beside her Dias cradled her newborn
son. The laundress was wearing a smart
gown, clearly a cast-off from her new mistress.
These two very different women had formed
a strange alliance.
Louise had saved Robyn a seat at the back,
for which she was thankful. She'd believed

herself to be fit and supple but that was before Bruno made her spend two hours lifting back-breaking rocks into heaps by the mangonels. Her shoulders ached as no one's had ever ached before, she was certain, since the Creation. 'Do the young nobleman good to get a bit of plain honest work in for once,' had been the cobbler's only comment as she begged for rest. 'Chess, indeed!' Satisfied at last, he'd said, 'We'll see how the Sire de Montfort likes those tumbling down on his head!'

Robyn saw Dias's eyes flicker over her then grow suddenly still, noting her shape, taking in the faint swell of her bodice with a sly smile and a small raise of the eyebrows. So she'd been rumbled at last. But Dias would say nothing. Secrets were a valuable currency and a secret once told was worthless. She smiled back and winked at the laundress who grinned and looked at the floor.

Bruno went first and then acted as acolyte for Hugues as he administered their sole sacrament to the rest of the postulants. There were women as well as men, since the Cathars, rejecting the material world as the work of Satan, held gender to be an illusion and gladly accepted women priests — another idiosyncrasy that didn't endear them to their enemies. Hugues didn't directly kiss the women as he did the men, but kissed the gospels then handed them to the postulant to kiss in her turn.

Jehane approached the white-clothed table next after her husband and genuflected three times, requesting a blessing and taking the gospels in her hand, although she couldn't read. She and Hugues then recited the Lord's Prayer together. 'We entrust this holy prayer into your keeping,' Hugues said when they'd finished. 'Receive it from God and us and the whole Church; may you have strength to say it in all the days of your life, night and day, alone or in company; may you never eat or drink without first uttering it.'

'I do accept it from God and you and the Church,' Jehane replied in her gruff mumble. 'I have the will; pray God give me strength.' She kissed the gospels and made way for the next postulant.

Pietre began to cry halfway through the ceremony and was rapidly soothed at his mother's breast. 'You're not receiving the sacrament?' Robyn whispered to Louise, stifling a yawn.

'Not tonight. I don't feel myself prepared for it, nor do I feel myself under the immediate threat that would excuse my taking it before I was truly ready, not like these people.'

'Can't your father take refugees into the safety of the Château d'Ambriers?'

She frowned, a faint look of shame crossing her regular features. 'He won't, since that would give de Montfort an excuse to attack him — an excuse that he would be only too pleased to take.'

'What happens,' Robyn asked, 'if you take the Consolamentum *des mourants* and then don't die?'

'It lapses,' Louise said, as if this were obvious.

'Learn to abide by God's commandments,' Hugues said, as the last of the new Perfects backed away from the altar table, 'and to hate this world. And if you do so steadfastly to the end, we have hope that your soul will attain everlasting life.'

'And 'the end',' a voice muttered in Robyn's ear, 'cannot now be far off.'

Robyn bit back a sarcastic retort, remembering Thibaut's suffering at Béziers. 'I thought you'd be gone by now,' she said instead. 'Like your friend Jaufré Piquier.'

'I leave tomorrow,' the barber said. 'I'm escorting the Demoiselle d'Ambriers back to her father's castle, after which I shan't delay one hour more.'

★ ★ ★

'May I join you?'

Janey sat down at the bar next to Dexter Mooney without waiting for his reply. 'They say you shouldn't drink alone,' she added.

'Only way *to* drink.' The American was sipping steadily on something brown, shiny and undiluted in a shot glass.

Janey signalled the barman and called, '*Un Scotch, s'il vous plaît.*'

It was a man's bar, she quickly saw, and she was the only woman there, but it couldn't be helped. No one took any notice of her, anyway, including the barman. They were absorbed in the TV set in the corner which blared out a football match in excited French. The patrons were uniformly middle-aged and working class, their hands rough with farm work, their faces brownish red from years of sun. They drank beer sparsely, smoked in plain defiance of the anti-smoking laws and argued about whether the last goal had been offside. Janey learned a new expletive she thought might come in useful. She wondered how it was spelt.

'If we're both drinking Scotch,' Mooney said, taking pity on her, 'it'd be cheaper to get a bottle. Bernard!' He called to the barman, who was apparently willing to allow *his* existence. A few words and some notes changed hands, and in no time a bottle of

Johnny Walker was sitting on the bar in front of them.

'Slàinte!' Mooney said, raising his glass in salute.

'Slarncher — whatever that means.' Janey asked for some mineral water too, in case it turned into a long night. Her glass wasn't clean, but she wasn't squeamish. There was no ice. 'Come here often?' she asked, when Mooney hadn't spoken for some time.

'No, as it happens, but when I do feel like a drink, this is my watering hole, as you were apparently informed.'

'Mmm. Simon said I might find you here.'

'I like it here, rough and ready. Like me.'

'Rediscovering your peasant-farmer roots?'

He wasn't offended, just the schoolmaster correcting a wrong answer from a pupil. 'My family haven't been peasants for generations. We've been in the States since 1905. We're not the Kennedys, nor yet the Kellys of Philadelphia, but we're not poor white trash either.'

Mooney had agreed reluctantly that they might search his room but had declined the offer to be there while they did it. Janey didn't blame him. It wasn't pleasant when someone made it clear they thought you might have done something pretty nasty, especially if you had. His room had told her little she didn't know about him except that he had a taste for the Western — that unique piece of American history — mostly translated into French with lurid covers. *Un homme, seul contre le désert.*

He was next door to Silvie at the back and had the same blessing of a small balcony. He'd added nothing to the hotel's furniture except the portable TV he'd mentioned at supper. As in Silvie's room, the only personal ornament was a photograph, this time of a dark-haired woman, too thin, but attractive in a severe sort of way, flanked by two unsmiling boys on the threshold of adolescence when you can never see much to smile about.

'Give my crib a good toss?' Dexter asked.

'Yes, thanks.'

'Find anything?'

'Nope.'

'Expect to?'

'Not really.'

'Thanks. If you want to know, I find the fact that you thought I might have hidden Robyn's bag in my room an insult to my intelligence.' Janey laughed. After a moment Mooney joined in. 'Where's the old man?' he asked. 'I thought you two came as a pair, like bookends.'

'Malcolm's gone off to bed. He's shattered.'

'Poor bastard,' Mooney said evenly. 'Who'd be a parent, eh? 'Specially of a girl.'

'I take it that's your family in the photograph,' she said, seizing the opening. 'The one by your bed.'

He answered readily enough. 'My ex-wife, Teri, and her sons, Ryan and John.'

'*Her* sons?'

'Okay, *our* sons. You're right. Guess with what I've paid for them over the years, they must belong to me by now.'

'Sorry. I didn't mean to pry.'

'No? That must be a first for you, Janey Silverman. Teri was one of my students at Harvard fifteen years ago. I was thirty and she was nineteen. I've steered clear of much younger women ever since, in case you were wondering if you're safe in this dive with me.'

The unspoken subtext was: Or if Robyn was safe from me.

'Harvard?' Janey said, not rising to the bait. 'You must be good, Dexter.'

'If there's one thing you can't make an intelligent man understand, it's that he should never get involved with his students. You either marry them or end up in front of a disciplinary committee.'

'You mean you *had* to marry her or get sacked?'

'Nope, I mean I was gagging to marry her. Head over heels in love. Lasted less than three years, and she was pregnant most of that time.'

'Maybe she didn't like the idea of you being in the field for years on end.'

'I wasn't. I was a stuffed-shirt, preppy college professor with a house in Concord and a lawnmower you could sit on. Nearest I got to a dig in those days was assiduous reading of the *Archaeological Review* each month. I was home by five every evening for a stiff G&T before dinner. I started going into the field *after* she left me.'

'Wow,' Janey said. 'Like joining the Foreign Legion.'

'Shit! Have you no feminine sympathy, woman?'

'You want sympathy, Dexter?'

'Damn right I don't!'

Janey didn't find Mooney attractive. His hair must have been red, even ginger, when he was younger but had now faded to something like dishwater, although he at least showed no sign of baldness. His eyes were such a pale blue as to be almost colourless. His mouth was small, his lips thin and suggesting no passion. It was odd how much pulling power being a teacher had; she'd noticed that even the most unprepossessing college lecturers had students with crushes mooning round after them, bleating about how sensitive they were.

Teri had fallen for *something* fifteen years ago, maybe the sharp mind and the mordant humour.

'Actually,' Mooney said, 'it's inaccurate to call Teri my *ex*-wife. We're not divorced. She's a good Catholic is Saint Teresa. Thus am I neither fish nor fowl: not married, not free.'

'That must be hard.'

'Makes me a misfit. We're a bunch of misfits. I've come to the conclusion that anyone who leaves home and lives in severe discomfort, scrabbling around in centuries-old earth for years on end, would have to be. I mean, does anyone outside the narrow world of archaeology give two hoots about Montprimeur and its relics and its people? When we're finished excavating that site — probably in another eight hundred years — half a dozen people will nod their heads and say, 'Hmm. Interesting' and go back to sleep.'

'I can see that you're a misfit, Dexter — '

'Thanks.'

'But what about the others?'

'Let's see now, the professor: a man of fifty-five who hasn't had a settled home since he was eighteen, unless you count a college room. A man who has, as far as I can make out, no sex life and never has had.'

'So he's a confirmed bachelor, a celibate; it's not a crime. He has more important things to think about. In an earlier age he might have been a priest.'

'Then there's Silvie; you saw what happened at dinner tonight.'

'So, she's a bit absent-minded, a bit . . . other-worldly.'

'She's living in another century with her famous ancestors. The blood line has decayed so much that there's nothing left in the veins but tap water.'

'Come on, our families are equally old, we just don't know who they were the way Silvie does.'

'Yeah, but we didn't all marry our cousins.' Mooney was starting to enjoy himself. 'You seen *Gone with the Wind*, Janey?'

'What do you think?'

'I think *everyone's* seen *Gone with the Wind*.'

'Okay. So?'

'So. Why is Ashley Wilkes such a fucking wimp?' He poked her arm with a pudgy finger. 'Because the Wilkeses always marry their fucking cousins. 'Scuse me.'

'You're excused, Dexter.'

'The boy, Peter, a little buttoned-up English public school boy; a virgin. He's another James Clements in the making. Meriel: a blue-stocking, brought up by a half-mad father, scared of life.'

'Oh, come on!'

'She is,' he insisted. 'She's such a perfectionist that it prevents her from ever doing anything. For instance, she speaks really good French, did you know that?'

'No, I haven't heard her say so much as a word.'

'Exactly! She won't open her mouth in case she makes a mistake! If she wants to buy a glass of wine in a café she agonises half an hour making sure she's got the sentence exactly right. Then there's Simon, of course, your archetypal Peter Pan, except that he gets older every year but the girls on his arm stay twenty-three.'

'Do you dislike all of them?'

'I don't dislike any of them. I *like* misfits. *You*'re a misfit.'

Janey didn't challenge this, wasn't sure that she could make a challenge stand up in court. Nor did she bother to wonder if it meant that Mooney liked her. 'Why don't you go home, Dexter?'

'To what? To be a misfit? I don't think so.'

'And Robyn?'

Mooney thought about that for a bit. 'She didn't belong with the rest of us,' he said finally. 'She had some of the symptoms, sure, raised without a woman in the house, like Meriel, plunging into a life in the field straight out of college, like James; but there was life in that girl, real life. She'd've grown out of it after a while, got married, produced a pack of dirty, happy, sane kids.'

'Not with Simon, I take it.'

'I like to think not. No, Robyn was no misfit.'

They drank on for a while in companionable silence as the home team scored a goal and the bar turned briefly celebratory. Janey had an idea she would regret this in the morning, but drink loosened tongues and she had to match him. Besides, she was having fun.

'Are you a native Bostonian?' she asked.

'Sure. It's one of the biggest Irish-American communities in the States.'

'How do you come to speak such good French?'

'French-Canadian grandmother on my mother's side. Slàinte.' He refilled both their glasses and put on an over-the-top English accent. 'Bottoms up, old thing!'

Janey decided she might as well put Dexter's considerable brain power to use.

'If it had been you,' she asked, 'where would you have hidden the bag?'

He looked at her suspiciously over the top of his glass. 'I was almost starting to like you. I never drink with hostiles.'

'Seriously. *If.* Put yourself in the shoes of the person who packed that bag and sneaked it away.'

'I hope they're clean and free from disease.' He thought for a while. 'Did I have transportation?'

'Maybe.'

'How desperate was I?'

'Dunno.'

'How pressed for time?'

'Dunno.'

'May I wear a blindfold, too?'

'Not much to go on, is there?'

Dexter filled his glass again and drank deeply. A Harvard-trained brain — even one fuddled by drink — was turning over at speed. 'Unless it was me or Simon, and I know it wasn't me and I don't think it was him — he's genuinely crazy about the kid — there was no transportation and time must have been very short indeed.'

'So?'

Dexter looked at her as if she was stupid. He spread his arms wide like a Jewish mother. 'So, it's somewhere at the hotel.'

★ ★ ★

'We're living in a time of great change,' Hugues said that night. It was late, the town elders had met, taken decisions, and dispersed again. He'd been sitting silently by the fire for some time and Robyn had thought he'd dropped off to sleep. 'An age of movement,' he continued. 'Ten years ago I could walk for five days in any direction and see no face to which I couldn't put a name. Even the itinerant shepherds were the same year after year. Now hordes of strangers fill our paths and byways and there's no knowing who is friend or foe.'

'Strangers like me?'

'I didn't mean that, although, yes, you are a stranger.' Hugues yawned and stretched. 'I'd best go up and try to sleep, and if I can't sleep, I'll pray.'

He got to his feet and placed a large log on the fire to see them through the night. It was damp and began at once to smoke, making Robyn's eyes sting. She moved over to the doorway for fresh air. 'What's that sound?'

'I hear nothing,' Hugues said, joining her.

She held up a finger. 'No, listen. It's like someone singing.'

Hugues strained his ears, then smiled

gently. 'It's Dias. She sings as she goes about her work. I'm so used to it, I'm hardly aware of it.'

'She's washing this late?'

'Oh, she doesn't mind when she works. She's often pounding linen far into the night.'

'What's her song about?'

'I don't know this particular one, but her songs are typically of love and courtship and are usually, as you might expect, a little indelicate. She's no troubadour with tales of courtly love, of gentlemen dying for their untouchable ladies. So a man is sturdy and well-equipped; she won't ask him to fight dragons for her.'

Robyn stood by the open doorway a moment longer. Dias's voice seemed strangely beautiful in the night, pure and unaccompanied.

'A fine time to be singing bawdy songs,' she remarked.

'She barely understands what's happening,' Hugues said. 'She's brought life into the world and has no thought of death. Tonight, she's immortal. Goodnight, dear Robert. Sleep well.' His cool hand lingered affectionately on her cheek, then he began to climb the ladder to the upper floor. It didn't creak under his weight. 'As long as I've known her she's lived only for the day,' he said, pausing outside his bedchamber, a muffled black shape against the night sky. 'Let the morrow look to itself! Dear simple soul. She doesn't understand that the day comes when you run out of tomorrows.'

* * *

Janey brushed her shining black hair a hundred times every night. It was strange that there were some childhood injunctions that stuck, she thought, the ones that mattered least. As she counted mentally she stood at the window of her room which overlooked the street.

She felt drunk, but only pleasantly so. She wondered if she should ring her mother, have a chat, but decided that she would wait until she was sober enough to work out which way the time difference went between here and the beach house in Florida. Last time, she'd woken up with a bad hangover and, racked with sudden filial duty, phoned her mother only to be asked, very coldly, if she knew what bloody time it was? Five o'clock in the bloody morning, that's what bloody time it was.

She smiled at the memory; she knew her mother thought she'd done it on purpose.

The brush slowed then stopped as she

became aware that a man was standing on the pavement opposite, staring up at the hotel. She could make out nothing in the cloudy night, the nearest streetlamp thirty metres away, except that he was a man of medium height, wearing dark clothing, and that he stood well back in the shadow of a doorway. He looked so deliberately furtive, like Orson Welles in *The Third Man*.

Janey stepped briskly across the room and switched off her bedside light before resuming her station at the window. She saw the man light a cigarette, his hand cupped to shelter the flame. It didn't conveniently illuminate his face. She pressed the button at the side of her watch and the digital face displayed 23:48.

She slipped her feet into a pair of black pumps and left her room. She wasn't accustomed to moving either quickly or quietly but somehow did both. The front door was locked and bolted by Madame Monami at eleven-thirty every night and was, Janey knew, inclined to be noisy, its hinges in need of oiling. She followed the corridor to the back door instead, unbolted that quietly and made her way through the car park and out into the street.

She had no idea what she was going to say to the loiterer when she caught up with

322

him, but was sure that inspiration would strike when the moment came.

Whisky courage?

When she reached the doorway opposite the hotel, it was empty. She stood uncertainly for a moment, torn between disappointment and relief. Perhaps the man had merely stepped out of the wind for a few seconds to light up and her imagination had supplied the rest.

Then a voice said, 'Meesse Seelvairmanne?' right behind her. She let out a small squeak of panic, pressing herself back into the friendly doorway, her hand to her throat, ready to scream if she could. She saw the glow of his cigarette, sinister now like some stinging insect.

'It's me,' the man said in French, 'Guy Laroche.'

As he spoke the moon emerged from behind a cloud and she could see him clearly, recognising the roughly handsome face, now in need of a shave. He was casually dressed in jeans and a loose black jacket, his white shirt open at the neck. 'Sweet Jesus!' Janey felt like collapsing on the doorstep. 'Inspector Laroche. You frightened the life out of me.'

'I'm sorry if I startled you. I heard someone moving stealthily around in the hotel car park and took cover to see who it was. My eyes are probably more accustomed to the dark than yours and it didn't occur to me that you wouldn't see me well enough to recognise me.' He inhaled deeply and blew smoke out through his nostrils. He made it a sensual act. 'By the way, is that fearful, three-wheeled, pink monstrosity yours?'

'Yes. I like it.' She added defensively, 'It's sort of eccentric.'

'You English, you have to be *different*.'

'If you mean we're not all anally-retentive conformists like you French, I agree with you.'

'Well, rather you than me. What happens if you get a sudden flat on one of the back wheels? You'll flip right over.'

'Oh! Does it matter?'

He shrugged. '*Ça m'est égal*. I don't want to be the one to have to scrape you off the tarmac, that's all.'

'What are you doing here?'

'I hardly know,' the policeman said.

'Are you watching the place?'

He laughed and shook his head. 'Even if I had the manpower, or a reason, to keep the hotel under surveillance, I wouldn't be doing it myself. Not an important inspector like me. No, I was on my way home — '

'At midnight?'

'From a social occasion, a dinner with a colleague, if you must know, when I suddenly found myself outside the Oustal Monami. It's a little out of my way, so I assumed that since, like Freud, I don't believe in accidents, my feet must have brought me by this route for a reason, so I stopped for a moment, to get the feel of the place.'

'Hoping for inspiration?'

'If you like.' He took a crushed packet of untipped Gauloises from his jacket pocket. 'Cigarette?'

'I don't smoke, thanks. What? No accidents at all?'

'No accidents, no coincidences.'

'What an ordered world! I envy you.'

He sniffed the wind. 'I hope you've not been drinking whisky alone in your room, Miss Silverman. The next step is talking to yourself.'

'No,' she said crossly, as if it was any of his business. 'At the *Bar du Marché*.'

'The Bar Machismo?' He raised his eyebrows. 'Alone? I'm surprised you got served.'

'I wasn't alone. I was with a . . . friend.'

'Ah, yes. Dr Mooney. Of course. The *yanquee*.'

'How did you know that?'

'It's a small town and it's my business to know things.'

'You heard what happened to Joachim Monami?'

'I heard, yes, although it's not my case.'

'Has anyone been charged?'

He hesitated. 'Strictly *entre nous*, the boy Eric Dussert has been charged with assault and GBH, but he won't name his accomplices.'

'What about the torn tee shirt?'

'Eric's.'

'Can't you do something about those young thugs?'

'Like what? You've heard of freedom of speech in England, I take it?'

'We invented it! Do you think it's connected with Robyn's disappearance?'

'Not at all.'

'A coincidence then?'

' . . . Apparently.' The inspector grinned. 'You win, Miss Silverman, since winning is clearly important to you.' He dropped his cigarette to the pavement and crushed it out with his heel. 'I must be on my way. My wife will be wondering where I've got to and she's a woman of imagination. Tell me, is the girl's father still here?'

'He's not going anywhere, not until he's found something out, one way or another.'

'Yes,' Laroche said, his voice grave now, 'one way or another. You've still got my card with my phone number on it, haven't you?'

'Yes, of course.'

'Goodnight, Miss Silverman. I should go indoors before you catch your death.' It was only as he turned and walked away that it dawned on Janey that she was wearing nothing but her pyjamas.

★ ★ ★

'Damn it!'

As Robyn used the only-too-public privy early the next morning, wiping herself with some rags Hugues had provided, she saw smears of blood. Of course — she hadn't been taking her contraceptive pills and was now experiencing withdrawal bleeding. Well, there wasn't much she could do about it — no quick trip to the chemist for a packet of Tampax — so she folded a rag carefuly into an oblong pad and stuffed it into her pants. Luckily her jeans were tight and would hold it in place.

The door opened as she finished and one of the refugees came in, grunting a greeting in a country accent so thick she couldn't hope to understand it. She smiled and nodded and left quickly as he dropped his hose and began to make contented straining noises over the pit. This was no place for the fastidious, but Robyn had never been overly fussy.

Despite the early hour, the streets were full of people, some running, heading for the south side of the town where the main gate was. Young Joachim brushed past her, his long arms swinging loose, clumsy as ever, almost knocking her over. He ululated what must have been some sort of apology. 'What is it?' she asked in vain. 'What's happening?'

Finally, somebody paused long enough to answer her. 'The crusaders are here.'

'What!'

'Well, in view, anyway.'

Robyn turned and followed the throng.

★ ★ ★

The professor spent one morning at the hotel each week catching up on paperwork and he'd invited Janey and Malcolm to join him that day. Janey's head felt a bit thick from the session in the bar and a quiet morning indoors suited her fine.

The professor's room was the largest Janey had yet seen in the hotel, necessarily so since this was the dig's primary workroom as well as his personal space, and half of it was taken up with his computer and other equipment. He had a four-poster double bed. Rather a waste, Janey thought, when he had no one to share it with. Perhaps this was the Monami version of the honeymoon suite since he also had a bidet. There was a fitted carpet in a rust-coloured floral pattern, like no flower seen in nature. The room was tidy without having the empty quality of Silvie's. Janey was prepared to believe what Dexter had said, that James Clements had no real home, only a set of rooms back at Balliol. He would probably be as happy in a tent.

An IBM PC stood on a purpose-built stand with a colour printer and a separate stack with two disk drives and a CD Rom. The adjacent table held cartons of paper and a cardboard box filled with items that been dug up in the last few days and not yet catalogued and sent home for safekeeping, which was one of the things James was going to do that morning. Because of this box, full of artefacts that were simultaneously worthless and priceless, the professor was careful to keep his room locked when the archaeologists were out at the dig. It was unlikely that Robyn's abductor had dumped her case here.

There were various jars and bottles. Janey

picked one up to examine the label: some kind of solvent to clear the rust of centuries away from metal. 'Careful,' James warned her, noticing her action, 'that stuff can give you a nasty burn.'

'May I?' Malcolm picked up two small but heavy discs from the box and turned them over in his hand. They had crude carvings on them, like pyramids. 'Coins?' he asked.

'Actually they're buttons,' James replied. 'Made of lead, which is why they're so heavy. You'd be surprised how little coinage there was in country districts in the thirteenth century. Trade was mainly by barter.'

Malcolm's hand went in again, as to a lucky dip. 'What on earth are these?'

'Tweezers, believe it or not, made of bronze. Probably considered classy, something to show off to your neighbours.'

They were cumbersome, more like tongs. Malcolm delved again. 'A belt buckle?'

'Sort of. You'd fasten it to your belt to hold your dagger. It's badly worn but you can make out the carving, look, a griffin, part of the d'Ambriers coat of arms.'

'Silvie has a brooch like that,' Janey exclaimed. 'I noticed it as it's the only jewellery she wears, apart from her wedding ring.'

'It was a common emblem for the nobility,'

James said, 'as it combines the lion and the eagle, the noblest beast and the noblest bird. It's supposed to guard hidden treasure too. *This* is a belt buckle.' He showed them a bronze circlet in the shape of a coiled snake, its forked tongue making the tongue of the buckle.

'Intricate workmanship,' Janey remarked.

'In its way it's beautiful,' the professor said. 'I think it's my favourite piece so far. That and the chessman.'

'The one Robyn found,' Malcolm said glumly.

'Yes.' James pulled at his nose with a hint of embarrassment. 'She's such an asset.'

There was also a scale model of the site of Montprimeur. Malcolm stood looking at the tiny community, his hands in his pockets. It seemed so much more real than the piles of dead stones which he hadn't the imagination to build into a living world. 'How many people?'

'The normal population of the town was about two hundred and fifty,' James explained, 'but that would have doubled at the time of the massacre with farm folk from the local countryside and refugees from other towns.'

'Five hundred people,' Malcolm mused, 'murdered in one day.'

'A bit like a plane crash,' Janey said.

James said kindly, 'If it helps put things in perspective, Mr Dawson, the Black Death wiped out one-third of the population of Europe little more than a century later, some sixty million people.'

'Oh, yes,' Malcolm said sardonically, 'that's a great help. I appreciate that the death of one young woman isn't statistically significant, but it's still a personal tragedy for her widowed father.'

'If we escape one horror,' James said, 'another is waiting for us. That's the way of the world, the history of mankind, since records began.'

'And we're still here,' Janey pointed out. 'We live, we breed, we survive . . . And we don't know yet that Robyn is dea — '

There was an enormous crash outside on the landing, the sound of crockery smashing, metal clattering and something soft and heavy hitting the floor. When the three of them had scrambled for the door, they found Joachim lying there, his head hanging over the top step of the staircase. He was surrounded by broken mugs and pools of steaming coffee in which spilt sugar cubes slowly dissolved. A tin tray lay by his feet. He was unconscious and his whole body was jerking in rhythmic spasms.

'An epileptic fit,' Malcolm said. He knelt down beside the boy, whose face was taking on a sickly bluish sheen.

'He's not breathing,' Janey said, aghast.

'That's normal. He'll start again in a few seconds.' Sure enough Joachim began to breathe, sucking in laboured, gasping breaths. 'Help me pull him a bit further onto the landing so his head isn't dangling like that.' They did so and Malcolm said, 'Now give him plenty of space.'

'Aren't you supposed to put something in his mouth?' James said.

Malcolm shook his head impatiently. 'That died out with the dinosaurs. We keep him comfortable and wait for it to pass.'

'There must be something we can do. Shouldn't we get a doctor?'

'It's not as dramatic as it looks, if you've never seen one before. I've got a cousin who has them occasionally. It'll be over soon.'

Madame Monami had appeared to investigate the noise. When she saw what was happening, she took the steps two at a time. 'Jojo!'

'*Ne vous en faites pas, madame,*' James said in his comically accented French.

The woman, determined that she *would* upset herself, whatever the professor said, knelt by her son and laid a tender hand on his forehead. The twitching was already beginning to abate and his limbs were contracting and relaxing at a slower rate. A strong faecal smell reached their nostrils as the young man's bowels spontaneously emptied and Madame Monami gave a further cry of distress.

'It's all right,' Malcolm said to her in English. 'You don't want to worry about that. It's nothing to be ashamed of and he'll clean up.' The woman didn't understand his words but caught something in the tone of his voice that soothed her.

'He hasn't had a fit in eight years,' she said. 'Not when he takes his pills. He said he was feeling fine and I let him bring you up your coffee.' She looked about in dismay at the fragments of wet china.

'Perhaps he's been forgetting to take his medication,' Janey said, 'in the . . . excitement.'

'That may be,' the woman conceded.

The spasms ceased as suddenly as they'd begun and Joachim lay still, his breathing gradually returning to normal. His mother took his head onto her lap and stroked his face as she might a baby's.

'Jojo,' she whispered. *'Petit ange.'*

His eyes opened and he sat up, looking about him in wary confusion. For a few seconds it was clear that there was nobody there he recognised and panic flickered into his dark eyes, then was gone. He looked about him at the mess and grunted something that might have been apology or distress. He got to his feet, his hands caressing the wet and darkened seat of his jeans. A clutch of tears formed in his eyes. Then he was normal again, or what was normal for him.

'Come along.' His mother held out her hand for him. 'Let's get you cleaned up and you can have a nice rest.'

He followed her obediently down the stairs. The others stood looking at each other. 'Do you think he really forgot his medication?' Janey asked. 'Or has the shock of Wednesday night aggravated his condition.'

'Only time will tell,' the professor said. He cleared his throat. 'You, um, did jolly well there, Mr Dawson.'

Malcolm shrugged off the compliment. 'If we can find a mop and bucket,' he said, 'I might as well clear this up, save Mrs Moonaymee the trouble.'

'I think there are some cleaning things in the cupboard in the bathroom,' Janey said. There were, and between them they soon cleared away the aftermath of Joachim's fit.

★ ★ ★

At first Robyn could make out no more than a cloud of dust on the horizon, a little thicker than usual, true, but not something that would normally have made her look twice. As she strained her eyes into the distance, narrowing them in an attempt to achieve a longer vision, she thought she could make out a thin procession of what looked like a circus or a carnival — a cavalcade of animals and machines.

'The siege train,' a grim voice said beside her. She glanced sideways to see Thibaut of Béziers, his broad face very pale. 'So many memories,' he murmured. The siege train; as soon as de Montfort had taken Lavaur he would have no further need of it and would send it, slow as it was, on to its next target, where it would wait for him.

The sun was higher now and another cloudless day promised. Jehane looked up at the sky and muttered something about rain, or the lack of it. 'The wells will dry up,' she said, 'just as they did at Carcassonne, and the disease will get us if the soldiers don't. God has no pity on his people.'

The bell began to toll once more. Small boys scrambled onto the flat roofs of the houses nearest the walls, the better to view the spectacle, their grubby little faces an amalgam of excitement and terror.

'My friends, my friends.' Hugues had appeared unnoticed among them. 'This isn't a time to stand staring; this is a time for action. We must send men into the countryside to bring in the rest of the farmers, as much livestock as we can manage and as much grain. There's no time to lose.' Robyn instantly volunteered but Hugues gave her a wax tablet and told her to stand at the gate and make a tally of the food, be it in sacks or still on the hoof, that came into the town. 'There are few enough of us who can read and write and reckon,' he said. 'That's how you will serve us best.'

From the gateway she had a clear view to the horizon as the enemy procession drew nearer. Louise's legend proved all too false: vultures circled high above the siege train.

'Will he send heralds to call for our surrender?' Robyn asked Hugues as he returned briefly to see how she was getting on.

Hugues pursed his lips. 'I doubt it. We've nothing to gain by surrendering since, as heretics, our lives are forfeit, and de Montfort knows that. My guess is that he won't waste his time. He will prepare himself for victory or defeat, as must we.'

Bruno, who'd overheard the last conversation, butted in scornfully. 'He won't keep his mercenaries happy by negotiating a surrender, and de Montfort needs to keep them sweet.'

The zigzag path was a rush-hour highway as men and women from the neighbouring areas who'd put off taking refuge in the town, hoping against hope for a miracle, hastened to whip their reluctant mules up the slope. Children as young as four shooed chickens and ducks before them like human sheepdogs, using small branches to keep the fowl in line. The swish of leaves and the clucking of offended poultry vied with the chatter of excited childish voices in the still air.

People brought their most precious belongings, however useless: their best clothes and drinking goblets, their linen wall-hangings and tabor pipes. Robyn had sometimes played the game where you had to say what one thing you would rescue from your house if it caught fire; she saw now how far she'd always been from such an extremity and how foolish her answers seemed.

There were useful objects too, of course: sickles and axes, spades with sharp cutting edges, billhooks and handsaws, any of which could deliver a lethal blow to a man's head. Robyn remained at her station for hours as the ribbon of refugees seemed to go on forever. Even the river down below brought a constant flow of barges from east and west.

Hugues kept an anxious lookout on the wall above her, fearing that soldiers on horseback would break loose from the cavalcade and gallop onward to challenge them; but the engineers of the siege train knew their job which, however despised, was the best-paid work in the army and they were as strict about demarcation as any trades unionist.

By the time the gates closed at dusk the enemy was no more than a mile away but had stopped for the night, out of the reach of pre-emptive strikes from the town. They would wait now for the foot soldiers, mostly mercenaries, and the mere handful of knights paying their feudal duty to the King of France or their pious duty to the Vicar of Christ. Great nobles, many of whom had been enemies for generations, were united to crush a handful of peasants in a foreign country, hundreds of miles from home.

Looking out in the red of the setting sun, Robyn would have laughed at their equipment had she not known how deadly it could be. It was like a Heath Robinson picture. She could see the trebuchet — like a child's catapult, but one made for a giant's child — which would hurl missiles 200 yards into the air. Then there were the ballistas — crossbows but, again, such as no human man could wield, wound back with winches to propel a missile perhaps twelve feet long into the heart of the town, a sharpened iron bolt or a flaming brand to bring fire and panic to the town.

There was no end, she thought, to the ingenuity man employed when it came to killing his fellow man. In an age where keeping disease and famine from the door was a constant struggle, man would still devote time and effort to creating new and more deadly weapons in an effort to make his neighbour cross himself and bow to the authority of the Pope and admit that good must triumph over evil. They had a cat, too, she saw: a mobile shelter which a dozen men would carry on their backs to gain access to the walls without being hit from above.

'Fortunately,' Hugues said, 'I don't think the sappers can mine under our walls. Our foundations are too strong, the rock too solid.'

'They won't get anywhere near our walls,' Bruno said. 'Not if I have anything to do with it.'

Which was all very well, Robyn thought as she smiled a tired and hungry acknowledgement, but unless her history books were very wrong, they wouldn't need to.

After lunch, when James had gone back to the dig, Janey poked her head round the door behind the reception desk, the one marked *Privé*, looking for Madame Monami. She found the middle-aged widow taking a rest, a small cup of black coffee to hand, her broad feet unshackled from their shoes. A half-smoked American cigarette dangled from her lips. She was watching *Dallas* dubbed into French.

She looked up as Janey coughed for attention, a weary, silent question forming on her face. Julie: the name of a much younger woman, surely.

'I'm sorry to disturb you, madame,' Janey said. 'I was wondering if I could buy a bottle of mineral water from you.' She was feeling dehydrated after her exertions in the bar the previous night. All in a good cause, naturally.

'Yes, of course.' Madame Monami got up. 'Come in, mademoiselle.' She stubbed her cigarette out in an ashtray which held the remnants of a dozen smokes. J.R. swelled, preparing to demolish someone or something, his French voice shrill and reedy. She turned down the sound of the TV, Janey sidled into the room and waited while the hotel owner disappeared barefoot into the neighbouring kitchen. An unexpectedly new, large and efficient washing machine was churning away the other side of the kitchen door.

The private sitting-room was about fifteen feet by twelve and had the same lack of cosiness evinced by the rest of the hotel. The sofa where the proprietress had been sitting was of black leather — possibly mock leather, Janey couldn't be sure from this distance. Both it and its matching armchair were shabby and the chair had a long tear down the back from which grey-white stuffing bulged.

An oak dresser, solid and dull, stood against the far wall. Some surprisingly pretty crockery was displayed on the shelves. Of the cupboards beneath, one door stood open to reveal a pile of towels and sheets with some tourist brochures escaping onto the floor. There was a fireplace with a gas fire fitted in it. A gilded wooden crucifix hung above the carved mantelpiece. Next to the kitchen door was a particularly ugly picture of the Sacred Heart, the Christ figure clutching at the huge, ruptured organ as it tried to burst from his chest.

A second door led into Madame Monami's bedroom. A big bed could be glimpsed, with a red plush ottoman at its foot. A black and white dressing-gown lay draped haphazardly across it. Neatly ranged beside it were a pair of fluffy mules.

'Still or sparkling?' the woman's voice called from the kitchen, raised to compete with the washing machine.

'Still.' Janey took the need to make herself heard as an invitation to move further into the room.

The older woman came out with a bottle of Evian and an automatic smile. Janey handed her a ten franc piece and told her to keep the change. Madame Monami put it in her apron pocket without demur.

'I hope you weren't too upset last night,' Janey said, 'about the business with the toadstools.'

The woman shrugged. 'I overreacted, I suppose, but Madame la Comtesse should know better, a countrywoman born and bred, than to bring that filth into my house, into a place where people are eating.'

'You know Silvie well?' Janey asked.

'My mother was in service with the de Chambertins all her life,' she said, 'as a maid first but later as the housekeeper, and my father was the groundsman. That was when they had the manor house, of course, a few miles from here, at Lautrec.'

'Ah, they lost their ancestral home?'

'You know how it was after the war,' she sighed. 'All those new taxes to pay for the social changes. I suppose they were for the better — I don't know. People fend perhaps best for themselves. That way the strong survive and the weak go under.' Janey murmured some uncommitted reply and the older woman continued. 'When Count Jean-Jacques died in 1952 the death duties were the last straw and the young Count Etienne sold up.'

'I suppose it is a pity,' Janey said.

The woman bridled. 'After hundreds of years, it is not a pity; it's a crime!'

'So you've known Silvie all your life?'

She nodded. 'I was born in that house, mademoiselle — in the gatekeeper's cottage, that is — and it was so beautiful then, dignified, you know? Perhaps it was a little shabby but it was *gentleman's* home. Now it's a country house hotel, with a swimming pool where the secret garden was and a nine-hole golf course in the park and a chef from Paris who scorns our local delicacies. It's full of rich tourists, businessmen, industrialists — half of them damn foreigners.'

She stopped, recalling a moment too late that she was talking to a damn foreigner. '*Pardon!*' she muttered.

'You must have been young when you left,

though,' Janey prompted her.

'I was six, old enough to remember. My mother was there when Mademoiselle Silvie came as a bride, so beautiful, just nineteen. That was in 1945, although of course she was often there as a girl, before the war. Who could have dreamt then that things would turn out as they did. Now she lives in that cottage in Cordes, nothing more than a peasant's house, smaller than the gatehouse where I grew up.'

'Did you and your parents come here then, when the manor was sold?'

'Yes.' Madame Monami looked about her, aware that her hotel didn't meet the exacting standards of modern travellers. 'And the de Chambertins did what they could to look after us. People like them, old families, understand that you have a duty towards your servants.'

'*Noblesse oblige.*'

'Which is why the archaeologists stay here and give me a steady income. Madame la Comtesse knows that things have been difficult, what with Joachim . . . ' She tailed off.

Janey took her cue. 'How is Joachim? Is he resting?'

'He's in the courtyard with his comic books. We thought it best that he shouldn't go out any more in the afternoons.'

'Well, not after this morning obviously, but — '

'Not any more,' the woman repeated fiercely.

'But then they've won,' Janey protested. 'The thugs who beat him up have won.'

'He's safe indoors, that's all that matters.' Her mood changed. She felt that she had said too much, revealed too much of herself to this young stranger, lulled into a false sense of security by the kindness of the two new guests that morning. 'Will there be anything else?' she asked brusquely.

'No. Thanks for the water.'

'Will you and the old gentleman be in to dinner tonight?'

'Um, yes. I should think so.'

'I need to know.'

'All right. Yes, then.'

'Will you be wanting the rooms much longer?'

'I don't know. Is it a problem?'

'People might come, now that Easter is over. Tourists.'

'Have you any definite bookings?' Janey was puzzled by the hostility.

'People might come,' the widow said stubbornly. 'Please let me know when you're ready to vacate.'

'Very well. Bye.'

Janey held up the water bottle in salute, but Madame Monami had already turned her attention back to South Fork and she left the room unnoticed.

★ ★ ★

'It's not the way of a man, a gentleman, a nobleman of France.'

Bisette laughed. Henri de Bresse had been talking like this all day. She had no idea what it was about, knew only that he and the other nobles had been summoned to de Montfort's tent that morning, had conferred there with him for upwards of two hours, and that Henri had returned in a foul temper.

She brushed his hot forehead with her lips but he pushed her away. 'I want none of your whoring tricks, slut.'

'Have I offended my lord?' She sat back on her haunches, thrusting out her chest so her white young breasts were clearly visible beneath her bodice. She gave him her most appealing look.

He got up and paced back and forth across the narrow confines of the tent. 'To take a town by force is glorious,' he said. 'Man against man, machine against machine, courage against stout walls. But this! This . . . treachery. It's unworthy.'

'They're not men,' de Montfort had said, reprimanding him with a look of iron, when he'd voiced these doubts. 'They're no more than the heathen Moor, less since the Moor knows no better. I won't risk the life of one of my men when this town has been handed to me by one who has seen the light.'

'I gave my son's life for chivalry,' Henri de Bresse told the uncomprehending Bisette, 'the last of my line, my hope of immortality. It seems that he died in vain.' He strode to the tent flap and bellowed for his squire. 'I'm going home,' he told Bisette, 'home to Orleans.'

She jumped up, alarmed. 'And me, my lord?'

'You can go to the devil with the rest of them!'

★ ★ ★

Janey and Malcolm found their way into the little courtyard garden at four o'clock that afternoon. Malcolm sat down on the seat that circled the well and relaxed his tired bones with a sigh. They seemed to have run out of things they could usefully do and Janey had sensibly vetoed his wild idea of driving around the country roads in the hope of spotting Robyn. 'Do you suppose there'd be any chance of a cup of tea?' he said.

'I'll ask.' Janey went back into the building and Malcolm examined his surroundings. The courtyard was twenty feet square and laid out haphazardly with paving stones interspersed with squares of a dry-looking soil and sad plants. A couple of slatted folding chairs leaned against the brick wall by the back door.

Some of the first-floor rooms had tiny balconies, only wide enough to take one person, or two if they were very good friends. He knew now that the shuttered windows above his head belonged to the old Frenchwoman and the American. Geraniums flowered in pots and white busy Lizzies. Impatiens: he was feeling a bit impatient himself.

He mentally counted his money. He realised, appalled, that he hadn't thought to ask how much the room cost and he'd already stayed three nights. And then there was Janey's room. He couldn't expect her to pay her way. He didn't see how he could possibly stay for more than a week. But surely a week would be enough, would see an end to this nightmare of uncertainty — one way or another.

Wouldn't it?

He bowed his head. Would it be better to know she was dead so that he could start the process of mourning which was also the process of healing? What if she never turned up, was never heard of again, so that he had no idea, perhaps until his own dying day, what had happened to her, with every knock on the door, every ring of the telephone, a hell of hope disappointed.

A man would go mad that way.

'Able if not exactly willing.' Janey reappeared, a welcome interruption to his gloomy thoughts. 'Madame Monami's spinster sister-in-law was bullied and threatened into making tea for us. I offered to do it myself but it seems that letting me into the kitchen would provoke some kind of cataclysm, possibly the wrath of God and the end of civilisation as we know it. She'll bring it out in a few minutes.'

'Oh, Janey Silverman,' he burst out, 'go home to your mother and tell her never to let you out of her sight again.'

She sat down next to him. 'It can't be that way, Malcolm,' she said gently. 'The end of good parenting is to let your children go, even if it's to hell in a handcart. Anyway, my mum's not at home at the moment; she's in Miami. And when she is at home, she's not much of a mum.'

'I'm sorry.'

'It's a matter of what you're used to. You don't miss what you never had. It makes you independent.'

They sat in silence for a moment then Joachim came out, laid a tray down on the flagstones at their feet and departed as wordlessly as he'd come. He was wearing shorts, revealing knotted ropes of muscle, and a sleeveless tee-shirt, his arms a smudge of healing bruise. The day was cloudy but muggy. 'He gives me the creeps,' Janey said, looking after him. 'I know he's had a rough few days and nothing could excuse what happened to him but the fact is he makes my flesh crawl.'

Malcolm looked faintly surprised. 'The poor boy was probably brain-damaged at birth. Or maybe his mother was too old when he was born. It's common enough in rural families. He's got a job here that he can do with his mum to keep an eye on him and make sure he doesn't get into trouble. See how she let him bring our tray out to show she still trusts him with little tasks like that. What would you do with boys like him, Janey? Stick him in a home where you don't have to look at him?'

'No. Um. No.' Janey felt ashamed.

'Or leave him out on a hillside to die at

birth, as the Spartans did?'

'No, of course not.'

'Or beat him to a pulp because he's 'unfit'?'

'Obviously not.'

'People like him are there to remind people like us how lucky we are.'

'Bit hard on him,' Janey commented, 'stuck like that to teach tight-arsed bitches like me a lesson.'

Malcolm laughed and leaned down to examine the tray. He was disappointed to see that there was no teapot but a tea bag hanging tagged from each cup of hot water. 'I use loose tea at home.'

'Yes, you would.'

He picked up the jug of milk and went to pour some into his cup when his hand was arrested in mid-air and a look of horror came over his face. He peered into the jug. 'This milk is hot! Look, there's skin starting to form.'

'Oh damn!' Janey took the jug from him and added some of the thin-looking milk to her own cup. 'I forgot to specify cold milk and they use hot otherwise. Can't you wait a minute for it to cool?'

'It won't taste the same,' he objected, a man abandoned among barbarians.

'Mmmm, I know. Why is that?'

'I suppose its . . . er . . . chemical make-up is changed by heating,' he said doubtfully. He tipped the rest of the hot milk over the nearest geranium and got up. 'What do I ask for?'

'*Du lait froid.*'

'Doolay frwa?'

'That'll do.' He went purposefully into the building. Janey, taking pity on the geranium, picked up the pot to examine it. In doing so she knocked against another pot which promptly disappeared down the well. 'Janey Silverman,' she said in an assumed upper-middle-class voice, which was presumably meant to be her mother's. 'Why are you so damn clumsy?'

She removed a couple more pots from the danger zone so that she could see clearly down the well, in case the lost geranium wasn't beyond hope. Between her, Simon and Malcolm there would soon not be a living thing left in this garden. She straightened up a moment later with a long-drawn-out 'Bugger me!'

The geranium was clearly visible because it was resting on something, a black leather something lodged about five feet down the narrow shaft of the well. Janey sat back on the bench and took a deep breath. This wasn't the time for her legendary clumsiness.

If she jogged the bag it might fall further down the shaft and pass beyond recovery.

Malcolm reappeared at that moment carrying a jug of milk and a look of achievement. 'Don't sit down,' she called out. 'In fact, don't come near the well. Stay over there. There's one bull too many in this china shop as it is.'

He hovered uncertainly. At home if someone told you not to come near a place, it usually meant it was about to go 'Bang!'

'What is it?' he asked.

'I've found it.'

★ ★ ★

After a supper of the thin pea soup and insufficient bread, Hugues got up and said he was going out for a few minutes after which he would offer his guest another game of chess. He'd seemed nervous all evening and Robyn guessed that something interesting was about to happen. She stood at the window, the shutter ajar, looking to see which way he went. It was an hour after sunset and darkness filled the town. She counted to sixty, then followed him. He walked swiftly and silently through the streets towards the western walls, not looking back, and she had to hurry to keep up with him, a slight black shape in the night.

She almost lost him as he turned down a narrow alleyway and she ducked after him, keeping against the sheltering houses. She paused at the end of the alley and watched the tableau that was forming beside a wooden hut built against the walls which looked like another privy. Thibaut of Béziers had a lantern which he kept partly darkened under his surcoat; Louise d'Ambriers stood a little apart, her pale face flushed with excitement, her nose red.

As Robyn edged forward, Hugues put one thin arm round each of them, his right reaching barely halfway round the barber. 'God bless and keep you both,' he said. He released them and, taking a bunch of keys from his belt, selected one and slid it into a hole in the wooden door. The three of them entered the hut and Robyn slipped into position one side of the doorway. She could see Hugues opening another door on the far side of the empty hut, a far heavier, sturdier door let into the wall.

'Take care on the slope,' he was saying. 'It's steep and may be damp. One false step and you're stewing meat on those rocks. Look after her, Thibaut. She is as precious to me as any daughter.'

'Don't worry,' the man said, his voice filled with emotion. 'She'll be safe with me.'

'I don't know if we shall meet again in this life, Louise — '

'Of course we will!'

'But there's better life to come — a life of the spirit that our Lord made, and not the miserable flesh of the devil. I know we shall meet again there, and know each other, and rejoice.'

Thibaut made a noise like 'Pah!' and, as the door creaked open, moved ahead with his lantern, taking the first danger upon himself. Louise gathered up her skirts in her right fist and stepped after him in her stout boots. Through the doorway Robyn could make out a flight of stone steps apparently leading into the town walls.

'I knew you were a spy!'

Bruno's triumphant hand fell on Robyn from behind. She would never have imagined that he could move so stealthily. She was immobilised by his grip as he propelled her forward into the hut, into the light of Thibaut's lantern as he turned back at the disturbance.

'Robert!' Hugues eyes were wet with reproach, like a scolded puppy. 'What are you doing here?'

'Spying, like I told you from the first,'

Bruno growled. 'I saw him follow you from your house and I followed *him*. It didn't occur to you, did it, Mr Clever Englishman, that two can play at that game? You thought you could pull the wool over our eyes with your smart clothes and your nice accent. Well, you didn't fool Bruno.'

'I meant no harm,' Robyn said. 'I was . . . interested.'

'I'll bet you were,' Bruno said.

'He asked me the day he arrived if there was another way out of the town,' Hugues said thoughtfully. 'Other than the main gate, I mean.'

'I'll bet,' Bruno said again. 'I'm surprised you didn't tell him, knowing you.'

Hugues looked hurt. 'I didn't tell him anything. I'm not a complete fool.'

'Well, he knows now!'

'I trusted you, Robert,' Hugues said.

'You were right.'

'The question is,' Hugues said, 'what are we going to do with him?'

Bruno had his answer ready and a keen knife in his hand. 'One thing's for sure. We don't need any extra mouths to feed in a siege.'

'Oh, no!' Louise exclaimed.

'No!' Hugues said simultaneously. 'I won't permit any bloodshed.'

'Very well,' Bruno said reluctantly, pushing the blade back into its sheath. 'Into the prison cell with him it is.'

'Hugues!' Robyn broke free from Bruno's grip with a strength born of desperation and darted forward, seizing her friend by his black robe. 'You must listen to me before it's too late. There *is* a spy in this town, a traitor, but I'm not — '

Bruno's fist fell on the back of her head, knocking her unconscious.

'You carry on here,' she heard him say as her senses deserted her. 'I'll see this one safely put away where he can't communicate with his paymasters.'

* * *

'The well goes down a good ten metres,' Madame Monami was explaining to Inspector Laroche about half an hour after the interrupted tea break. 'Normally we keep it covered, but the wooden cover was damaged a few weeks ago and we didn't get round to fixing it yet because . . . '

She rambled on but the inspector wasn't listening. He'd equipped himself with a hook on the end of a pole and was now leaning his long body uncomfortably over the well, moving the hook with almost infinite slowness towards the handle of the bag. Janey, Malcolm and the other policemen stood hardly daring to breathe. Janey wished there was some way of shutting Madame Monami up since she was as annoying as a road drill outside your window.

'Gotcha!' Laroche said a moment later.

He fed the pole back up through his hands until the bag became visible at the neck of the well, where it stuck briefly. Malcolm moved forward to take it. 'Don't touch it!' the inspector snapped.

Even Malcolm managed to understand that burst of French; he fell back, stuttering an apology.

'Fingerprints,' Janey said.

'All right! I've got the point now. Thank you.'

The inspector gave an extra heave on his pole and the bag came clear of the well and fell to the ground where it lay, a little damp, a little dirty, on its side. He clicked his fingers at one of his constables who handed him a torch. He switched it on and peered down the unobstructed depths, moving the beam into the darkest corners. He muttered something inaudible to himself, then pulled out a piece of loose brick and dropped it.

'*Un, deux, trois,*' he counted. Just as he got to fifteen there was a faint and distant splash. 'It would've been well hidden down there if it hadn't stuck,' he remarked. 'I think you'd better get the cover mended, madame, before you lose a guest, especially a small one.'

'Of course. Of course.' Madame Monami was flustered. 'At once.'

They stood looking at the bag in silence for a few seconds. 'I take it, monsieur,' the inspector addressed Malcolm directly, 'that you have no doubt that this is your daughter's bag?' Janey translated.

'None at all!' Malcolm said. 'Look, those are her baggage labels.'

The inspector didn't seem to need this translated but nodded gravely. 'That would have been too much of a coincidence,' he conceded.

'And you don't believe in coincidences,' Janey reminded him.

'Quite so.' He spoke brusquely to one of his men who manoeuvred the bag into a large polythene sack with gloved hands and took it away. 'Let's hope the person who threw it down there has left prints,' he said. 'She would probably have been acting in a hurry, a panic, and may not have taken the necessary precautions.'

He used the words *la personne* and then referred to this person as *elle* — she. That confused Janey for a moment until she remembered that in the French language a person, like a film star or a victim, is always female.

'My superintendent likes proof,' Laroche said. 'That little bag is the proof I needed.'

'What now?' Janey asked.

'The bag will be fingerprinted. Everybody in Professor Clement's party will give me their prints, or I shall want to know why not, and — ' he gave a faint smile as if pleased with himself ' — I'm going to get a search warrant, and not the professor, nor all his important friends in the Ministry of Defence, nor his precious archaeology, are going to stop me turning that hillside upside down and inside out because — ' he gave a covert glance back down the well and lowered his voice ' — her body is not down there.'

'You think she's dead, don't you?' Janey said.

'*Cela reste à voir.*' His voice and words were noncommittal but his eyes said Yes.

'Oh, Robyn,' Malcolm said, mercifully not understanding. 'My darling. Where are you?'

'Madame Monami . . . ' Janey turned to look for the woman but there was no sign of her. 'Oh! Where did she go?'

'She slipped away a minute ago,' Malcolm

said, 'after you found the bag.' Janey and Laroche exchanged glances and the inspector nodded his head at one of his men who disappeared into the hotel after her. 'You don't think . . . ' Malcolm said, 'you can't think it was her? I mean . . . why?'

'No,' Janey said. 'I don't think she put the bag in the well, but I think she's got a pretty good idea who did.'

6

'I know who speaks with courtesy,
yes, and who seeks to injure me,
the one who smiles beguilingly.'
Guilhem de Poitou

Robyn, as so often, was poring over the facsimile of Louise d'Ambriers's diary in her spare moments. There were times when the poet, dead in 1255 at the — for those days — ripe old age of sixty-six, was more real to her than her colleagues. She liked the feel of the book, bound in old leather that had creased and even broken with the decades, printed on yellowing paper. It dated from the final years of the nineteenth century, a limited edition paid for by one of de Chambertins, and was hard to come by.

How she'd coveted Silvie's copy when she'd first arrived and the old lady had shown it to her. How she'd stood with her tongue hanging out as Silvie pointed things out to her in her ponderous way. She'd placed queries at every antiquarian bookshop in the Midi to lay hands on this one and it hadn't been cheap, despite its rough condition.

On each left-hand page was the black script of the diary, all but illegible to modern eyes; opposite a welcome translation into modern French. Arpaïs de Chambertin had dedicated half her life to it after an early and childless widowhood. There was half an hour to go before supper and she was curled up in the dining-room on the window seat, her cheek resting against the comfort of the red velvet curtains. She let the book open at random and read an entry for the winter of 1210.

'*It is strange to see the difference between Hugues and Bruno although they're both good men in their way and devout. They argue often, in particular, although without anger, about crime. Hugues insists that there's no such thing as a born criminal, that crime is the result of poverty and deprivation and that kindness and reason can bring an end to it.*

So when a man is taken for petty pilfering or house-breaking, Hugues asks that he be brought to the Perfect's house that he may talk with him. Often he will converse with such a malefactor for hours, long into the night. He asks him about himself, his parentage, even for details of his childhood although I know not what their relevance may be. He questions him even about his dreams. He shares his food (such as it is) with the man.

Meanwhile Bruno is stamping around impatiently outside convinced that the one sure cure for a cutpurse is a good beating, followed by a few days down in the cold darkness of the prison cell with only the rats and worms for company.

And the threat of hanging if he reoffends.'

Robyn let the book fall closed on her lap. The prison cell. Louise's diary gave it as a certain fact that there was such a place in Montprimeur, apparently underground, but the archaeologists had yet to find it. Even aerial photos and X-rays had revealed no clue to its whereabouts.

'There you are.' Simon came into the room with a smile and ruffled her hair. 'I was looking for you. Oh, no! Not the smelly old book again?'

'I like it.'

'It's social history,' he said sitting next to her. 'That has nothing to do with archaeology.'

'Some of us have enough brains to take an interest in two things at once,' she replied tartly.

He laughed good-naturedly, put his arm round her and began to kiss her with a delicate thoroughness. 'Robyn?'

'Yes?'

His nerve failed him. 'Nothing . . . It doesn't matter.' His lips nuzzled against hers again.

The door opened and they drew apart as Joachim came in and began to lay the table for supper. He glanced at them briefly with his heavy eyes but didn't smile — although Robyn was one of the few regular recipients of his rare smiles — hardly seeming to acknowledge their existence.

'Want any help, Joachim?' Robyn asked. He didn't reply, apparently not hearing her, and she jumped up and put her hand on his arm to get his attention. He jerked back as if she were a wasp that had stung him. 'Joachim? You all right?'

'No need,' he muttered. 'Joachim no need help.'

'Please yourself,' she said, hurt.

The boy slapped a clean cloth on the table and left the room again.

'What do you suppose he does for sex?' Simon asked.

'Oh, really, Simon.'

'Seriously. He's clearly seething with hormones, you've only to look at how hairy he is, and those dark, brooding features. Testosterone overkill.'

'I don't expect he thinks about it.'

'You can be naive, Robyn,' her lover said. 'All men think about it, an awful lot, especially at his age. The fact that no woman could possibly fancy him doesn't alter that.'

'What are you trying to say?'

'That you ought to be a bit careful with him, that's all. Not give him ideas.'

Robyn's thin Irish lips set in irritation. 'I'm not giving him *any* ideas. I only try to be kind to him, which is more than anyone else does. No one except Silvie takes the trouble to try to talk to him. You can usually get what he's saying if you concentrate.'

'Kindness can be misplaced,' Simon said. 'Or misunderstood.'

★ ★ ★

She was still annoyed with Simon after supper and took herself off to James's room to study the plans and the model of Montprimeur, while the others lingered in the dining-room over wine. Her finger traced the lines of the map but her mind was elsewhere. Plans had their uses but there were times when only a personal inspection would do.

367

She could scrabble over the site for months without getting close. What was needed was thought, a simple, logical train of common sense.

★ ★ ★

'Bruno let me look in his famous prison cell yesterday since it is at present unoccupied. I had been nagging him to see it. He laughed and said that I should be the next to occupy it if I wasn't a good girl.

I don't think I could spend so much as an hour in it. There's a window, of sorts, perhaps nine inches square, but it's high up and little light penetrates. The prisoner isn't allowed the luxury of a candle unless he can pay for it himself. The sleeping place is a stone ledge with not so much as a handful of straw.

I know a poem by Dias de Muret, written many years ago, in my grandfather's day, before the wars, in which she likens the castle of Muret to a prison. She can't have been in a real prison, I think, or she wouldn't have written so foolishly.

When I remarked that it was a cruelty to confine anyone so, Bruno said that it must be harsh if it is to deter people from crime, or stop them from sinning again.'

★ ★ ★

The following day as the others stopped for lunch and began in ones and twos to descend the hill, Robyn called out to Simon that he should go on without her, that she would follow in a few minutes, that she wanted to finish this. Once she was sure of being alone on the summit, she stood in the centre of the market square, thinking. If she was building a medieval town, where would she put the prison? Where was the safest, the most impenetrable place to keep a criminal secure?

The walls, surely — a double thickness. She turned the problem over to her subconscious mind and let her feet lead her where they would. She crossed to the north side of the site where the cliff fell almost sheer to the ground a hundred feet below. Here were the remains of a flight of steps that had puzzled her in the past although she would have been hard put to it to say why. Now she examined them with renewed vigour.

There were other stone steps to the top of the wall within a few feet either side, making these seem superfluous. The bottom step was only half the height of the others, perhaps four inches from the ground. She'd jarred her foot coming down it once, miscalculating the expected drop.

She brushed centuries of accumulated dirt and dust from the edges of the stone at the bottom of the steps. As she did so, some of it began to trickle down around the edge of the stone, indicating that it didn't lie flush against the ground. Eagerly now, Robyn's deft fingers worked at the edges. Then she fetched an iron bar that Peter had left lying on a ruin and inserted the sharp end into the gap at the edge, pressing down with all her strength and then sideways for leverage. The stone began to move, then stubbornly stuck, then came free with a heartfelt sigh.

She saw how the bottom step, the half-sized one, continued to its full depth in the hole at her feet. She could make out another step below that one. She'd found it. She'd found the entrance to the prison cell.

Half of her wanted to call for help but the other, the more dominant half, said that this was *her* find and that no one was going to take her moment of glory away from her. She hurried back to the main gate and looked down. The others were busy below, lolling under trees, eating, reading, talking, listening to the minibus radio.

Returning to her find, she took a torch from her bag and stood, fearful, on the topmost step. If there was one aspect of her chosen profession she didn't like, it was bones, human bones. Had there been anyone in this cell when the town fell? If so, had the crusaders found him or had he been spared the massacre, only to endure another, slower, even more horrible death by starvation? Would the skeleton have survived these many centuries?

It was no good, she had to be brave. She took a deep breath and began to descend the steps into the hidden chamber.

Her torch showed her a room perhaps six feet square, roughly hewn out of the limestone. A certain amount of light came from a window which was, as Louise had described it, less than a foot square, high in the wall on the steep slope of the hill. It wouldn't be visible from outside: too high to be noticed from below, at the wrong angle to be seen from above. You would need to abseil down the cliff to find it.

The air tasted stale, no breeze had circulated here for centuries. It smelt damp; she could feel the coldness of it on her nose and lips. She sensed movement about her as if this was a universe of insects, not of humankind, but insects didn't bother her. The rats would have left a long time ago, with no humans to provide for them.

She clicked her torch off, the better to drink in the atmosphere, and sat down on the bench-come-sleeping-platform hacked out of the far wall. It ran the length of the cell and was about two feet wide and two feet high.

'You wouldn't get much sleep on this,' she said aloud and the words echoed round the chamber.

'This, this, hiss, ss.'

She was, she was thankful to find, alone. There were no bones, no sign of occupation, no ghosts here. Her foot brushed against something and she bent, groping in the darkness, and picked up a metal goblet, a drinking cup, wonderfully preserved and not at all rusty. She placed it on the sleeping-shelf beside her. She switched on her torch again and played it across the floor. She saw a piece of wood, worked into a circle six inches in diameter: a crude plate. She retrieved it and added it to her collection.

'I agree with you, Louise: I wouldn't like to spend many hours in here,' she said to herself, but in a low voice, thwarting the echo.

She leant back against the wall, deeply satisfied with her find. In a moment she would go and fetch Simon and the professor and ask them to come with her. She smiled as she imagined the looks on their faces.

She could hear James congratulating her — or congratulating himself, more likely, on having chosen her for his team.

But not yet. She wanted a few more minutes in her secret place, savouring the thought that she was undoubtedly the first person to set foot in here since 1211. How many people could better such a claim? Sir Edmund Hillary? Neil Armstrong? Howard Carter? You could probably count them on the fingers of one hand. She felt like part of history. A small step for a woman; a giant leap for Cathar studies.

She flicked her torch idly along the walls. There was a niche opposite, holding what looked like a chamber pot. Obviously there would be a need for such an artefact but she didn't feel up to examining its mummified contents. Then there was what looked like a fat stub of candle, almost fossilised in the far corner. The last occupant had been rich enough to have light and food sent in, or hadn't wanted for friends.

As the torch circled the rough slabs of rock she realised that someone had been carving in the wall above her head, to the right. Early graffiti? The writer had evidently knelt on the sleeping-platform to leave his immortal words. Guillaume was here? She scrambled onto her knees, ignoring the rough tug of the stone against her blue jeans. The words were faded with the centuries but they'd been well protected from the elements here and she could make out almost all of the letters.

L U S DAMBRI R TRA T R MUR E E A OST T

She puzzled at the words for some minutes, as with a crossword puzzle shorn of its clues. Then it came to her in a rush. She fell back on the hard platform. It was as if the breath had been knocked out of her by a savage blow to the solar plexus.

'Louise d'Ambriers,' she murmured. 'Traitor, Murderer, Apostate.'

★ ★ ★

She left the goblet and plate on the sleeping-platform and struggled back up the steps, her mind numbed by what she'd seen. She put the doorstone carefully back into its place and sprinkled handfuls of dirt round the edges to hide where she'd lifted it. She'd barely finished when she heard Simon's voice, out of sight but not far away. 'Robs? Where are you?'

'Over here.'

'You're a bit keen today. Don't you want any lunch?'

'Just coming.'

'Not like you to be off your food.'

She darted to meet him, resisting the urge to look back, and he caught her in his arms and, glancing round to make sure they were alone, kissed her soundly. 'Hey, what've you done to yourself?' He held her away from him the better to inspect her. She followed the line of his eyes and saw that the right knee of her jeans was ripped open in a four-inch gash, while the left one was pitted with holes. Her grazed knees were clearly visible. 'And your hands.' He held them in his, turning them up to the sun. They were dirty and scratched.

'I lost my footing.' She reclaimed her hands and pushed them into her pockets.

'I'll say. Looks like you took a nasty tumble. Where did it happen?'

She nodded her head vaguely in the direction she had come. 'I was on the walls.'

'You want to be careful up there. You know bits of it aren't safe.'

Her mind wasn't on her lover; in truth, she scarcely heard him, making up her answers on automatic pilot. She had to think about what she'd seen, what she'd read. It mattered to her. She felt that she'd come to know Louise, to see the long-dead woman as her friend and suddenly that friend was a different person, a monster.

'Are you sure you're all right?' Simon asked, puzzled, folding her in his arms again. 'You're a bit distracted. You didn't hit your head?'

'No, no. I was thinking about something.' She wriggled out of his embrace. 'Come on. I'm starving.'

★ ★ ★

She lay awake that night with her secret, aching to share it, glad that Simon's regular breathing and occasional snuffles made it clear that he was sleeping soundly and out of temptation's way, since secrets imparted in bed in the dark didn't seem to count, and she knew that she would have told him and regretted it in the morning.

There was one person who deserved to know the truth before anyone else. Robyn had a deep respect for Silvie de Chambertin and was willing to be guided by her in this matter of her revered ancestress.

Louise d'Ambriers — Traitor, Murderer, Apostate.

★ ★ ★

When Robyn came round in the prison cell her head hurt badly, as it had done in Hugues's house a few days ago. Whatever she was lying on wasn't as comfortable as Hugues's straw pallet and that was saying something. She lay awkwardly, one arm under her body and as she shifted, she winced at the burn of pins and needles as the limb came back to life.

She straightened herself, feeling for the back of her head. There was no fresh bleeding, which was just as well as there was no Jehane ready with a bowl of egg white, although she might easily, she reflected, have run to a spider's web in this place. Bruno's blow had been well aimed and effective but hadn't broken skin.

'Damn!' she muttered to herself. 'What a complete and utter cock-up. I can't believe I let myself be jumped from behind *again*.' Was it the second blow in the same place that had brought her memory back, or the passage of time, or had being back in the prison cell jolted her reluctant brain cells? No matter: she'd remembered. That was the main thing.

She could see by the paltry light from the window that it was the middle of the night. How long had she been out? It was a clear night and the stars shone cold in the sky but there was scarcely any moon, the merest crescent, a last gasp. It had been in the dark quarter, then, that de Montfort's men had come in through the secret doorway to their revelry of slaughter. That made sense.

She moved swiftly up the steps and pushed at the entrance stone, knowing that she was wasting her time. Something heavy would be weighing it down and, even if it wasn't, it had taken all her strength to open it from above, with a lever; few men would be able to push it up from beneath, let alone a young woman.

She gave up, angry, frustrated.

Was it tonight, or tomorrow night? It must be tonight. Were the crusaders already on their way? They'd sent the siege train on as a decoy, a bluff, knowing the townspeople would take it to mean that they had a day or two in hand. Meanwhile the cavalry would come up under cover of night.

Was it too late to change things? Had she been mad to think she could, to think that the tapestry of history, once woven, could be unpicked?

She lifted the flap on her belt bag, feeling for her penknife in the dark. She opened the blade and ran her finger along it. It was blunt and fit for few practical purposes, like all penknives. She knelt up on the sleeping-platform, pressing the blade into the rock at head height. Her arm ached with holding it at that level and her hand stung with the effort of digging into the limestone. At the end of an hour the blade was ruined, but she'd carved the necessary words.

A message to her future self.

Louise d'Ambriers — Traitor, Murderer, Apostate.

Her work done, she sat back on her heels, filled with misgiving. Wasn't it reckless to try to change history, foolhardy? The people of Montprimeur had died that night. Was that not their destiny? Even if it wasn't too late to do anything about it, could she take responsibility for the additional men and women, perhaps many thousands of them, who would be born over the next eight hundred years as a result of her actions? Geniuses? Perhaps; or monsters.

She consoled herself. She must have been sent here for a purpose, and what could that purpose be, if not to prevent a hideous crime? She'd no way of knowing if she was doing the right thing, and she had her own life to save. She wasn't ready yet to say goodbye to that.

She lay down, exhausted, to sleep.

'Hello, Robyn. Have you come to give me a hand?'

Silvie was her usual self, friendly but reserved, as Robyn came to find her on the summit after lunch. Her brisk walk round the site had cleared her mind and resolved her on the right course of action. She'd slipped quietly back up the hill without being seen by any of the others and sought out her elderly colleague.

'Not exactly, madame. There's something I wanted to talk to you about, something I wanted to show you.'

Robyn could hardly restrain her excitement and Silvie smiled at her with genuine amusement and said, 'How young you are! How well I remember that youthful enthusiasm. How much I regret its passing.'

'I think you'll be excited too, Silvie.'

'Well?' She put down what she was holding — an implement less than a spade though more than a trowel — and made herself comfortable on a rock. She patted for Robyn to sit beside her, which she did.

'I've found the prison cell,' Robyn began. Silvie cocked her head to one side quizzically. 'The one Louise mentions in her diaries. You must know the passage I mean . . . '

'Not so well as you, apparently.'

'When she talks about how Bruno liked to lock miscreants up until they'd thoroughly repented.'

'It rings a bell,' Silvie said. 'I haven't read the diaries closely for many years, you know. I grew up on them, as it were, and lost heart.'

'Well, I've found it.' Robyn hugged her knees to her chest. 'Lost in the walls for all these centuries.'

'Where?'

Robyn pointed. 'You know where there's that odd step in the north wall, not as big as the others?'

'I know the one you mean.'

'There.'

'Bravo! You must be pleased with yourself.'

'But that's not all. It . . . it solves the riddle, madame, the riddle of Montprimeur, of why the town fell to de Montfort as it did, without a fight.' Her voice rose in childish triumph. 'I've solved the mystery of Montprimeur — me, Robyn Dawson, after all these years!'

'Tell me,' Silvie said.

She did.

★ ★ ★

381

Robyn heard a creaking, the noise of the entrance stone to the cell being quietly lifted, or as quietly as anybody *could* prise a heavy stone from its bedding. A light flickered above her. She sat up as a black-enveloped figure made its way down the rough-hewn steps, picking each one out with care. 'Hugues?' she said.

The figure threw back its black hood with a shake of its head, since its hands were full. The cadaverous face was now as familiar to her as her own father's, its expression grim but thoughtful. She felt a surge of affection for him, this man who, in the face of the evidence against her, hadn't deserted her. He indicated his left hand which held a wooden platter. On it was a hunk of black bread, an apple, a slab of cheese and a cheap metal goblet half full of red wine, the same one Jehane had used to give her water on the first day, the one she'd found so miraculously preserved eight hundred years hence. His voice was flat, without expression.

'Bruno said you weren't to be fed, but I don't think it right to starve you, whatever you may have done or proposed to do.' In his other hand he had a fat stub of candle which he held out in front of him, the better to light the squat room. 'Besides . . . '

'You wanted to know.'

'Yes.' Hugues put the plate down on the platform next to Robyn and squatted on his heels in front of her, unafraid. He held the candle up to illuminate her face. A trickle of hot wax reached his hand but he didn't seem to feel it. 'Am I such a poor judge of character, my young friend?'

'No. I didn't betray you to de Montfort, but I know at last who did.'

'You speak as if it was a thing done,' Hugues said, 'a past event.'

'It is for me.'

He smiled kindly. 'You've had one too many blows on the head, I think, Robert. It's true that the crusaders are now gathered about our hill, thousands of them, but we're not done for, not by any means; the odds are firmly on our side. Although . . . '

'Although you yourself said you had a bad feeling about it.'

'Yes. That's true. I did. I have.'

'Hugues, listen to me. The odds will be overturned by foul means. Tonight, in the small hours, Montprimeur will be betrayed. Someone will lead the crusaders up the secret path and in at the door where Bruno caught me. You will be put to the sword. Not one soul will survive the massacre — not even Pietre who is two days old.'

383

'It's not given to mortal man to see the future, Robert.'

'Sometimes — perhaps once in a generation — it is. When a great wrong has been done, a wrong that cries out to heaven for vengeance. Oh, I don't claim to be anything special, I'm not a great seer. I'm a tool. I don't know how I came here or why, but I know that I have a duty to perform tonight, if I pay for it with my own life.'

Despite her brave words she began to tremble as death came close and seemed to breathe his icy breath on her neck.

'This is foolishness,' Hugues said, shakily. 'I've heard such talk from poor, deranged creatures.' Perhaps he was right, Robyn thought. Perhaps she was a poor, deranged creature who had imagined hundreds of years of implausible future. 'If Bruno knew I'd come . . . ' Hugues said.

'I can't promise to prevent the massacre. What I can promise you is that if nothing changes we shall die tonight.'

Hugues reached out and clutched her arm, squeezing so hard that she let out an exclamation. 'You're no spirit,' he said, 'unless you are illusion for the hand as well as the eye. And yet when the image of the Christ came on earth, his followers must have taken him for solid flesh and embraced him.

Tell me, are you a man?'

'I'm not a man,' Robyn said truthfully, 'and I'm not of your world.'

'If you can see the future it may be the gift of God or the curse of the devil. How am I to know which?'

'You can't. You can only trust, only listen to your instincts and obey them. Help me, Hugues. Let me out of this cell. Keep watch at the door tonight with all the armed men you can muster. You'll see the truth of what I say. What have you to lose by doing that?'

'Do you know also,' Hugues said slowly, 'who the traitor is?'

'May I?' Robyn took the candle from his yielding fingers and held it to show him the inscription on the wall. She watched his face collapse into horror.

'But this is fresh carving,' he said, collecting himself, accusing. 'You wrote that yourself. You *must* have.'

'Yes. Just now. A message to the future. It will stay there for hundreds of years until a young woman stumbles on it one day by accident and finally learns the answer to a riddle that has baffled history.'

Hugues stared at her yellowed features in the candlelight, at her beardless face with its soft cheeks and lips, at the swell of her breasts, understanding at last. '*And the light shineth in the darkness,*' he breathed, '*and the darkness comprehended it not.* But it isn't possible.'

'I promise you.'

'I mean it isn't possible that she, the demoiselle d'Ambriers, Louise . . . ' His voice was anguished, a father who has learnt the full iniquity of which his child is capable. Even as he spoke, he believed it. 'For the rest,' he said, 'God is unfathomable and will be until the Day of Judgement.'

'It was her, Louise. I mean it will be. I don't know why. Only she can tell us that, if it's not too late. What time is it?'

He shrugged. In an era without formal clocks and watches, time was measured by daybreak, dusk, day or night; yesterday, today and tomorrow. 'Well past midnight, I think, perhaps an hour or two.'

'Then we may not have long.'

Hugues reached a decision. 'Quickly. Take this.' He stripped off the hooded cassock he was wearing and handed it to her, leaving himself only a thin shirt and some threadbare hose. She saw once more the bones of his arms, the puckered, dying flesh. 'Yes,' he said, following her eyes. 'I'm dying anyway. It makes little difference to me if it is tonight by fire or the sword, or in six weeks from starvation, but I can't believe that God wants my loyal and loving friends to die this night for, strong as my beliefs are, I know and understand that man *clings* to life. Put the robe on.'

She obeyed. It reached to the ground and she wrapped it round her.

He said, 'Bruno has set a guard above. He let me in because it was me and because I begged him, but he won't let you out. You must be me.'

'I shall need you with me, Hugues, to help convince the others.'

'You overpowered me and stole my clothes.' He pulled the hood up for her, letting its ample folds fall over her brow and shadow her features. 'It will hide your face. No one will doubt that you're me. Say as little as possible. I'll give you a good start then shout for the guard. I shall follow behind you as fast as I can. Trust me.'

'There's no one I trust more. You told me once not to call you Father. May I do so now?'

'My dear child.' He handed her an iron key, a rudimentary two-pronged affair, oiled and free of rust. 'Here. This is the key of the secret door.'

'Does anyone else have a key?'

'Only . . . the demoiselle d'Ambriers. I gave it to her this night. Oh, God forgive me!

Go, Robert of Durham. Do what you came here to do, if it can be done. Good luck.'

She said, 'God bless you, dearest Hugues.' She kissed his cheek and felt him shrink back, ashamed of a woman's embrace.

'Wait! So,' he asked wistfully, 'the end of the material world is not at hand?'

'Not yet.'

'Ah!'

As she moved quickly back up the steps and into the night she heard him fall to his knees and begin to pray.

And God shall wipe away all tears from their eyes; and there shall be no more death, neither sorrow, nor crying, neither shall there be any more pain: for the former things are passed away.

★ ★ ★

'Poor Louise.'

Silvie's words were mild and regretful. There were tears in her voice. Robyn turned her head tactfully away and looked out across the blue-green river valley. 'The d'Ambriers and the de Chambertins,' the older woman went on. 'It has never been an easy heritage. We are a selfish people — proud, insular, sometimes cruel.'

'She must have had a reason,' Robyn said.

'It's that, above all, that baffles me. These people were her friends, her neighbours. She was of their communion. Why did she betray them to de Montfort?'

'Will you show me the place?' Silvie asked.

'Of course.' Robyn jumped up. Silvie picked up her bag of tools and followed her to the prison cell, watching as she prised up the stone once more. A cold seemed to emanate from the cell, as from the open door of a fridge. 'Let me go first,' Robyn said, 'then I can break your fall if you lose your footing. The stone steps are badly worn. Careful now.' She descended slowly, holding her hand up behind her to steady her companion.

The old lady said, 'How good you are, Robyn. How thoughtful.'

'Here.' They were both standing now on the floor of the dim cell. Robyn pulled out her torch, switched it on and played it on the damning inscription. Silvie moved forward as though in a trance and stepped up onto the stone sleeping-platform, the better to view the evidence. Her bag slipped from her hand onto the bench. 'It's still clearly legible,' Robyn said. 'Isn't it exciting, Silvie? After all those centuries, the truth can be known at last.'

The old woman traced the letters with her mottled fingers, as if to assure herself that they were real, murmuring them — L–O–U–I–S–E. — like a child reciting some mad alphabet. 'My husband, Etienne,' Silvie told her, 'is the last of the de Chambertins. There have been few children in recent generations, as the bloodlines decay, and we are childless.'

'I thought you were a widow.'

She slowly shook her head. 'The Comte de Chambertin lives in a nursing home.'

'Oh, I'm so sorry. Was it a stroke?'

'Not that sort of nursing home.' Silvie turned back to face her. 'This one has bars on the windows and guard dogs in the grounds and nurses in prison uniform. He's been there since he was thirty-three — more than thirty-five years. He killed someone — two people in fact, two little girls. It was a capital offence, of course, in those days, but the court accepted a plea of insanity.'

'How awful for you!' Robyn was genuinely moved and a little embarrassed. It was a personal tragedy beyond her imagining. Suddenly she wanted to get out of this dungeon as fast as possible, but she didn't want to appear feeble. 'How . . . how did they die?' she asked.

'The destroying angel came for them.'

Seeing that Robyn didn't understand, she elucidated. 'Amanita Verna, a fungus, a toadstool, one of the deadliest toxins known to man.'

'I see.'

'Only I knew that they, those two girls, hadn't been the first, and I didn't talk. He must have had his reasons . . . like Louise.' Silvie's voice went on, slightly monotonous, as French voices may be, rising only at the end of a phrase, falling to end the sentence. 'You must understand, my dear, dear child, how this discovery of yours can't be allowed to become public knowledge, for Etienne must be protected from this last desperate blow.'

'I'm afraid that's not possible,' Robyn began, 'although there seems no reason he should have to know. Would he understand if he is . . . ?' She jibbed at the word 'Mad'. It sounded too strong in her mind, medieval in its judgement. Too harsh for this woman who was his cousin as well as his wife. She turned, looking with longing at the square slab of light at the top of the steps, a distant normality.

She heard Silvie step lightly down from the platform, picking up her bag as she did so, a faint chinking coming from it as archaeological implements danced together inside it. 'No one must know! I may be a humble epigone of the great house of de Chambertin but I can do this last service for them.'

Robyn, catching movement out of the corner of her eye, turned her head a second too late to avoid the skull-splitting blow from the tool that was more than a trowel and less than a spade.

'I'm so sorry.' She heard Silvie's words like a ghost's voice hovering somewhere above her consciousness. 'So very, very sorry.' The old woman picked up the torch and clicked it off so as not to see the inscription further, or not to see her own handiwork. She made her way nimbly back up the steps. Then, after what might have been moments or hours, Robyn heard the doorstone drop into place, robbing her of the last of her light, as she lost consciousness.

★ ★ ★

The key turned at last, although it had taken all her effort, the lock warped by the spring rains. No one had taken any notice of her as she progressed through the streets in Hugues's clothes, emulating as best she could his hunched walk. As the thick door creaked awkwardly open she knew that she'd never felt such fear. There was no knowing where the besiegers were now, how far up the path. She might be granting them admittance herself without need of Louise's complicity.

She breathed a long breath of relief as the path ahead proved empty and her keen ears picked up no sound from below. The secret path was narrow, scarcely trodden by human foot, and wriggled between the rocks like a snake. She crept to the first corner of the winding gully then almost screamed as she stumbled over something large and soft and not yet completely cold.

There was no doubt that Thibaut of Béziers was dead; she had no need to feel for a pulse. His jugular had been cut and he lay in a pool of his own drying blood, pints of it. Robyn found the sticky stuff on her feet, the hem of her cloak, then, somehow, on her hands. The barber's extraordinary luck — or his instinct for survival — had run out at last.

'You poor sod,' she muttered. 'What had you ever done, other than be in the wrong place at the wrong time?' She needed no further proof of how ruthless Louise was prepared to be. She looked up at the familiar stars, unchanged in their dance in eight centuries, and drew her own penknife. It was better than nothing, but not much.

'Lord,' she said uncertainly — she hadn't been to church since she was eight, after her mother was no longer there to take her. 'If it be your — I mean thy — will . . . I'm not good at this. Look, if you're there, then help me. Please. It doesn't matter about me but . . . Shit! Yes it does. I'm as unprepared for death as any of them. These people have never harmed anyone. All they ever asked is to be left in peace with their beliefs. Even if you don't agree with those beliefs, I can't believe you want them to be burnt alive, unless you're some sort of bastard sadist in which case — '

She heard a hiss behind her — a furious intake of breath — and suddenly Bruno was there with Hugues right behind him.

'Bruno came the moment you'd left,' Hugues said apologetically. 'I can't make him listen.' He shook his head at his friend in exasperated tenderness. 'When was it ever different?'

The cobbler knelt by Thibaut's body and rose with blood over his hands. 'Do you need any more proof?' he demanded of Hugues, holding his hands up to the other man in demonstration. 'When will you admit that the Englishman is a spy and now a murderer? I've known you half my life, Hugues, and I've gladly tolerated your eccentricities, but

I never before took you for a fool.'

'I just this minute found him,' Robyn protested.

'Indeed!'

'How am I supposed to have cut his throat?' she asked. 'With this?' She showed him her penknife, ruined by her carving.

'No need,' he said. 'Poor Thibaut was murdered with his own razor, or my name's not Bruno Vuissane.'

'The man has been dead for some time,' Hugues pointed out. 'His body is cooling, Bruno, his blood isn't fresh. Robert was in the cell until a few minutes ago.'

Bruno looked grudgingly at the blood on his hands, but he was a fair man at heart and finally conceded, 'He's not new-dead, it's true.' He wiped his hands clean on the barber's tunic, then used his thumbs to pull the man's startled eyes closed. Legend had it that a murdered man's eyes reflected the last thing he had ever seen — the face of his murderer — but the light wasn't good enough to reveal the truth of this.

Hugues spoke on. 'In fact, this corpse tells us the truth of Robert's claim: that Louise has betrayed us. Who else could have done this? Who else could have taken Thibaut unawares and stolen his razor and used it to such ill effect? And where is the razor now?'

'It is here, in my hand, still sharp and eager for blood — even your thin and meatless blood, Hugues.'

The voice was cool, merry. She was laughing at them. The hand that held the razor was steady and the other hand held a dagger, its hilt emblazoned with the griffin of the d'Ambriers. A flat rock gave her height, ascendancy over them. Her skirts were tucked up some six inches to reveal muscular calves in stout boots. Robyn could smell her cologne, the fierce odour of jasmine, on the thin breeze.

She said, 'I underestimated you, Master Robert.'

'That's because you didn't know what I know,' Robyn acknowledged. 'Otherwise you would have got away with it.'

'I still will 'get away with it'. I have a rendezvous with de Montfort himself at the foot of the hill in less than an hour. Who's going to stop me? You three? A half-starved priest, a beardless boy and a stupid peasant?'

Hugues stood shivering in his thin shirt, his teeth chattering as he said, 'I have to understand, Louise. Why?'

'I've listened so long to your preachings, old man. I'm sick of them. You're free to starve yourself to death if you choose — to renounce the world and the flesh — but did you seriously imagine that I would too?'

'No one has asked you to,' Hugues said, sadly. 'No one is pushed to take the final step, to renounce earthly pleasures, a moment before they're ready and that readiness can only ever be a personal decision.'

'I'm to marry my cousin, Aimeric de Chambertin. It was agreed between us on his last visit. He's a nobleman, a wealthy man and a Catholic. He will take me away from this godforsaken land, to Paris, to the court of the King of France. There will be dancing and merry-making. I will wear fine gowns and priceless jewels. My children and grandchildren — '

'Are you mad?' Hugues interrupted. 'You cannot marry your cousin, Louise. It's against the law of God as laid down in the Bible, against the law of both Church and state. Even the corrupt Catholics know that.'

'The Pope,' she said, 'is Christ's vicar on earth, God's representative, and he can give me dispensation. He alone.'

'He gives such dispensation only to those of royal blood!' Hugues argued. 'Those who are too powerful for him to gainsay. He won't hear your plea. You, who are no more than a fly buzzing round his head.'

'He will give it to me,' she said haughtily.

'I am a d'Ambriers. My mother's a de Chambertin. What is royalty? Who are the Capets and the Plantagenets? De Montfort will intercede for me. Aimeric has spoken to him and he's promised it. The Pope is grateful to de Montfort and he, tonight, he will have cause to be grateful to me!'

Hugues said quietly, 'I wish I had died yesterday, and not lived to see this moment.'

Robyn felt sick. 'Is that it?' she said. 'The lives of five hundred men, women and children, in exchange for a papal dispensation so you may marry your cousin and wear fine jewels and dance at court?'

'Don't mock those things,' Louise spat back. 'It's all very well for you, with your father who has King John's ear. I bet you've danced at court many a long night. Have you any idea what my life has been these last years, as war raged over the Albigeois? I'm young and strong and beautiful, and I've been left here to rot with a brood of filthy peasants.'

Her voice was hungry, her eyes mad. The de Chambertins, Robyn thought, had always been slightly mad and inbreeding hadn't helped. Their insistence on marrying their cousins, generation after generation, on the grounds that no one else was good enough for them had concentrated those genes into the pure and introverted insanity that was Silvie and her husband.

Robyn measured the distance between herself and Louise with her eyes. Thibaut had taken pride in his profession and his razors were stropped to a lethal perfection. One slash was all Louise needed to disable any assailant. Surprise was the only weapon that could hope to succeed.

She shifted her weight noiselessly onto her front foot, her knees bent. She was nearer than the others, stronger than Hugues and faster than Bruno. Logic said that she stood the best chance, but fear had a grip on her throat like a blacksmith's hand and she knew that in the moment of truth her courage had failed her.

Then a real hand, Hugues's hand, was on her arm. He'd felt her movement, her fearful readying, and was warning her off. 'I've lost a daughter tonight,' he whispered in her ear, 'she shall not take another from me.'

'What are you whispering about, old man?'

'Louise, let us go back inside the town and talk about this.'

'It's too late.'

'What was that?' Hugues barked, starting as though at a noise below them on the path. Louise looked away for a second and the priest was upon her. He weighed little now, skin and bone as he was, probably less than she, but he had the benefit of surprise and the impetus of his assault sent them both flying from the rock on which she stood, into the nothingness beyond the cliff.

Bruno and Robyn huddled close together, united at last in fear for their friend. She found herself taking his arm as Louise let out an inhuman scream — more rage than fear — as her body hit the first of the rocks below her, Hugues's weight above her driving her flesh into the knives of limestone. There was another scream a few seconds later, as they tumbled together further down the cliff, then a third, then silence. There was nothing left on the air but the lingering scent of jasmine, a smell Robyn knew she would hate for the rest of her life.

Hugues, throughout it all, emitted not a sound.

Bruno had his arm round Robyn by now. She was trembling, shaking, her last frugal meal coming back up into her throat in burning vomit. She still wore Hugues's cassock and clutched it round herself as if it would armour her against what she had witnessed. She was screaming, crying, aching, all at once. The horror of it was beyond her knowledge.

Bruno's hand stroked her hair, soothing

her into a calmer sorrow, like a vet tending a sick animal.

'I can't look,' she sobbed, when she could speak again.

'I will look. Wait here, boy.'

He stood for a long minute on the rock where Louise had been taunting them only seconds earlier. The drop was almost vertical. He could make out two broken and motionless shapes lying halfway down on an outcrop. 'We won't get them back,' he said. 'The vultures must have them. So be it.'

'Hugues?'

'He was dying anyway. *Greater love hath no man than this, that he lay down his life for his friends.*'

'He deserves a hero's burial.'

'There's nothing you could have done for him. He'd taken the Consolamentum; he was ready. It was what he wanted, the end of earthly suffering and transition to the life of the spirit. Especially now, tonight, when the one person he loved above all others had betrayed him.'

Bruno looked up at the sky where the stars were spread out across the Milky Way, undimmed by competition from aircraft or ground neon. 'We must look to our own lives,' he said. 'Time is running short. We must prepare for battle. Come.'

401

'What about Thibaut?'

'Of course! He at least shall have a Christian burial.'

They dragged the barber's heavy body back through the door. Robyn handed Bruno her key and he made it fast, drawing the heavy iron bolts across doubly to secure it. 'De Montfort won't find his way safely up the path without her guidance,' he said, 'and if he does we shall be ready for him.' He clapped her on the shoulder. 'Robert of Durham, it half kills me to say this, but you did well. I was wrong, and I thank you.'

Before Robyn could reply, a drop of something wet fell on her bare head and she turned her face up to the sky in surprise. A brisk wind was blowing pale clouds in from the west, dozens of them, chasing each other like excited children to blot out the stars. More and heavier raindrops fell on her face, dribbling into her nose and mouth as she drank them in, inhaled them in all their cold beauty.

'Rain!' Bruno exclaimed. 'Now our wells will be filled.' The heavens opened and torrents began to pour down upon them, soaking through their thick cloaks. They didn't mind the wet and both began to laugh.

'Thanks be to God,' Bruno said. 'Thanks

be to God and to mad Hugues who has rushed to his throne demanding rain for his friends.' His voice began to fade in Robyn's ears and she heard him say sharply, 'Are you all right, boy?'

Exhausted, she felt consciousness slip away.

7

*'Al cap des set cens ans
verdego le laurel.'*

*'After seven hundred years
the laurel will be green again.'*

There was a hand on her forehead, cool, still.
Simon, she thought. *Please let it be Simon.
Please let me be home.*

'Robyn!' A voice, urgent, loving, known
to her. 'Can you hear me, darling?'

'Dad?'

'Robyn.'

She opened her eyes. Her father's face
came slowly into focus. She stared at the
familiar features. She looked around for
Simon but there was no one else in the
room.

'I'll ring for the nurse,' her father said, and
pressed a button on the clean, pastel wall.

'Dad. Is that really you? How did you get
here?'

'How do you think? I hopped on a plane
to Toulouse as soon as Professor Clements
rang me about your accident.'

'You did? All by yourself?'

'I'm not a child,' he said, laughing. 'I can catch a plane. And they met me at the airport.'

She tried to hoist herself into a sitting position but her limbs wouldn't obey her. 'Are you all right? How . . . ?'

'Don't try to sit up yet. Don't talk if you don't want to. Of course *I*'m all right. I'm staying at the hotel in Réalmont with the rest of the archaeologists.'

'Réalmont!'

'Of course. Don't you remember? The *Auberge Fleurie*.' He pronounced the words self-consciously badly. 'It's very comfortable.'

She murmured. 'Where am I?'

'In the hospital in Albi. You've had a nasty bang on the head and they say you might be a bit concussed, but otherwise you'll be fine.'

She blinked about her. 'A private room, no less! What happened?'

'You fell when a bit of the wall collapsed under you. It was only a few feet but you hit your head. Lucky not to have any broken bones. You've been unconscious for the last three days. They kept saying you'd come round any minute but you didn't!' He gave a sheepish smile. 'To tell you the truth I was starting to get worried.'

'I . . . it's a bit hazy at the moment.'

In fact nothing was hazy. She remembered with the utmost vividness the recent — the far distant — events of the last few days, or centuries; but since she couldn't begin to explain them to her father, a further bout of amnesia seemed her best course. She raised her hand to the back of her head and was dismayed to find that a patch of hair had been shaved away, the better to tend her wounds. She must look as if she'd been tonsured.

'Egg white,' she muttered. 'That's the thing.'

'What, sweetheart?'

'Nothing.'

A nurse bustled in, exclaimed with pleasure at seeing her awake, and fussed about, taking Robyn's pulse and peering into her eyes.

'How many fingers am I holding up?'

'Three,' Robyn said dutifully.

'Now?'

'Still three.'

'And now?'

'Two.'

'She seems fine,' she said eventually. 'I'll get the doctor to pop by later but I don't think we need worry. The X-rays were clear. Is there anything you need, mademoiselle?' Robyn shook her head and the nurse left.

'Do you think it's all right to hug?' Malcolm asked. 'Or are you too fragile?'

'I think it's always all right to hug.'

He pressed her to him for a moment. He was trembling. Neither of them spoke. He released her.

'Can we come in?' Professor Clements's head appeared disembodied in the doorway. 'The nurse said Robyn was coming round.'

'Come in,' Malcolm said.

The rest of the professor entered the room, followed by Peter Finlay, Dexter Mooney and Meriel Richards. 'How're you feeling, kid?' Mooney asked. 'You gave us a fright.'

'Simon?' she asked weakly. She longed to see Simon now that it seemed she was safely home in the time and place where she belonged. She wanted to see his face and hear his cynical laugh.

'He's actually in the hospital,' Meriel said, 'as Conchita was due for a check-up. They'll both be along in a minute.'

Robyn was baffled. Who was Conchita and why did she need checking? She felt too woozy to ask. 'Silvie?' she queried, a flutter of fear in her belly.

It was their turn to look baffled. 'Who?' James said.

'That bang on the head was worse than we thought,' Dexter whispered to Peter Finlay, more loudly than he imagined.

'Silvie de Chambertin,' she murmured. 'The old Frenchwoman who was . . . who was . . . ' She tailed off. *Who was descended from Louise d'Ambriers.* Except that she'd left Louise a bag of bones halfway down the cliff, unmarried, childless. It wasn't possible for Silvie to have been born, nor her husband Etienne. Somewhere in the world were two little girls, maybe more, who'd never met Etienne de Chambertin and had lived. Somewhere in the French equivalent of Broadmoor there was a vacant cell where Etienne de Chambertin had been.

She heard Simon's light tenor voice out in the corridor; she could hear that he was happy, laughing, no doubt relieved by her quick recovery. She struggled into a sitting position, ignoring her father's remonstrances that she should take it easy. Simon came in without knocking, followed by a woman with black hair and olive skin and a grand — an awesome — beauty, whom he held tightly by the hand.

The woman was small, not above five feet, although her abundant hair was coiled smoothly onto her head to give an illusion of greater height. It wasn't so much black when you got close as a shining depth of deep brown and purple, like the peel of an aubergine. She was perhaps thirty years old. Her skin was free of make-up but very clear and her huge black eyes looked at Robyn with great affection. She would have been slender had she not been several months pregnant.

'Robyn, they told us you're awake at last!' She spoke in excellent English but with a slight Spanish accent. 'We've been so worried.' She released Simon's hand and leant over her huge bump to kiss the younger girl firmly on the lips, her hand tangling with tenderness in Robyn's matted fringe. She smelt faintly of jasmine and Robyn wanted to gag.

'Who are you?' she asked in dismay.

Simon laughed and put his arms round the Spanish woman's thickened waist. 'You're still concussed, I see. You must remember Conchita, my wife.'

Robyn started. She felt her lip begin to tremble as she fought back tears. *I know every inch of your body*, she thought. *I've cupped your tight little balls in my hands and heard you moan. I've kissed you from head to foot — that tender place on the back of your neck, your ticklish toes, your smooth thighs — but you don't remember that and wouldn't believe me if I told you, since, for you, my darling, it never happened.*

She was relieved when Meriel spoke, drawing attention momentarily away from her. 'How was the check-up, Chita?'

'Oh, fine,' Conchita said. 'Young Simon is growing fast, it seems, and is lively, but I could have told them that.'

'Here,' Malcolm stood up. 'You must have my seat, Mrs Guzman. I mean Dr Guzman. Sorry. So confusing to have *two* Dr Guzmans.'

'No, no. You stay there, by Robyn. I know how precious she is to you.'

'I insist. I can't let a pregnant woman stand.'

'No, you stay put, Malcolm,' Simon said. 'We're off — back to the hotel, to let Conchita get a siesta. We only wanted to put our heads round the door to say welcome back to Robyn.' He waved an indifferent hand at the invalid. 'See you later, kid,' and left the room with his arm round his wife's waist.

'Don't they make a lovely couple?' Meriel said to no one in particular.

Professor Clements chuckled. 'I have to say I never thought I'd live to see any woman tame Simon, let alone get him to the altar. He'll be learning to change nappies next. Still, the ones who sow the most wild oats often make the best husbands in the end.'

'You'd know, would you?' Meriel teased. They were in high spirits, relieved to have their young colleague restored to them in one piece.

'I've had my moments, I can promise you, my dear Dr Richards,' Clements said with a twinkle, then added ruefully, 'Not recently, of course.'

'Whirlwind romances are the best,' Mooney said, with a hint of what might have been nostalgia in his voice.

Robyn wanted to scream. Instead she asked, 'How long have they been married?'

Meriel looked at her in surprise. 'Well, you were at the wedding too, sweetheart. Eight months. One month to the day after they met at the dig.'

Robyn struggled to comprehend. Silvie de Chambertin had never been born, so James had had to find another seventh member for his dig, this Spanish woman, evidently, this exotic beauty, and Simon had fallen head over heels in love with her and never so much as noticed Robyn while she, unencouraged, had probably not thought twice about him either.

And, with this woman, Simon hadn't hesitated for an instant.

She put her hand to her head. 'Does it hurt?' Malcolm asked anxiously.

411

Yes, she wanted to say. *It hurts very deep and very bad, but not here; in my heart.* To try to take her mind off it, she turned to the professor. 'You must have been furious at having police and ambulancemen trampling over the dig like that, James. I'm so sorry.'

He shrugged, a little surprised. 'Just two men with a stretcher and there was no need for the police. It's not as if there's much left to excavate there. It's hardly a site of great historic importance — an ordinary farming community, like a thousand others, that eventually died out when people didn't need the safety of the hills any more and moved down onto the plains. That would probably have been depopulated anyway by the famines and plagues of the fourteenth century. I can't wait to move on to St Pierre des Bois, personally.'

'Montprimeur has one claim to fame,' Mooney objected. 'That it survived a siege during the Cathar wars and preserved the faith for another century or two.'

'If you believe that old story,' Clements said with a smile. 'There's no historical evidence for it at all. Nothing but anecdote and local legend. Well . . . ' He'd been standing with his hands in his pocket, but now reached one out to place it paternally, if heavily, on Robyn's shoulder in a gesture which didn't seem natural to him. 'We'd better let you get some rest, young Robyn. We shall want you back at work soon, you know. Not too much of this lolling about in bed.'

'No,' she agreed. 'I'll soon be earning my keep again.'

'We'll have to talk about that!' Malcolm said grimly.

The archaeologists filed out, leaving Malcolm and Janey in the room. Was it her imagination, Robyn wondered, or were her colleagues more light-hearted than they had been, as if they no longer carried the weight of the tragic history of Montprimeur on their shoulders?

'You'll be fine when you've had a bit of a rest,' Malcolm said, turning back to his injured daughter with determination. 'Then we'll go back home, the two of us, to Belfast.'

It was tempting. The thought of staying to work with Simon and his beautiful hateful wife flickered a spasm of pain across her face. But she was an adult, a woman who'd changed history. She couldn't run for cover at the first sign of trouble like a lovesick adolescent. She'd saved five hundred lives and lost Simon: was that a fair exchange?

Would she undo what she'd done if she could?

It was academic.

'I'll fly back to Belfast with you, Dad,' she said. 'See you safely home, even stay and rest for a few days, but my work is here, my *life* is here. I can't stay home with you forever. You understand that, don't you?'

After a brief pause he said, 'That's my girl.' His voice quavered. 'That's her mother's daughter.'

'But we'll . . . see more of each other in future, spend more time together. Okay?'

He said joyfully, 'You're on!'

It seemed that the Catholics had been right all along, Robyn thought good did triumph over evil in the end — even it took nearly eight hundred years to do it.

Author's Note

I first became interested in the history of the Albigensian crusades when working as an English language assistant at the Lycée de Muret near Toulouse in 1976. Muret was the site of one of the last and most decisive battles in the crushing of the heresy, which destroyed the Occitan civilisation and led to the establishment of the infamous Inquisition. I always meant to write about them.

I've given Janey Silverman my job and my car but she bears no other resemblance to me.

I've invented the village of Montprimeur, its people and their fate, although it's typical of the medieval fortified hill towns of the Cathar country which are still — where they have survived — among the most picturesque in Europe. The roll call of shame of such villages would include Béziers, Bram, Lavaur, Minerve, Cabaret, Fanjeaux, Cassès, Lasbordes, Castelnaudary, Montmaur and Montségur. Others yet have slipped completely from the memory of history.

SK

Other titles in the Ulverscroft Large Print Series:

THE GREENWAY
Jane Adams

When Cassie and her twelve-year-old cousin Suzie had taken a short cut through an ancient Norfolk pathway, Suzie had simply vanished . . . Twenty years on, Cassie is still tormented by nightmares. She returns to Norfolk, determined to solve the mystery.

FORTY YEARS ON THE WILD FRONTIER
Carl Breihan & W. Montgomery

Noted Western historian Carl Breihan has culled from the handwritten diaries of John Montgomery, grandfather of co-author Wayne Montgomery, new facts about Wyatt Earp, Doc Holliday, Bat Masterson and other famous and infamous men and women who gained notoriety when the Western Frontier was opened up.

TAKE NOW, PAY LATER
Joanna Dessau

This fiction based on fact is the love-turning-to-hate story of Robert Carr, Earl of Somerset, and his wife, Frances.

McLEAN AT THE GOLDEN OWL
George Goodchild

Inspector McLean has resigned from Scotland Yard's CID and has opened an office in Wimpole Street. With the help of his able assistant, Tiny, he solves many crimes, including those of kidnapping, murder and poisoning.

KATE WEATHERBY
Anne Goring

Derbyshire, 1849: The Hunter family are the arrogant, powerful masters of Clough Grange. Their feuds are sparked by a generation of guilt, despair and ill-fortune. But their passions are awakened by the arrival of nineteen-year-old Kate Weatherby.

A VENETIAN RECKONING
Donna Leon

When the body of a prominent international lawyer is found in the carriage of an intercity train, Commissario Guido Brunetti begins to dig deeper into the secret lives of the once great and good.

A TASTE FOR DEATH
Peter O'Donnell

Modesty Blaise and Willie Garvin take on impossible odds in the shape of Simon Delicata, the man with a taste for death, and Swordmaster, Wenczel, in a terrifying duel. Finally, in the Sahara desert, the intrepid pair must summon every killing skill to survive.

SEVEN DAYS FROM MIDNIGHT
Rona Randall

In the Comet Theatre, London, seven people have good reason for wanting beautiful Maxine Culver out of the way. Each one has reason to fear her blackmail. But whose shadow is it that lurks in the wings, waiting to silence her once and for all?

QUEEN OF THE ELEPHANTS
Mark Shand

Mark Shand knows about the ways of elephants, but he is no match for the tiny Parbati Barua, the daughter of India's greatest expert on the Asian elephant, the late Prince of Gauripur, who taught her everything. Shand sought out Parbati to take part in a film about the plight of the wild herds today in north-east India.

THE DARKENING LEAF
Caroline Stickland

On storm-tossed Chesil Bank in 1847, the young lovers, Philobeth and Frederick, prevent wreckers mutilating the apparent corpse of a young woman. Discovering she is still alive, Frederick takes her to his grandmother's home. But the rescue is to have violent and far-reaching effects . . .

A WOMAN'S TOUCH
Emma Stirling

When Fenn went to stay on her uncle's farm in Africa, the lovely Helena Starr seemed to resent her — especially when Dr Jason Kemp agreed to Fenn helping in his bush hospital. Though it seemed Jason saw Fenn as little more than a child, her feelings for him were those of a woman.

A DEAD GIVEAWAY
Various Authors

This book offers the perfect opportunity to sample the skills of five of the finest writers of crime fiction — Clare Curzon, Gillian Linscott, Peter Lovesey, Dorothy Simpson and Margaret Yorke.

DOUBLE INDEMNITY — MURDER FOR INSURANCE
Jad Adams

This is a collection of true cases of murderers who insured their victims then killed them — or attempted to. Each tense, compelling account tells a story of cold-blooded plotting and elaborate deception.

THE PEARLS OF COROMANDEL
By Keron Bhattacharya

John Sugden, an ambitious young Oxford graduate, joins the Indian Civil Service in the early 1920s and goes to uphold the British Raj. But he falls in love with a young Hindu girl and finds his loyalties tragically divided.

WHITE HARVEST
Louis Charbonneau

Kathy McNeely, a marine biologist, sets out for Alaska to carry out important research. But when she stumbles upon an illegal ivory poaching operation that is threatening the world's walrus population, she soon realises that she will have to survive more than the harsh elements . . .

TO THE GARDEN ALONE
Eve Ebbett

Widow Frances Morley's short, happy marriage was childless, and in a succession of borders she attempts to build a substitute relationship for the husband and family she does not have. Over all hovers the shadow of the man who terrorized her childhood.

CONTRASTS
Rowan Edwards

Julia had her life beautifully planned — she was building a thriving pottery business as well as sharing her home with her friend Pippa, and having fun owning a goat. But the goat's problems brought the new local vet, Sebastian Trent, into their lives.

MY OLD MAN AND THE SEA
David and Daniel Hays

Some fathers and sons go fishing together. David and Daniel Hays decided to sail a tiny boat seventeen thousand miles to the bottom of the world and back. Together, they weave a story of travel, adventure, and difficult, sometimes terrifying, sailing.

SQUEAKY CLEAN
James Pattinson

An important attribute of a prospective candidate for the United States presidency is not to have any dirt in your background which an eager muckraker can dig up. Senator William S. Gallicauder appeared to fit the bill perfectly. But then a skeleton came rattling out of an English cupboard.

NIGHT MOVES
Alan Scholefield

It was the first case that Macrae and Silver had worked on together. Malcolm Underdown had brutally stabbed to death Edward Craig and had attempted to murder Craig's fiancée, Jane Harrison. He swore he would be back for her. Now, four years later, he has simply walked from the mental hospital. Macrae and Silver must get to him — before he gets to Jane.

GREATEST CAT STORIES
Various Authors

Each story in this collection is chosen to show the cat at its best. James Herriot relates a tale about two of his cats. Stella Whitelaw has written a very funny story about a lion. Other stories provide examples of courageous, clever and lucky cats.

THE HAND OF DEATH
Margaret Yorke

The woman had been raped and murdered. As the police pursue their relentless inquiries, decent, gentle George Fortescue, the typical man-next-door, finds himself accused. While the real killer serenely selects his third victim — and then his fourth . . .

VOW OF FIDELITY
Veronica Black

Sister Joan of the Daughters of Compassion is shocked to discover that three of her former fellow art college students have recently died violently. When another death occurs, Sister Joan realizes that she must pit her wits against a cunning and ruthless killer.

MARY'S CHILD
Irene Carr

Penniless and desperate, Chrissie struggles to support herself as the Victorian years give way to the First World War. Her childhood friends, Ted and Frank, fall hopelessly in love with her. But there is only one man Chrissie loves, and fate and one man bent on revenge are determined to prevent the match . . .

THE SWIFTEST EAGLE
Alice Dwyer-Joyce

This book moves from Scotland to Malaya — before British Raj and now — and then to war-torn Vietnam and Cambodia . . . Virginia meets Gareth casually in the Western Isles, with no inkling of the sacrifice he must make for her.

VICTORIA & ALBERT
Richard Hough

Victoria and Albert had nine children and the family became the archetype of the nineteenth century. But the relationship between the Queen and her Prince Consort was passionate and turbulent; thunderous rows threatened to tear them apart, but always reconciliation and love broke through.

BREEZE: WAIF OF THE WILD
Marie Kelly

Bernard and Marie Kelly swapped their lives in London for a remote farmhouse in Cumbria. But they were to undergo an even more drastic upheaval when a two-day-old fragile roe deer fawn arrived on their doorstep. The knowledge of how to care for her was learned through sleepless nights and anxiety-filled days.